Defenders of Destiny

Book One

The Discovery of

ASTROLARIS

By

Brenton Barwick

I dedicate this story to Joseph, who inspired me with:
"I love you daddy. Tell me a story about me and the robot."

*"Remember, a person's inability to verify the existence of
something in no way disproves the reality of its existence."*
Joseph and Sharianna's dad, Thomas.

CONTENTS

Acknowledgments

I give a very special thanks to my wife, Kjerstin, for her essential support, and remarkable ideas. She encouraged me to write the story and inspired me to flavor the adventure with a little mystery.

Thanks to my mom, Donna, my dad, Ken, and my sisters Kenda Barlow, and Keva Wardell for their thoughtful critique and invaluable suggestions.

I am grateful to my brother, Stott, for the robot and the obelisk on the cover art.

I thank my brother, Valdon, for his help in book layout and arrangement, and who always helps me with technical computer solutions.

I extend my sincere appreciation to the following, for giving me incredibly useful feedback and encouragement:

Kelly and Nathan Nuttall and their children: Rebekah, Kampton, and Kayla.

Denice Cannell, Mike Cannell, Kayson Barwick, Logan Malmstrom, Steve Rasmason, Melinda Diamond, Mitchell Gillette, Parker Costa, Aspen Curtis, Nancy Nielsen, Vanessa Nuttall, Gary Dazley, Carter Bryant, Danielle Finlay, Rodger and Connie Brown, Alex Dewsnup, Richard Malmstrom.

CHAPTER ONE

The Viper

"LOOK! THERE!" JOSEPH LEAPED FROM THE RUSTY OLD flatbed pickup truck as it rolled to a stop at the bottom of a gully, and ran to the spot where he saw the sun glinting from the ground.

"Did you find a geode?" Joseph's dad asked, as he climbed out of the truck.

"No." As Joseph turned, he held up a large piece of shiny black obsidian shaped like an arrowhead. "Even better." A huge smile crossed his face. "It was sitting on that flat rock. Sharianna's going to be sorry she didn't come now." Joseph and his sister were born less than a year apart. Joseph was about the oldest student in the seventh grade, while Sharianna was probably the youngest.

"Wow, a spearhead," his dad, Thomas, marveled. "Let's look around and see if there are any more."

While searching the area, they found along the rim and scattered down the slope of the gully several geode fragments, but none that were whole. Joseph suddenly heard a sound that made him freeze.

"Don't move!" Dad whispered fervently from several yards away. "Now, very slowly, move away; don't make any sudden movements." Directly in front of Joseph, in the shade of a sagebrush bush, was a large rattlesnake, coiled and ready to bite. Its rattle was at least four inches in length. Joseph was easily within striking distance of the five-foot diamond back. Joseph's

1

heart seemed to stop momentarily; when it resumed its function, it did so with a furious pounding. His mouth felt suddenly dry as he held his breath, while beads of sweat rapidly formed on his brow. He was startled and scared, but he knew he had to act carefully. Slowly, he moved his left foot backwards and cautiously shifted his weight to that foot.

The snake's head was moving from side to side slightly, with its tongue flicking in and out, testing the air for the scent of an enemy. A large bead of sweat rolled off Joseph's forehead and into his eye. The salt from the sweat stung as he blinked, but he resisted the involuntary urge to wipe it away. One more step backward and Joseph would be safely out of the viper's striking range.

"Slowly..." whispered Dad.

The serpent hissed as its head rose above the coils of its body, even higher than the quivering rattle.

Joseph carefully, and very slowly, moved his right foot behind his left.

"Okay," breathed Joseph's dad with obvious relief. "I think you're safe..."

Suddenly, the coiled viper hissed loudly and lunged toward Joseph in a blur of movement.

Joseph's reflexes caused him to instantly jump back, catching his heel against a rock, and crashing to the sand. As he fell backwards, his arms swung wide in an instinctive attempt to break his fall. His eyes were riveted on the serpent's head with its fangs distended as the toe of his worn out tennis shoe came up to meet it. Joseph's mind perceived his surroundings as if he were in slow motion; he could see his sock through the hole in the top of his tennis shoe as the fangs sank into the end of his shoe. At the same time, Joseph felt a painful prick in his hand as he hit the ground.

There must be two of them, he thought frantically, as he jerked his arm back and scrambled backwards like a crab.

The snake recoiled and continued to shake its rattle.

Joseph felt his dad's hand on his shoulder as he scrambled to his feet.

"Did it bite you?" Thomas asked anxiously.

Joseph held up his hand and saw, with a strange kind of painful relief, several cactus spines stuck in his flesh.

They retreated several yards away. Joseph sat down on a boulder and pulled off his shoe and his sock. They examined his toes, looking for any puncture marks.

Thomas looked at Joseph's shoe, and held it up for him to see. "That was close."

Joseph looked at the rubber on the toe of the shoe and saw two small marks, then looked back toward the serpent.

"Why did it try to bite me?" Joseph asked when he began to breathe again.

"I don't know – rattlesnakes will usually only bite things that are too big for them to eat if they feel threatened, maybe this one is just mean," answered Dad, as he picked up a softball size rock and hefted it in his hand.

Joseph grabbed Dad's wrist, "I think we should let it go. I heard on Animal Planet that they really don't want to waste their venom, or risk getting injured by attacking large animals."

"I guess you're right, they do help balance the ecosystem in the desert by eating rodents and keeping them from overrunning the environment," agreed Dad.

Joseph pulled the cactus spines from his hand, as they watched the graceful reptile from a safe distance until it slithered over the hill and disappeared.

The sun began to set, and finding no more spearheads or whole geodes, they decided to make camp right there, with plans to dig for geodes in the morning.

After dinner, they spread their sleeping bags on top of their camping pads in the back of the pickup.

"We'll be safe from rattlers and scorpions up here," Dad commented confidently, as he lay down on his comfortable bed and fluffed his pillow.

Joseph plopped down on his sleeping bag with a big, "Ahhhh, I'm sooooo tired." He caught sight of the first star. "Star light, star bright, first star I see tonight; I wish I may, I wish I might, wish upon this star tonight." After a long pause gazing into the

3

night sky Joseph said quietly with a sigh: "I wish…" A big yawn made the rest of his wish incomprehensible.

As the other stars began to appear in the clear desert night, Dad asked quietly, almost to himself: "Have you ever seen so many stars?"

"Nope, I can even see the milky way," was Joseph's nearly inaudible reply, full of awe.

He pointed to what looked like a red star, "Is that Mars?"

"I'll bet it is," replied Dad. "See how it doesn't twinkle?"

"Yep."

"That means it's a planet," continued Dad. "Stars twinkle, planets don't."

"My star chart!" Joseph rummaged in his backpack and pulled out an earth and astronomy fact book that Uncle Jared had given him on his last birthday. He reached into his pack again for a flashlight. Opening the book up to the northern hemisphere star chart, he held it up to the sky and rotated it until he had the big dipper lined up and all the other stars fell into place.

"It must be Mars," observed Dad, "there is no red star shown on the chart in that spot."

A bright speck of light appeared and slowly made its way across the sky. Another speck of light approached the first and seemed to connect. "That is the space shuttle meeting up with the space station," announced Joseph.

"How did you know that?" marveled Dad.

"Mr. Lato described it to us."

"Ah, your science teacher?"

"Yep, he's pretty cool."

The desert night sounds were as beautiful as the sky. "Listen," entreated Dad, as he put his hands behind his head and relaxed contentedly onto his pillow.

Joseph could pick out the individual sounds of a cricket as an owl hooted from a nearby snag and a coyote howled from a faraway hilltop.

Joseph and his dad lay quietly for a long time, enjoying the solitude and beauty of the desert. A shooting star flashed across the sky.

4

"Joseph, what did you wish for?"

"I wished that..." his voice trailed off as he drifted into sleep.

Joseph was snuggled deep in his sleeping bag as the sun tentatively approached the jagged mountain peaks along the eastern horizon, casting a faint golden aura across the desert-scape.

Dad arose, and glanced at the lump in the bottom of Joseph's sleeping bag. *He had a long day yesterday*, he thought to himself, as he quietly fired up the small propane stove for a large breakfast.

The morning was still cool and pleasant when the lump began to move. Slowly, it moved up the sleeping bag until finally, a blonde pillow head with light blue eyes emerged.

With a yawn and a slow stretch, the sleepy boy mumbled: "What time is it?"

"Morning time – time to find those geodes we came for."

"I hope we find more than yesterday." Joseph breathed down a pancake smothered in real maple syrup, quickly followed by two more and topped off with a pile of scrambled eggs and a small carton of milk.

"How were geodes formed, anyway?" inquired Joseph.

"Geodes were originally bubbles in lava rock and over a very long period of time minerals seeped into these bubbles in the rock and crystallized, forming the beautiful crystals in the geodes. This process made the geodes harder than the surrounding rock; as the rock eroded, the geodes were freed and rolled down the mountain and eventually ended up being deposited in the sand at the bottom of a great lake. In time, the lake evaporated and became a desert."

"Think we'll find something worth keeping today?" Joseph asked.

"I'm thinking that since we found so many geode fragments along the edge and sides of the gully, maybe we ought to dig right into the side of the gully."

A strange thought suddenly occurred to Joseph. "Maybe the

5

spearhead is an ancient Native American good luck omen." He couldn't explain why, but Joseph suddenly felt impressed to say: "We should dig here in the bottom, right where we found the spearhead."

Joseph grabbed his digging tools and the shade umbrella.

"I think the digging would be easier in the side of the hill," pressed Dad.

"But this *feels* like a lucky spot," replied Joseph, as he set up the umbrella with its precious shade directed over the flat rock.

"That's good enough for me," agreed Dad.

As they dug, they fell into a routine. Dad picked, and then Joseph shoveled. Every now and then Joseph picked up a large geode fragment from the sand he was shoveling and put it in a bucket.

"This one is very pretty; but why are we only finding broken geodes?" asked Joseph, with some disappointment.

"Don't know," huffed Dad, as he put down the pick.

Joseph picked it up. "Spell ya?"

"Thanks." Dad climbed out of the hole and sat down on the bucket of geode fragments.

Joseph's first swing of the pick bounced right back with a loud clang.

"Ugh. What is that?" questioned Joseph, his hands stinging from the vibration of the pick handle.

"Quick, get out of the hole!" exclaimed Dad in an urgent voice.

"Why?" asked Joseph, as he scrambled out of the hole. They quickly clambered up the steep slope at the end of the gully and Dad explained between great breaths: "This area is close to the Dugway military firing range; it might be an unexploded artillery shell!"

As they climbed out of the gully, they dove behind a large rock outcropping that leaned away from the gully, creating a cave-like shelter. They peered around the edge of the rock and could see the hole they had dug, the truck parked next to it at the bottom of the gully, and the gentle slope they had driven down leading away and out of the gully. The outcropping of rock they were hiding behind was on top of a small hill about fifteen feet higher than the edge of the gully. They looked all around and noticed for the first time that the edges of the gully also seemed to be mounded up slightly more than the surrounding desert, which sloped gently to the south for what looked like several miles toward a great flat plain, with very little vegetation.

"From up here, it looks like a big scrape in the desert," mused Joseph.

"That's odd," observed Dad, as he looked down at their dig site. "That gully slopes the wrong way."

"What do you mean?" inquired Joseph.

"Gullies and canyons are created by erosion, right? As water flows down them, it cuts them deeper, until it flows down into a river or valley. This one slopes down, alright, but it cuts crossways across the main slope, and it ends in a pit instead of emptying out onto lower ground."

Joseph looked at the gully thoughtfully. "Erosion is slowly filling it in, rather than cutting it out."

A thought suddenly occurred to Dad: "This must be a meteorite crater! See the shape of the depression: it's long and sloping from one end to the other. The trajectory of the meteorite must have been almost parallel to the ground; and its velocity..."

"Wow!" Joseph interrupted excitedly. "A meteorite is even cooler than geodes!" After a short pause, "So, you don't think it's an unexploded artillery shell?"

"Nope, this pit is way too big..."

"That must be one big meteorite!" exclaimed Joseph, as he began to stand up. He glanced up at the outcropping of rock that hung over them.

"Look at that, Dad."

Above them, etched into the rock were strange looking drawings.

"Pictographs," stated Dad.

"Do they mean anything?"

"Who knows," Dad laughed. "I guess you might consider them ancient graffiti."

"What about these," asked Joseph, pointing to some type of

7

ancient inscription etched into the rock.

"I wish I had Mom's knowledge of ancient languages," said Dad.

"She wouldn't know what this says anyway; didn't she study Latin and Greek?" responded Joseph.

"I guess you're right, I don't think she knows any Native American languages."

"Oh well, meteorites are a lot cooler than old rock art," said Joseph, as he ran back down into the pit.

Joseph and his dad resumed their excavation with renewed vigor. Joseph didn't even pause to save the broken geodes. His shovel was flying so fast that Thomas decided it would be safer to watch from the edge of the hole. The shovel struck the metallic object several times, but the sand continued to pour into the bottom of the hole. Finally, enough sand was removed; Joseph threw his shovel onto the edge of the hole and, bending down, began to brush the sand away from the metal object.

As Dad was climbing into the hole he heard Joseph: "Wow, no way! Look at that, it's not like the meteorites at the natural history museum—it's too smooth."

Joseph had exposed about a foot of the strangest material he had ever seen. On the surface it was dark and shiny and yet not reflective. "That's definitely no artillery shell," whispered Dad.

"Then what?" queried Joseph as he raised his hands slightly for added emphasis.

"Let's find out." They began removing the sand in an attempt to find the edges of the object.

The sun quickly moved across the desert sky; the shade from their sun umbrella no longer fell upon the team as they worked. Oblivious of the heat, beads of sweat glistened and danced, then rolled to the ground, leaving tracks in the dust on their faces.

More of the object was now exposed; it seemed spherical and they estimated it to be about twelve feet in diameter. Kneeling down, they brushed away the sand with their hands. It felt smoother than glass and cool to the touch, even in the hot desert

8

sun. The surface was absolutely flawless – no cracks, rust, pits, or scratches at all – even where they had scraped and banged it with the pick and shovel.

When examining the metal from slightly varying angles, the color seemed to be a changing, blending combination of different shades of midnight blue and subdued dark purple to black, accented with hints of deep dark reds and yellows, almost like swirls of different colors of oil floating on water, blended together, but not fully mixing.

It seemed to draw them toward it until they had their faces pressed close up with their hands cupped to the side as if peering into a window. The metal appeared to be of infinite depth, small silver flecks of varying intensity and size were interspersed throughout the vastness, as if looking at the stars in the expanse of deep space.

CHAPTER TWO

"IT'S from SPACE!"

"IT'S BEAUTIFUL," DECLARED JOSEPH. "IT LOOKS KIND OF LIKE the pictures of space on the NASA web site."

Slowly, Joseph and his dad raised their heads from the incredible sight and climbed out of the now large hole.

Handing Joseph a jug of water and a camp chair, Joseph's dad flipped open another chair and put it in the elusive shade of the umbrella and with a long sigh, relaxed into it, as if it were his favorite lounge.

Chugging the water straight from the jug, Joseph handed it back to his dad nearly half empty, and sank into the other chair. "So." This was Joseph's signature invitation to his dad for his thoughts.

There was a long pause as Thomas finished off the jug of water. "So..." he drawled contemplatively. "I think we should finish digging it up and then figure out what it is." After a thoughtful silence, "We should go get the backhoe. I'm too tired to keep digging by hand; besides, even if we could dig it up, it's too big for the pick up truck, and no telling how heavy it is.

Thomas operated a one-man excavation company; they owned a backhoe and a dump truck.

"We *are* going to keep it, aren't we, Dad?"

"Yeah, this is the find of a lifetime. Let's put a little sand over it, in case someone comes by while we're gone. I think we should leave the umbrella and the cooler, to mark it as our spot."

Joseph couldn't wait to see his mom's face when he showed

10

her the spearhead. As they pulled down their long tree lined gravel driveway, he saw Percy come out from under the porch. With a couple of barks and his tail wagging furiously, he ran to greet them. Joseph could see his mom look out the kitchen window. She came out onto the porch as Joseph came bounding up the steps.

"I see by your face that you must have met with success," she observed, smiling.

Joseph pulled the spearhead from his pocket as if performing a magic act, "Ta da..."

"Wow, that *is* an interesting geode," his mother responded, a little bit teasingly.

"It's an ancient Indian spearhead!" Joseph exclaimed. "But that is nothing; wait till you see what else we found," he declared, as he handed the spearhead to her.

She turned the spearhead over, noticing how beautiful it was. "What else did you find that could top this?"

"We found a giant metal meteorite-thing...from space!" he burst out.

"It's the 'thing' part of your description that intrigues me," she said with interest.

Standing at the bottom of the front porch steps, holding the bucket of broken geodes, Dad explained: "We don't really know what it is but it *is* at the bottom of an impact crater."

"We are going back out there with the backhoe to dig it up and bring it home!" exclaimed Joseph.

"Not till I've had a meal, a couple hours rest, and a hot shower. Oh yeah, and a kiss," proposed Thomas, as he leaned over toward his wife, Sophia.

"I think you ought to start with the shower, *everything* else can wait till after," she countered, as she bent down to look at the bucket of geodes. "You too," she directed, looking at Joseph."

"Where is Sharianna?" asked Dad.

"She's sleeping over at Kim's house. She couldn't wait to show off her new clothes from our little shopping expedition," Mom replied with a smile, as she thought of the great deals they had found at the factory stores.

11

Weeks before, when Joseph and Dad were planning their trip to the desert, Mom suggested that they make it a father and son camping trip while the girls went to Park City for an adventure among the many shops and art galleries. Sharianna enjoyed the outdoors and loved to go camping, but digging holes out in the hot desert simply did not sound as fun as shopping along the streets of the old silver mining town.

Joseph and Dad arrived at the pit before dawn the next morning. It looked like no one had visited the site. They began digging with the backhoe. Ever since Joseph could remember, he loved working with the backhoe with his dad and today was no exception – except that today he was more excited than ever. The four o'clock wakeup call that morning from his dad would normally have been unbearable, but today it was no problem.

As they continued digging, they discovered that the sphere appeared to have a large tube extending from one end. They continued to dig.

Suddenly, Joseph exclaimed with extreme excitement, "It's a robot!"

They had now uncovered what looked like the back of a giant metal head, neck and shoulders.

"Oh, I don't know about that," reasoned Joseph's dad, "it could be an ancient sculpture or monument."

"Yeah, right," Joseph's voice contained a hint of sarcasm. "It doesn't look like copper, bronze, or even iron to me." Joseph had been studying the stone, bronze, and iron ages in his world history class at school.

"But how could it be a robot if it doesn't have any seams or joints? How would it move?" queried Dad. "Look, here where the head meets the neck and where the neck meets the shoulders, it looks like one solid piece. Right? Who knows what kind of advanced metallurgies ancient people may have had and lost?"

Joseph quickly responded. "I'll bet they can't make metal this hard, even today. There is still not a scratch on it, even after digging and scraping with the backhoe."

"Maybe it's not ancient, maybe it's modern," Dad continued, without conviction but interested to see what other observations Joseph had made.

"Then how do you explain the crater it's lying in, and all those broken geodes? And why is it buried so deep? And why is there so much cactus and sagebrush growing over it? I'll bet it's been here for hundreds of years! Maybe thousands," Joseph reasoned proudly.

As the last word left Joseph's lips, Dad realized the folly of his own argument. He knew what Joseph would say next.

Simultaneously, Dad conceded thoughtfully, while Joseph announced victoriously with finality, "*IT'S* from *SPACE*!"

Suddenly, Joseph remembered the pictograph on the rock above the pit.

"Dad, this is in the rock art. Remember, it was flying through the sky, and lying in the ground."

"Someone must have seen it land!" exclaimed Dad with excitement, as he leaped from the backhoe and clambered up the hill to have another look at the pictograph.

As they looked at the rock art, they realized that it was a series of pictures depicting the events of the crash landing of the robot. The second to the last one showed the robot lying under the ground.

"What about this last one?" Joseph paused, "Something feels strange."

"Déjà vu," whispered Dad, as he looked at the last pictograph of the robot lying in a hole with the primitive drawings of two men, one a little shorter than the other, holding spears and standing on top of the giant robot.

"They must have defeated it with their spears," speculated Dad.

"Those aren't spears—they're shovels, whispered Joseph, "...it's us."

Dad leaned a little closer to the rock, "They do look like shovels; I think you might be right...but how could that be?" he pondered soberly, almost to himself.

Joseph answered the question, "It was probably drawn by an

13

ancient medicine man, maybe he had a vision—don't forget the déjà vu."

"Forty seven feet, head to toe," called out Joseph, as he looked at the tape measure he was holding. The figure now lay at the bottom of a huge pit, fully exposed, still lying on its face with its arms to the side and fingers together, pointing down toward the feet.

Thomas ran his hand along the flawless surface as he walked toward Joseph, who was winding up the tape. He could not stop marveling how cool to the touch the figure was, even in the blistering desert heat.

As they approached each other, Joseph asked, "How are we going to get it home?"

"We could put it on the backhoe trailer. It would hang over the sides at the shoulders, and out the back quite a bit, but I think we could strap it down; I've got the big tarp and the wide load sign in the truck's tool box."

"How heavy do you think it is?" asked the boy.

"I don't know. Let's see if we can move it with the back-hoe." They put the bucket of the backhoe under one of the shoulders and lifted while pushing.

"It's rolling," observed Joseph, as one side came a few inches off the ground.

"It's still too heavy and too bulky to lift with the backhoe," concluded Dad.

"What about hiring a crane?"

"I think we better keep this to ourselves for now," cautioned Dad. "I've got an idea…"

They used the backhoe and dug a ramp down along one side of the giant figure until they could back the trailer down into it, with the deck of the trailer a couple of inches below the level of the giant. They unhitched the trailer from the truck and drove out of the gully up onto the desert and backed it up to the edge of the pit, perpendicular to the figure. The truck was now above the giant and about forty five feet away. They strung a chain from

14

the truck, over the trailer and across the back of the giant and wrapped it around the far arm.

"Now, Joseph, I think it is going to take both of us working as a team to load the robot onto the trailer. With the truck up here pulling, and the backhoe down there lifting and pushing, I think we might be able to roll the giant over on its back right onto the trailer."

Joseph was not old enough to legally drive, but at thirteen years he was already pretty experienced with the backhoe and he definitely knew how to drive the dump truck. "Okey dokey, Dad," answered Joseph, with a huge grin.

"I'll honk when I want you to go and then I'll honk again to stop," instructed Dad.

Joseph put his foot on the brake pedal and pushed in the air switch that released the parking brake. When he heard the backhoe's horn, he slowly began to pull. The wheels on one rear axel began to spin, so he engaged the interaxel differential lock, which made both rear axels pull together. Suddenly, the truck moved forward and almost as suddenly he heard another honk. Joseph stopped, put the truck in neutral, pulled out the park brake button and jumped out. As he ran to the edge of the pit he heard his dad yell, "Ya Hooo!" He looked down to see the giant figure lying on its back right on top of the trailer. Dad climbed across the front of the backhoe and jumped from the bucket onto the top of the giant.

"Yaaaa Hoooooooo!" Joseph echoed his dad, with a little added emphasis, as he ran down the steep bank and clambered onto the backhoe and then onto the giant to join his dad.

"So," contemplated Dad, staring down at the giant's face.

"So..." was Joseph's reply.

The facial features were very subdued, almost imperceptible, except the eyes: they were distinctively peculiar and arresting. From their point of view, standing on the chest, it looked like the eyes were portals into the galaxy with a view of two nebula set against the backdrop of deep black space; beginning with translucent swirls of the most vibrant blues on the outer fringes, then turning to yellows, then reds with the deepest darkest red at the center as if it were a red giant star shining from beyond the nebula.

"Beautiful, yet powerful," Joseph breathed softly.

"My sentiments exactly," responded Dad. "What an amazing work of art. The Smithsonian may have to build another wing."

"More like area 51," countered Joseph.

"Well, let's get it home, then we'll figure out what to do with it. We'd better hurry, if we want to get it ready to go before dark," observed Dad, as he looked across the desert toward the sun hanging low over the western hills.

"That should do it." Thomas tied the last rope on the tarp while Joseph attached the WIDE LOAD sign to the back.

Dad looked over at the huge excavation in the bottom of the pit, "I think we should fill in the hole before we leave because tomorrow is a holiday and there might be geode hunters and people on four wheelers all over here. We'll come back early tomorrow with the other trailer to get the backhoe."

Joseph found several whole geodes as they filled in the large hole, several of them the size of basketballs, but as he looked toward the trailer and the figure of the giant under the tarp, they just weren't as exciting as they seemed the day before.

They had to drive very slowly over the rough terrain until they got back to the gravel road. They stopped to tighten the straps.

"Look at that sunset," Joseph marveled. They stood there, looking back the way they had come as the sun settled behind the mountains.

Dad put his arm around the shoulders of the boy. "What a vacation, Huh?"

"The best," replied Joseph.

Joseph watched the yellow lines in the middle of the road appear and disappear in the headlights in seemingly endless monotony as they drove through the darkness. Joseph leaned his head against the window of the truck to rest his weary eyes for a moment.

Slowly, Joseph became aware of flashing red and blue lights; he looked out the window of the truck into the night sky to see a giant spacecraft with red and blue lights flashing above them. He heard an ominous deep female metallic monotone voice: "Release my baby!" Joseph perceived that the truck was no longer moving. He felt the truck and trailer being lifted off the road toward the alien craft. He felt powerless to do anything. He looked down toward the ground and closed his eyes, then slowly opened them. When he looked up again the spacecraft was gone, but the flashing red and blue lights still illuminated the interior of the cab.

"Don't you know you can't haul wide loads after four pm?" the highway patrolman demanded.

The flashing red and blue lights from the patrol car reflected off the mirrors and lit up the inside of the truck.

I must have been dreaming, Joseph thought with great relief as he pinched his cheek to make sure he was really awake.

"I'll need your commercial driver's license, your wide load permit, proof of insurance, and the registration for the truck and the trailer. Oh yeah, I'll also need your over length permit – your load is hanging over the end of the trailer at least ten feet," the officer directed, as he walked to the back of the trailer and began untying the rope holding the tarp. He flipped the tarp back and shined his flashlight at the feet of the robot hanging over the end of the trailer.

Thomas watched him in the rear view mirror with dread as he got his commercial driver's license and insurance card from his wallet and the registrations from the clip on the sun visor.

"What's your story?" asked the patrolman, when he returned to the driver's door.

"We found this giant space robot out in the middle of the desert and we're going to take it to Area 51," announced Joseph, with a tone of sober seriousness.

The officer paused for a moment as he involuntarily pursed

17

his lips, as if he were trying to hold in some invisible force. Suddenly, a burst of air escaped, followed by an explosive thunder of laughter so powerful that tears were rolling down his cheeks by the time he finally, partially, regained his composure.

"Actually..." began Dad, as the officer held up his hand.

"I know..." interrupted the officer, still laughing a little. "Tomorrow is the 4th of July and you are going to Salt Lake City for the parade and you couldn't get your float ready in time."

"Well..." continued Dad, as the officer raised his hand again.

With another chuckle, the officer said, "It's okay I've heard that half the floats aren't ready until the parade starts. Good luck and drive safe." As he turned back toward his car they heard him say to himself, "Area 51!" Then they heard another restrained burst of laughter, "I love it."

After tightening the tarp and the straps, they resumed their journey and were soon pulling onto the gravel country lane where they lived. Their place was a little twenty-acre farmlet. Thomas loved trees so he had planted several hundred of them on the property years before, so now they had a nice secluded mountain feel to the place.

"I think we'll back the whole trailer with the giant on it into the barn," said Dad. Thomas had built it with a woodshop in the east wing, a truck shop in the lower portion of the center with a large loft above it, and a tinkering and welding shop in the west wing.

Joseph jumped out of the truck to guide it into the barn. "Ho!" he yelled when it was in the perfect spot.

"We'll take a closer look at it when we get back tomorrow," said Dad, as they closed the doors to the barn.

CHAPTER THREE

"Human...oid?"

JOSEPH WAS AWAKENED BY THE FABULOUS AROMA OF breakfast wafting through the house. As he entered the kitchen, Sharianna turned from the fridge and put a gallon of milk on the table. "We thought you were going to sleep all day."

"Where is Dad?" Joseph asked, as he looked out the window toward the barn.

"He left early this morning to get the backhoe, saying that you needed some sleep. Sit down and have some French toast," answered Mom.

Sophia put the source of the exquisite aroma on the table and sat down next to Joseph. "Tell us about your adventure," she encouraged, with authentic interest.

"You have to come out and see this giant statue-thing we found," Joseph declared, as he began to rise from his chair.

"I want to see it!" exclaimed Sharianna, as she headed for the door.

Mom put her hand on Joseph's shoulder. "It will still be there after breakfast. Come and sit down Sharianna. Now, tell us everything," she entreated with earnestness. She didn't tell Joseph and Sharianna that Thomas couldn't wait to tell her everything and had even drug her out to the barn long before dawn to unveil the figure with all the excitement of a five year old on Christmas morning.

They ate, and the girls listened intently.

Finally, when breakfast was done and the whole adventure was fully expounded, Mom said: "Well, let's go out and see this strange thing."

"Prepare yourselves..." Joseph admonished with great drama,

19

as he opened the man-door next to the two large main doors of the barn. Sharianna and Mom stepped into the dim interior. "The aberration!" announced Joseph, as he dramatically turned on the lights.

"Wow..." Sophia had meant to let out an exaggerated gasp to go along with Joseph's theatrical introduction, but she realized that her amazement was as strong now, as when Thomas had shown her the giant hours earlier.

Joseph walked all around the figure showing them every detail. "See, it doesn't even dent or scratch." He took a hammer from the workbench and banged it on the side of the figure.

Joseph grabbed a stepladder off the wall and leaned it against the giant. "You have to look at it close up." He swung a step stool over and climbed up. Putting his face against the side of the figure, he held his hands up to the sides of his face and peered into the depths. "Like this."

Sophia climbed the stepladder and peered into the metal. "It does look never-ending," she concurred with amazement.

"Let me see," demanded Sharianna, as she pulled on Joseph's pant leg. He climbed down and let her have the stool.

"I wonder what could be inside," Mom mused mysteriously, as she climbed down the ladder and looked up at the figure. "Maybe some treasure, or a message from another world." She smiled as Joseph's face lit up. She knew he loved mysteries, treasure, and adventure.

"You think it might be from outer space?" questioned Sharianna, with excitement overflowing in her voice.

"It might be," whispered Mom furtively.

"Let's see if we can cut it open," proposed Joseph, as he prepared the welding torch and put on the goggles and gloves. He was proud that he was the only seventh grader he knew who could use a cutting torch and a welder. After about five minutes of holding the flame to the side of the figure, Joseph turned off the torch and looked at the metal. "It's not even red."

Sophia waved her hand over the metal, and then tentatively touched it. "It's still cool," she observed with wonderment.

They heard the sound of wheels rolling over the gravel

driveway.

"That sounds like Dad in the dump truck," announced Joseph.

They turned and looked when the door opened and Thomas stepped through. Looking at Sophia in her nightgown he whistled loudly. "You pretty...."

Suddenly, his mouth dropped open as his eyes became riveted on the head of the giant figure lying on the trailer. Joseph, Sharianna and Mom turned to see a four-foot round door silently slide open on the side of the giant's head where there had previously been no seams or other indication that a door existed. They could see light emanating from the interior.

Thomas stepped forward and put a hand on Sharianna's shoulder and the other on Joseph's.

After a few moments of anxiously staring at the doorway, Joseph deduced: "I think Dad's whistle activated it."

"I think you're right," responded Mom.

Dad leaned the ladder up into the doorway. "Stay here," he commanded, as he began to climb the ladder.

"Wait, what if there is something in there?" Mom questioned tensely.

"I doubt it, it must have been buried for hundreds of years," Dad replied with a casual tone, while his heart pounded in his throat as he continued up the ladder.

"It looks like some kind of control room, and it is empty," called out Dad, from the top of the ladder. "I'm going in." He disappeared from their view as he stepped over the top rung of the ladder into the control room.

"I'm coming up!" called out Sharianna and Joseph, almost simultaneously.

"No," countered Mom, as she caught them each by the arm, "It could be dangerous."

Dad stuck his head out the door. "It will be alright. You can all come up. I think it is safe as long as we don't touch anything."

Joseph wanted to fly up the ladder to see what was inside but he stepped aside: "I'll hold the ladder for you, Mom."

Joseph's mom was so proud of him, she almost forgot her

apprehension. She stepped up eagerly. She couldn't believe how curious she was to see the inside.

"Thank you, Joseph. Will you hold the ladder for Sharianna too?"

"Okay," agreed Joseph, reluctantly.

Sharianna smiled sweetly at Joseph. "Thank you," she condescended surreptitiously, as she paused with her foot on the bottom step and nodded her head as if she were a privileged royal princess, delighting in her preeminence over her subjects, and knowing that even the slightest delay was practically unbearable for Joseph.

Joseph was so excited to see the inside of the robot that he could hardly wait for Sharianna. She seemed to climb so slowly that he felt as if she might never reach the top. He could bear it no longer when she paused near the top and glanced down at him with her smile. Joseph shook the ladder slightly and she scrambled quickly over the top. Joseph flew up the ladder so fast that he almost passed her in the doorway.

The interior was small, only about twelve feet across with two control chairs side by side, with joysticks on each armrest, positioned on the same level as the doorway. Directly behind the captain's chairs, and two steps higher were two other chairs right against the back of the sphere, with the outline of an oval door between them. Directly in front of the control chairs and four steps lower was another small level with a sofa-like bench.

There was a wide screen directly in front of the captain's chairs, angled slightly like a desktop, with a beautiful display of earth's solar system, the sun, and each of the planets with their moons. Earth was lit up. It even showed the asteroid belt and the position of many comets. Below these screens were several lights labeled with strange symbols and pictures.

The entire wall in front of the chairs, from the midpoint of the ceiling all the way to the floor of the lower level and from the door on the left around to the right of the control chairs, was a huge curved view screen. The view was so perfect that at first they thought the hull of the ship must be transparent from the inside. In the exact center of the screen was a small red dot.

"Look." Dad pointed to the view screen. They saw Percy stop in the doorway of the barn and look in. With a slight whine, he laid down.

"That's remarkable, I could hear Percy whine as if I were standing right with him," Mom observed. Percy was black with a white patch on his chest and white paws. Their best guess was that he was half Labrador Retriever and half Border Collie. They had found him a few years earlier, as a lost pup in the hills.

Joseph sat down in the left control chair, then quickly stood up again and looked on the chair. Reaching out, he grabbed three beautiful, smooth, rounded stones and held them out for his dad to see.

"Interesting," Dad commented.

"Look." Sharianna held out a similar stone. "I found this one right by the door."

"What could they mean?" puzzled Mom.

A disconcerting thought occurred to Joseph. "How could these round stones be sitting on the seat?"

"Someone left them there." Sharianna's tone intimated: 'why do you ask such stupid questions?'

Joseph looked at his dad while rolling the stones around in his hand.

Suddenly, Dad's jaw dropped and his eyes widened as he looked around the room a little nervously.

Witnessing this strange interchange, Mom's penetrating look captured Dad's eye. "*What*?" demanded Mom with unquestionable authority.

"The stones would have fallen off the seat during the crash landing," he explained.

"Maybe they were placed there after it landed," theorized Sharianna.

"But we rolled the robot completely over when we loaded it onto the trailer," countered Joseph. "And the robot was lying on its face when we found it—the chairs would have been hanging upside down."

"They must have landed on the chair when you rolled it over," proposed Sharianna.

Joseph looked up at the smooth, domed, ceiling. "When we found the robot, it was on its face; if they were lying on the ceiling, then they would have slid along the curved surface as we rolled it over. All four of them would have ended up on the floor by the door."

This time it was Sharianna who looked around wondering who could have put the rocks on the chair since the day before.

"Well, I don't see any aliens in here now," Mom stated, "Surely, if the ship was buried for hundreds of years there couldn't be anyone still on board. Could there?"

"I wouldn't think so," replied Dad.

Dad sat down in the right control chair at the same time that Sharianna made an attempt to slip past Joseph and take the left. Joseph was slightly faster, and besides, he had been anticipating her move.

Joseph set the stones on the console, as he settled into the chair.

"Every button and switch has some kind of symbols labeling it," observed Sharianna.

"Yeah, but what do they mean?" asked Mom, as she leaned over Joseph to get a better look. As she looked at the console something occurred to her: "If this...ship? Was buried for hundreds of years, then why is everything in here so clean? Shouldn't it be all dusty?"

"The door was perfectly sealed," reasoned Joseph.

"Then wouldn't the air be stale?" she persisted.

"That's a very good point," responded Dad. "I think this..." he gestured at the ship with his hand while he looked at Joseph, searching for the right descriptive word.

"Robo-ship," interjected Joseph.

"Yes, I think this Robo-ship has been fully functional the whole time it was buried. It must have been maintaining a breathable atmosphere."

"I can tell what these mean," declared Joseph, pointing to the labels in front of the left joystick on his chair.

"And these are exactly the same," observed Dad, pointing to those on his chair.

24

Surrounding each joystick were arrows pointing in different directions. In the top of the joysticks, next to a roller button, were drawings of the robot's hands. On the console in between the seats was a switch with two drawings, one of the robot in a vertical position and the other horizontal. Joseph flipped the switch.

"Hey, don't touch anything," reiterated Dad.

"Okay," replied Joseph.

"Here's another one I can understand." Dad pointed to a large toggle switch between the chairs labeled with line drawings of a chair on each side of the switch. "I'm sure this one switches control from one chair to the other." As he pointed to the switch, he reached out and flipped it in the direction of his chair.

"Hey!" Mom tried to muster her scolding voice: "You said not to touch anything." But her heart was pounding with the excitement of the adventure and new discovery and she realized that she liked it. She really wanted to experiment and see what some of the controls and buttons would do. A myriad of thoughts raced through her head all at once: *What if this ship really does work? Where did it come from? Who built it? Why did it crash in the desert? Where is its crew? Were they really aliens?* With this last thought, she looked at her husband and her son comfortably sitting in the control chairs. "They must have been humans, because the chairs and the controls fit you guys so well."

"Maybe they're just human...oid," posed Sharianna, as she looked at Mom to see her reaction. Turning to look at the outline of the doorway between the rear seats, she said with a little trepidation: "Do you think there could be *remains* of any of them in other parts of the ship?"

"That would be cool!" Joseph exclaimed.

They made their way to the door, "Look at the seal on this door," marveled Joseph, as he ran his hand around the edges. "If it weren't for the outline on the door and this push button you would never know there was a door here. It looks like it is one continuous piece."

Sharianna reached around Joseph and pushed the button.

"Careful..." Mom cautioned.

CHAPTER FOUR
The Creature

THE DOOR SEEMED TO DISAPPEAR AS IT SLID INTO THE WALL. Sharianna didn't want Joseph to think she was scared, so she quickly slipped past him and entered the small corridor.

"Wait, Sharianna," directed Dad. But she was so fast and the corridor was only a few feet long that she was already in another room when she stopped. Dad quickly bent down and followed her through the door. This room was larger than the control room, about twelve feet wide and about twenty feet long. It was illuminated in the same manner as the control room, and like the control room, the source of the illumination was a mystery. It seemed to originate from everywhere and yet nowhere, and there were no shadows.

Thomas stopped in the doorway, still bent over as he gazed into the room. Joseph was right behind, with his head bent slightly to one side. He was not yet as tall as Dad, but the ceiling of the hallway was still a little low for him.

"Hey, I can't see a thing," exclaimed Joseph. "Dad, you're blocking the whole door."

Sophia's heart leaped wildly when she heard Sharianna suddenly scream. Her instincts flashed into action as she grabbed Joseph from the corridor and flung him into the control room. Thomas was still blocking the doorway to the next room as she tore through the corridor. They both went sprawling into the room as she collided with him in her headlong rush to save her daughter from unimaginable horror. The world seemed to slow down as Sophia flew through the air. She turned her head to see Sharianna standing to one side smiling. Sophia saw Sharianna's smile morph into an expression of consternation and the words, "Oohhh, Oohhhh," in slow motion escape her lips. Unfortunately, Sophia's world resumed its normal speed as the words faded and she crashed on top of Thomas with a thud.

"Sharianna! What in the world..." demanded Mom with displeasure.

Joseph entered the room and looked at Sharianna.

"So sincerely sorry," stated Sharianna seemingly somewhat sadly; slightly sheepishly. Soon, she suddenly sensed some singularly surreptitious, shrewdly subtle silliness swiftly saturating said smile-soliciting situation.

"You're in trouble now," whispered Joseph from the corner of his mouth, as they both stepped forward to help Mom up.

"Are you okay Mom?" inquired Joseph gallantly, as he reached out his hand.

Thomas rolled over on his side in a relaxed position and, while bracing his head with his hand, watched the interaction with interest. A restrained smile began to spread over his face and his cheeks puffed up as he tried to control the humor welling up inside of him.

Joseph glanced past his mom as they were helping her up and was the first to see his dad still lying on the floor, nearly bursting with comedy. He glanced over at Sharianna, who was holding Mom's other hand and, catching her eye, motioned back at Dad with a small movement of his head. As Sharianna's eyes met her dad's all her apprehension fled and was replaced with his contagious emotion. Simultaneously, all three inadvertently allowed a small laugh to escape, making the suppression of further laughter impossible.

As Sophia stood up amid this raucous uproar she looked at her two children with consternation, then turned to see Thomas attempting to maintain his unlikely appearance of complete composure on the floor, while barely able to keep his head propped up on his elbow, due to the involuntary convulsions of laughter. Sophia was suddenly infected by the mysterious pathogen of mirth—most of her aggravation was swept away.

"I guess it may have been funny, *this* time, but you realize that it could have easily turned out quite bad and someone could have gotten seriously hurt, don't you Sharianna?" Mom

27

questioned, when she regained her composure.

Dad continued to lie on the floor. "We'll have no more screaming or yelling, unless the house is on fire or someone's life is in danger, okay?" Dad's voice carried less than a convincing sternness as he looked from Joseph to Sharianna.

"Okay," agreed Sharianna meekly.

"Hey, I was a victim here too," insisted Joseph, feigning seriousness.

"Remember it for the future," warned Mom.

"I don't think I'll forget this," smiled Joseph with a final chuckle, as he thought about the hilarity of the event. He looked at his mom in amazement and marveled that a woman so small could have such strength.

Dad rolled over onto his back with an imperceptible moan and lay looking at the curved ceiling.

"Are you hurt?" asked Sharianna furtively, as she knelt down next to Dad.

"Look," Dad pointed at the curved ceiling. He rubbed his knee and paused to answer her question: "No, I'm okay."

"I'm so sorry Dad, I didn't mean for you to get hurt."

"I know, it's okay," he consoled her. "Now, look at the ceiling. What do you think?"

"It looks like another door, except it practically takes up the whole ceiling. This must be a cargo area."

"I think you're right," agreed Dad.

Joseph and Mom had been looking at the walls of the room with interest. They were smooth but were covered with the outlines of various sizes of square, rectangular, and even round shapes; and each shape was labeled with a peculiar type of writing.

Mom touched the label of one of the rectangles and out of the wall slid a drawer. "Ah, storage space – I like it." She touched two more and they silently and smoothly slid out of the wall like the first.

"Whoa, hold on there," cautioned Dad, as he stood up and stepped over to look at the drawers.

"If we don't investigate, we'll never learn how it works,"

reasoned Mom.

"Oh, so now you want to learn how it works? Maybe we should even learn how to fly it?" questioned Dad.

"Of course, this is the most exciting thing we have ever done. Besides, as Sharianna said, this is a cargo area; how dangerous could it be?"

"There's another door over there." Sharianna pointed to the far end of the oval room.

"It must go into one of the robot's legs," speculated Joseph.

Mom touched another label. A crack appeared in the floor and a section of it began to rise up. They stepped aside and the section of floor began to unfold into a counter. On one side of the counter five strange shapes began to inflate.

"They're couches," guessed Joseph, as he saw the long horizontal cylinders with one flat side for the seat and another, smaller cylinder for the back.

"And lounge chairs," added Sharianna, as three soft luxurious chairs emerged from the floor.

Under the counter were many more drawers like the ones on the wall, except the fronts of them were transparent. Mom opened one and noticed that cold air flowed from it. She opened several more and found some of them also to be refrigerated.

"It's kind of small in here, but it is organized very efficiently – reminds me of the combined kitchen and living room in our first apartment," commented Mom.

"I'd say it was more like the motor home we rented when we went to Yellowstone," Dad added, "except maybe a little bigger."

As they continued to investigate, they found strange looking containers in some of the drawers. "I think these are cooking or food storage containers," theorized Mom.

"This one is shaped like a frying pan, but it is not made of metal." Sharianna tapped it with her finger.

"These are probably eating utensils." Joseph held up what looked like a pair of chopsticks made of an almost clear plastic type of material, except that they were hinged in the middle and had rings for the thumb and forefinger and the ends that picked up the food were flattened instead of round. Joseph used them deftly as he pretended to pick up and eat some food. "They work quite well, and they are easy to use."

"This must be a kitchen," concluded Mom. "But where are the sink, and the stove?"

Dad sat down in one of the comfortable looking lounge chairs. "Better than my recliner," he commented. "In fact, I have never been so comfortable in my life," he mused. "As if I am suspended in tangible comfort."

"You know what I think is the strangest thing?" Mom pondered thoughtfully.

"What?" replied Dad, from his supernal resting place.

"There are no provisions."

"Maybe they had a machine that created their food for them," speculated Sharianna.

"Or maybe they ate pills," theorized Joseph.

Mom would have put Sherlock Holmes to shame with her analysis of detail and her unsurpassed deductive abilities. "Now, concerning Joseph's premise: If they ate pills there would be no need for all this cooking equipment."

"Maybe they ate reconstituted food made from pills," countered Joseph.

"If they had the technology, and went to all the trouble to reduce their food to miniscule proportions, why not make it ready to eat when it is reconstituted? The same argument applies to Sharianna's premise—no need for a kitchen if your food is produced miraculously. Besides, there aren't even any pills here."

Mom continued her detective work: "And look here, these drawers are cold inside, like a refrigerator, and yet they are empty...and perfectly clean."

"So...?" Joseph queried for further explanation of her conclusions.

"I think this ship was lost by mistake or by accident, even before its first planned trip," deduced Mom.

"What makes you think it was its first trip?" marveled Dad.

"Well, first off, it looks brand new, and second, if I were stocking the kitchen, I would have a variety of foodstuffs, some perishable and some not. Even if you cleaned out the kitchen after each trip, you wouldn't remove the long lived items like salt and pepper."

"And the ship was unmanned when it was lost!" exclaimed Joseph.

"Now it's getting interesting. And how do you deduce that?" asked Dad, looking at Joseph.

"There is nobody here...alive or dead," he replied.

"Maybe they left when they landed," suggested Dad.

"But the ship did not land, it crashed, remember the crater?" argued Joseph.

"Maybe they buried their escape route when they left the ship. Or maybe it was covered by erosion," continued Dad.

"Why would they leave their ship when it was still perfectly functional?" Joseph's logic appeared to triumph.

Sharianna seemingly shattered Joseph's logic when she pulled the smooth stone from her pocket and waved it in front of Joseph's face: "Who moved the stones," she said mysteriously.

Mom had moved over to the other door. "You forget, we haven't searched the whole ship yet, there could still be aliens on board." Sophia wondered how she could feel two conflicting emotions so strongly and yet simultaneously. *Why am I so apprehensive, and yet filled with such an overpowering need for more adventure?* she thought to herself. With that, she touched the large flat button on the door. It slid into the wall, revealing a narrow hallway; it was taller and narrower and longer than the first corridor. In fact, it was tapered – smaller at the floor than at the shoulders – but it was tall enough for Thomas to stand up straight. Along the walls of the corridor were more storage compartments and at the end was another door with a round window in it.

"What do you see?" asked Dad, from the end of the line.

Mom walked to the end of the corridor and looked through the small window in the other door: "A small room with two more doors, one at the end and one in the ceiling," she called back.

"That one has to lead outside," concluded Sharianna, pointing

31

to the one in the ceiling. "We are in the leg of the robot, so the other door must go into the foot."

Sophia opened the door and at that very moment she had the most unusual desire to scream. She could not explain this adolescent desire for drama even if she had to. She capitulated to the desire at the very same time she told herself it was ridiculous and irresponsible, especially after the tongue lashing she had given Sharianna. She tried to suck it back in, but some of it had escaped; more like a loud gasp than a scream.

This time Thomas' heart leaped but before he had time to act he heard Sharianna, who was right behind Mom and could see into the doorway, "Mom! I can't believe you!"

"Sorry. I couldn't resist," confessed Mom.

"What's the punishment for crying wolf? Huh Dad?" demanded Joseph in a loud stern voice, as he looked back at Dad with a smile.

"I'll have to think of a good one," replied Dad loudly, with a wink.

Mom stepped across the small room and opened the oposite door.

"I think it might be a bathroom," called Mom, "but it has a steeply sloped floor." She stepped into the small room expecting to climb up the floor; but to her surprise, the floor suddenly seemed level to her. The upper part of one wall was as reflective as a mirror, but it seemed to be a continuous part of the wall. It was the seat jutting out from the wall with an elongated hole in it that gave it away as a bathroom. At the far end of the room was a strange looking gold dial on the wall. *But where is the sink?* She thought to herself.

"Mom," said Sharianna in an apprehensive voice.

Sophia turned and looked back into the hallway to discover that while the bathroom floor was now level from her perspective, the hallway floor now seemed inclined.

"Mom, you're leaning."

"No, *you're* all leaning."

"That's weird," declared Joseph, as Sharianna stepped into the room next to her mom and he saw her orientation shift.

"Come in," said Sharianna, with a wave of her hand.

Joseph also stepped into the tiny room, expecting something strange, but he experienced nothing; it all seemed normal – like stepping through any other doorway.

"Okay, Mrs. Detective, explain that," challenged Dad, as he stood in the doorway.

Joseph began to develop a theory by stating the facts: "We are in the foot."

"And the foot is pointed rearward with the bottom of the foot sloping upward," added Mom.

"The ship must be able to manipulate gravity so that we are always standing straight up, no matter what our orientation to the earth is," concluded Sharianna, with smug satisfaction.

"How old are you?" asked Dad with a smile.

"Then it must have artificial gravity when in space!" Joseph deduced.

"That must be why the round stones were still on the seat. The ship maintained the gravity according to its orientation, not the earth," reasoned Mom with obvious relief, as she realized that the stones on the seat did not mean there were aliens on board. "But why were they there in the first place?" she wondered.

Dad crowded into the small room.

Joseph stood looking at a gold-colored pipe that curved downward from the lower part of the mirror section. "That must be the faucet."

"But there is no sink…" argued Sharianna, as Joseph reached out and put his hand under the pipe.

Water suddenly gushed out onto his hand and he jerked it back in time for everyone to see the water miraculously "flow" through mid air and disappear into the wall below the faucet.

"Whoa," said Joseph softly. "I guess you don't need a sink." He elbowed Sharianna discretely for emphasis.

"Wow!" exclaimed Dad. "It must be able to manipulate gravity in a very specific way."

Sharianna reached out and touched one of the labels on either side of the faucet. A wide shallow drawer silently slid out of the wall. "More storage."

Mom stepped to the back of the room and turned a strange looking gold dial on the wall. To her surprise, she was suddenly getting soaked with water spraying directly out of the ceiling and the wall, even though there were no spray heads.

Sharianna saw the water spraying on Mom and stepped back instinctively. As the water sprayed toward her it seemed to be hitting some kind of transparent partition. She reached out her hand to touch it, but only felt the water spraying on her hand as it passed through where she thought the partition was. She quickly pulled her hand back in surprise, and was shocked to discover that it was dry.

Mom quickly turned the dial back to its original position and turned to look at her family.

"I think I found the shower," she said, looking very humble, and soaking wet. "I think I'll go get some dry clothes. She took a step toward Sharianna, but as she passed the point where the invisible barrier had been, she was suddenly dry—even her hair was dry and fluffy. Sophia felt her arms in amazement: "You don't even need a towel!"

"Incredible!" exclaimed Dad. "There must be some kind of invisible barrier that prevents only the water from passing through, keeping it in the shower area."

Mom looked at the floor of the shower area that was now completely dry. "There is not even a drain; where does the water go?"

"The water seemed to be absorbed directly into the floor," explained Joseph.

"Shhh. Listen," whispered Dad earnestly, with his finger to his lips.

They could hear sounds emanating from the control room. Dad turned to face the intruder down the hallway, his body blocking the family's whole view. They could hear the faint sound of rapid breathing and a strange clicking sound.

"It sounds like claws on the floor," whispered Joseph.

"It's getting closer." Sharianna breathed nearly silently while her heart seemed to make a loud racket, pounding in her chest. *Quiet*, she thought silently to her palpitating heart.

Dad stepped to the corridor, hands clenched into tight fists, his knees bent, ready to attack anything that should appear at the other end of the corridor.

Sophia looked at his back as he filled the narrow corridor. Suddenly she felt a great swelling of love for this man who would fight for his family.

At that moment the creature creating the sounds came into Thomas's view at the end of the corridor. Thomas charged down the length of the hall, with Joseph at his heels. He tackled the creature and rolled off to one side.

It all happened so fast that Sophia didn't have time to react. When Joseph disappeared around the edge of the doorway, she suddenly sprang to life. Pushing past Sharianna, she raced down the hall amid the sounds of ferocious battle and terrible growling.

Sophia burst upon the scene of battle and leaped toward the rolling mass of flashing teeth and black and white fur, and Thomas.

She suddenly stopped. "Percy! Thomas!" she yelled, when she saw Dad and Percy rolling around in mock battle, both of them growling like wild, ferocious beasts.

"I think there is just a little too much goofing around in this family!" scolded Sharianna, as she stood in the doorway with her hands on her hips.

CHAPTER FIVE

The Neanderthal Twins

JOSEPH WOKE WITH THE SUNLIGHT STREAMING THROUGH HIS window; it split and refracted into different colors as it struck his crystal collection on the windowsill. The morning was particularly quiet; all he could hear was the occasional raspy cry of a magpie in the tree in the yard.

From his window, Joseph could see through the trees, across the backyard, to the barn.

On his way to the barn he made a compulsory stop in the kitchen. On the counter was a note: "Went with Grandma to the doctor—I'll be back this afternoon. Mom."

Joseph opened the cupboard and stared blankly at the granola, cheerios, and cornflakes. As he stood, wondering why they couldn't have something that tasted better, he suddenly seemed to hear his mom's voice in his head: "You might as well give your kids a candy bar for breakfast as feed them those sugar cereals."

He opened the pantry, but there were no candy bars, so he turned to the fridge. There, on the middle shelf, was a huge piece of carrot cake with thick cream cheese frosting. *Just as good as a candy bar*, he thought, as he reached for the cake.

Taped to one of the rungs of the ladder leading to the control room of the ship was a note from Dad:

Don't touch the controls.

Joseph sat down in one of the comfortable chairs in the lounge area of the cargo bay and enjoyed the last of his cake. He felt so relaxed, as if he were almost floating in the air.

He glanced down the hallway toward the bathroom that they had discovered the day before. As he looked, he noticed that a section of one side of the hallway wall was not covered with storage compartments. Instead, there was a single label. He got up and pressed the label. The wall rolled back and revealed eight strange looking overalls hanging from a rack. They were clear and seemed quite large. They reminded Joseph of the huge overalls that painters sometimes wear, except that these were almost transparent and had a strange looking hoodie attached to them.

No, they look like some kind of one-piece haz-mat suit, he thought to himself. At the wrist, elbows, knees shoulders, hips and feet were pieces of the same metal as the hull of the ship. The pieces on the wrist were about three inches long and two inches wide. The rest of the pieces were about the size of an old time silver dollar.

"Maybe they are spacesuits!" commented Joseph out loud. He looked around for air tanks but could not find any. He pulled one of them off the rack and began to try it on. He felt like he was putting on a giant pajama sleeper because it was open from the hood all the way down to one ankle. But he could not see any zipper, snaps or other way to close it. He pulled the edges of the suit together where the zipper should have been.

At that moment, Sharianna appeared in the doorway. She gasped at what she saw: as soon as the two edges of the suit touched each other, they stuck together, like two magnets. It seemed to Joseph that there was a magical, or invisible, zipper automatically going both directions.

Sharianna screamed as she saw the suit zip up by itself. At the same time it began to shrink, until it fit perfectly snug on all of Joseph's body; with the exception of his head, which had about a half-inch clearance all around. The more it shrunk, the more clear the material became until it was virtually invisible, except for the small pieces of metal.

"Hey, it fits," proclaimed Joseph, apparently calm, except for an almost imperceptible squeak in his voice that gave away some of his nervousness.

"Can you breathe?" questioned Sharianna.

"Yes."

"Can you move?"

"Yes," he answered, as he took a step toward her.

Without warning, his mouth dropped open and his hands shot to his neck; he mouthed the words: "Help me."

Sharianna instantly jumped toward him and tore at the invisible suit, pulling on the material where the zipper should have been, only to have it stretch and flex, but not come apart. Suddenly, Joseph burst into laughter.

"That's not funny!" she scolded, as she gave him a shove.

"Yes it is," Joseph replied, still chuckling.

"It feels like I'm not even wearing it!" exclaimed Joseph, as he moved his arms and jumped up and down.

Joseph pulled on the material with both hands where it had gone together and it easily pulled apart. When he let it go, it resealed itself.

"How come it wouldn't come apart when I pulled on it?" demanded Sharianna.

Joseph pulled the seal apart again. "I don't know. Maybe it only responds to itself." Joseph held up his hands and Sharianna pulled on one of his fingers. As the material stretched she observed: "It's like a latex glove."

"Except that it's clear," responded Joseph.

Sharianna touched the invisible material that covered Joseph's face. "It's hard. How come I can hear your voice like normal? It isn't muffled or anything."

"I don't know."

"Do you think it's a spacesuit?" she asked.

"I couldn't find any oxygen tanks," he replied. "I don't know if it takes the air from outside, or if it uses what is already in here."

Sharianna began to put on one of the other suits. "I know how to find out."

"How?" asked Joseph.

"Follow me."

They got their bikes from the garage.

"Where are we going?" asked Joseph.

"To the lake." They called it a lake even though it was really a reservoir.

As they rode down the road, Joseph noticed that he couldn't even tell that Sharianna was wearing the alien suit over her regular clothes, except that her hair looked kind of flat and did not blow in the wind.

"Wait!" called Joseph, as he stopped on the side of the road. "Let's take the bike trail along the creek."

"Yeah, less chance of being seen," Sharianna concurred.

They were about halfway to the lake, riding side by side, when they noticed two motorbikes coming the other way.

"Oh no. It's the goony twins," moaned Joseph.

"I hate those bullies." Sharianna shared Joseph's contempt for the twins.

"Just keep on riding and ignore them," cautioned Joseph.

As they approached each other, the riders on the motorcycles suddenly slammed on their back brakes and skidded sideways, blocking the entire path. Joseph and Sharianna could barely stop before they plowed right into them.

"Look, it's the wash rats." Don spat into the dust as he spoke the derogatory words.

"Hey, where did you find those old pieces of trash?" Dan sneered, as he looked at their bikes. "The thrift store?"

"No, the landfill," countered Don. "Didn't you know that's where they get everything?"

"Yeah, your parents drive old junk, so why wouldn't you?"

Joseph felt a surge of anger. It was true, that their bikes were old, but they were still in good shape. Sophia and Thomas had bought them new with the intent to ride them regularly even before Joseph and Sharianna were born, but they had sat idle in the basement until Joseph and Sharianna were old enough to ride.

"I thought we told you that this was our personal bike trail," mocked Dan.

"I guess you'll just have to pay," echoed his brother.

"Leave us alone!" commanded Sharianna sharply, as she tried to ride around the bullies.

Dan gunned his motorcycle and bumped into her front tire, knocking her down. "Or what?" he taunted, laughing.

Joseph was fuming mad now as he got off his bike. "Leave her alone!" he yelled.

"Oooh, look at the big tough man," jeered Don, as he flipped his kickstand and got off his motorcycle. "What'cha gonna do about it?" he scoffed, in a challenging voice with a disdainful upward nod of his chin. He stepped toward Joseph with his elbows out, fists clenched and his chest puffed out.

Joseph looked up at the twin that dwarfed him by more than a foot in width as well as height. He wondered if David was this scared when he stood up to Goliath. The difference was that David had a sling and didn't have to grapple with the giant, while Joseph had nothing. Joseph glanced at Sharianna, still on the ground. He saw her hand curl around a baseball size rock with a long jagged point as she stood up and faced the other hulking twin.

Dan got off his motorcycle and came toward Sharianna, but stopped when he saw the jagged shard protruding from her fist.

"What are you gonna do? Stick me with that?" he asked.

"Yes I am," she retorted calmly, with determination flashing from her eyes.

Dan took a step back. Bullies, even big bullies, are usually only bullies when others cower.

By this time, Don had covered the distance to Joseph with a couple of giant size steps.

"I don't want to fight," insisted Joseph.

"Good," replied Don, as he faked with his left while swinging a ham-sized right that caught Joseph square in the face. In the split second before the impact Joseph winced in anticipated pain...but he felt nothing. Instead, he heard Don groan in agony. Don stepped back as he cradled his injured hand.

The encounter was so intense for Joseph that he had momentarily forgotten that he was wearing the alien suit. Immediately, he realized that the 'helmet' had reflected the force of Don's punch.

Dan turned from Sharianna toward Joseph.

40

Sharianna picked up her bike and looked at the front tire, it was a little bent but looked like it would still roll. She pushed it between the two motorbikes and jumped on.

"Come on Joseph! Let's go!"

Joseph jumped back on his bike and made for the gap between the motorcycles. Dan leaped over and gave Joseph a shove on the shoulder. As Joseph fell, he crashed into one of the motorcycles, knocking it down. Both the hulking Neanderthals now leaped toward Joseph with the intent to really teach him a lesson. In desperation, Joseph swung as hard as he could at Dan's gut. Dan doubled over in pain as his feet lifted off the ground and he landed on the other motorcycle, knocking it to the ground.

Realizing that the suit must be enhancing his strength, Joseph turned with a little more confidence as Don swung at him with his good hand. Joseph caught his fist as if it were softball, pulled Don toward him and grabbed him by the belt and tossed him onto the heap that was his brother.

Sharianna had stopped and witnessed the interchange with amazement.

"Are you going to leave us alone?" Joseph demanded, pointing at the pile of bully with a squeak in his voice from the adrenaline.

The two bullies meekly nodded.

As Joseph rode away with Sharianna, Dan said with a moan: "I think he's been taking Karate lessons."

Don rubbed his hand. "He's got a hard head. Let's keep this to ourselves."

"Wow!" exclaimed Sharianna, as they rode down the trail. "How did you do that?"

"Adrenaline."

"You don't think it was the suit?"

"Probably," Joseph replied. "Dan did feel a lot lighter than I expected, when I threw him on top of Don."

"Wasn't it Don you threw onto Dan?"

"What's the diff? Goons are goons," quipped Joseph, as they both laughed.

41

When they approached the lake, Joseph turned onto a barely discernable trail that appeared to lead away from the lake, but in reality doubled back to a secluded alcove nestled between some low cliffs. The trail was strewn with rocks, branches and the occasional fallen tree.

Sharianna could see her front wheel wobbling, and wondered if it would hold up as she bunny hopped over the logs that blocked the path. She was impressed by her own ability to climb, without even stopping, right up the big rocky hill that protected the alcove from most other casual explorers. Usually, she had to push her heavy bike up the hill – it really wasn't that heavy, only when compared to the new super light composite bikes some of the other kids had at school.

Sharianna loved to shop with her mom and still enjoyed imagining that she was a princess, but she also loved the outdoors and this was her favorite swimming spot on the whole lake; it was worth the trouble it took to reach it.

"How about that? I didn't have to stop, even once," Shariana bragged, as she probed for a compliment.

"Yeah, I didn't have to either," commented Joseph, as he stashed his bike in some bushes.

Sharianna hid her bike too, and followed Joseph to the edge of the small cliff that overlooked the alcove. It was only about ten feet high, but always looked a little too formidable to her. She was a good swimmer, but the water was so clear in this spot that she could see the rocks on the bottom, and she had to admit, *that* was a little *too* scary.

Joseph stepped to the edge and looked down at the rocks on the bottom. They looked very close to the surface, but he knew they were over twelve feet deep, because one time he had tied both his and Sharianna's fishing poles together and probed the depths with it.

"If you can beat the Cro-Magnon twins then why are you scared of a little cliff?" he silently asked himself. Joseph's heart was pounding as he took a few steps back and, with a quick run, leaped off the cliff. As he was flying through the air, it occurred to him how strange it was to be jumping in fully clothed.

Normally, when they came to the lake on a warm summer day they would wear their swimsuits. Joseph took a deep involuntary breath and closed his eyes a moment before he plunged into the water. It was a very odd sensation for Joseph as he felt the water flow over his body without feeling its wetness. He opened his eyes and exhaled; then he forced himself to take a small breath. The euphoria that flowed through him was a singularly unique emotion. He realized that he *really* could breathe under water. He wanted to explore the whole lake.

Sharianna watched as he splashed feet first into the water. The splash and the ripples momentarily made it so she could no longer see the bottom. As the ripples cleared, she looked and saw Joseph swimming around among the large boulders on the bottom. Finally, after what seemed like a long time, he made a lazy ascent. When his head slowly broke through the surface, she could see an enormous smile.

"*Well?*" she inquired.

"See for yourself," proposed Joseph, with a wave of his hand. "I dare you."

The call of exploration, and Joseph's challenge, was too great for Sharianna. Overcoming her fear, she took a running leap and screamed, with both exhilaration and trepidation, as she flew through the air and plunged into the cold water—except that it didn't feel cold.

Sharianna involuntarily held her breath until she reached the surface, and then she took a deep breath.

"You don't have to hold your breath, you know," Joseph informed her.

"I couldn't help it."

Sharianna was an excellent swimmer, so she dove down and swam toward the bottom, and then without stopping she began to swim toward deeper water. Joseph was hard-pressed to keep up with her.

Sharianna stopped and pointed to a hollow under a large boulder. "Look," she mouthed the word. There, resting in the shade, sat an enormous catfish. Joseph swam toward the huge whiskered beast but it darted swiftly away into deeper water.

"Whiskers, come back here," coaxed Joseph.

"Hey, I can hear you, even though we're under water," Sharianna exclaimed.

"Cool! There must be some kind of walkie-talkie built right into the suits," replied Joseph.

As they swam along the shore, they could hear splashing and discovered that five of their friends from school were playing near the shore. The water was a little murky from all their splashing about. Sharianna smiled as she got a mischievous idea. She motioned to Joseph and reached out as if she were grabbing some imaginary legs. Joseph smiled wide and with a nod swam toward their unsuspecting friends.

Pandemonium reigned when Alison screamed in utter terror.

"Something has a hold of me!" she screamed, as Joseph grabbed onto her ankle and didn't let go.

Slowly, he dragged her a couple of feet toward deeper water, before relinquishing his grip. As she scrambled to get away, he momentarily grabbed her other ankle, creating even more panic.

At about the same time, Sharianna grabbed Cameron, who also panicked. The others had no choice but to believe that something was attacking their friends because their screams were so real and unexpected. They all stampeded for shore.

Joseph and Sharianna swam away right on the bottom, until they got behind a boulder a short distance away, where they surfaced to watch their panicked friends scramble out of the water.

"Cameron screamed like a little girl," Joseph commented, in between laughs.

"So did Alison," giggled Sharianna.

"She is a girl."

"I know, but she sure did scream, didn't she?"

"I can't wait to hear them tell the story of how they were almost dragged down into the lake by some horrible monster," laughed Joseph.

"Yeah, me too!" agreed Sharianna. "We'd better be getting home; I forgot to leave a note for Mom and Dad."

CHAPTER SIX

"A Test Try, Not A Test Fly."

"WHEN ARE WE GOING TO TAKE THE ROBOT OUT FOR A TEST try? Huh Dad?" queried Joseph.

"Yeah, Dad. You said we'd take it out after investigating the interior," pressed Sharianna.

Mom looked across the breakfast table at Dad as he looked up from his notes. "Why not today?" she asked. "I don't think we can learn another thing until we experiment some more."

Dad glanced out the window toward the tarp covering the big hole in the side of the barn and the hole in the roof that resulted from his last attempt to experiment with the cabin controls.

A wry smile spread across Joseph's face as he interrupted Dad's pondering: "At least we know two of the controls: The arm...and firing the laser beam."

"And it's a good thing the robot was on its back and facing the sky, or someone's house might have been destroyed with that laser," observed Dad.

"But it only put an eight inch hole in the roof," argued Mom.

"*Only* an eight inch hole?" Dad got a worried look on his face as he contemplated the damage that could be done with the robot, if the wrong people gained control of it.

"Let's take it out of the barn and experiment in the yard. That way it won't destroy the barn," Sharianna suggested.

"It's forty-seven feet tall! Someone would surely see it," Dad countered.

"That's with its toes pointed. I'll bet it's not more than... forty-two feet standing flat footed," returned Joseph. "That's only about the same length as our school bus."

"That's still taller than a three story building," argued Dad.

"But our trees give us some privacy. Besides, our nearest neighbors are a quarter of a mile away. And the robot does not make any noise when it moves," reasoned Mom.

Dad declared, with a tone of finality: "Unless you smash something; besides, I'm sure you could still see the head through the tree tops. What if someone were to come over? It's just too risky."

Joseph looked at Mom, then back to Sharianna with a look of: 'do something.'

"What about at night? The robot looks almost black. Nobody could see it unless they were right here in the yard...and we could lock the front gate," begged Sharianna in her sweetest voice, while looking at her dad with her big green eyes and her beautiful smile.

He melted: "I guess that would work," he conceded, all his defensive posture now dissipated. "Think you kids can stay up till two am?"

"Dad, this is more exciting than Christmas!" exclaimed Sharianna.

"And you can't stay up for that," Joseph teased.

"You're not supposed to," she retorted.

At dusk, Thomas locked the front gate, then hitched up the trailer and pulled the robot out of the barn. He didn't want to take the chance of waking any neighbors with the noise of the dump truck in the middle of the night. He looked around and was glad they had planted so many trees years earlier. The large barn blocked most of the view of the neighbors from one side, while the trees created a pretty good screen with only a few gaps on the other sides. He was pretty confident that with the cover of night they would not be detected.

Sophia came out of the house carrying grocery bags, with Sharianna carrying her sleeping bag and a large soft body pillow, almost as large as herself.

Dad looked at them with a quizzical look.

"If we have to wait till two, then *I'm* going to be *comforta-*

ble," Sharianna emphasized.

"There's four more bags on the kitchen table," directed Mom, "and grab my purse."

"We're just going to experiment a little with the controls," groaned Dad.

"Just a few snacks and some food for breakfast; I'm going to try out the kitchen in the morning," she replied, as she walked past him without pausing. "What use is a kitchen if there is no food in it?" she reasoned.

As Dad was heading for the house, Joseph emerged carrying a huge fluffy beanbag. Dad held out both his hands with a silent expression of: 'Now what are you doing?'

Joseph tossed the bean chair into his hands. "Thanks Dad," he said, as he turned back into the house to get his iPod.

"This won't even fit through the door!" exclaimed Dad.

"You just have to stuff it through. It'll fit," called Joseph, as the screen door closed behind him.

Finally, everyone had everything they thought they might need for the night. Dad slipped into one of the captain's chairs and continued to study his notes, comparing them with the buttons, switches and controls.

"What's first?" asked Sharianna, as she sat in the other captain's chair.

"I think I have figured out how to make it stand up. Then we will try taking a few slow steps and maybe try out the hands to see if we can pick something up."

"Then we'll fly?" she asked eagerly.

"NO. No flying."

"*Daaaaad...*"

"Nope. *Nooo* flying."

"Awwww," she moaned in a disappointed, begging voice.

"We need to master ground travel first."

"Hey, what about Percy?" asked Joseph, through a mouthful of Doritos as he emerged from the hallway.

"I'm not going to carry him down the ladder again," complained Dad.

"You only carried him about halfway down," retorted Shari-

47

anna, with a tiny restrained laugh.

Dad smiled, "Okay, I'm not going to *fall* down the ladder with him again."

"You won't need to. Once the robot is off the trailer, we'll be able to walk right out the ankle door, onto the foot," Joseph replied.

Dad looked at the view screen on the wall where he could see Percy with a very sad looking face sitting at the bottom of the ladder. "Okay, but you're in charge of him."

Joseph stepped to the doorway. "Here boy, come on Percy!"

Percy seemed to smile as he jumped up and began climbing the ladder. Thomas always marveled how easy it was to read Percy's emotions. "And some people say animals don't have emotions!"

When Percy reached the top, Joseph tossed him a Dorito.

"I think that dog eats more people food than dog food," observed Mom from the doorway. "Anyone else want some more *people* food? Nachos? Chips?" Three 'yes's' and one bark told her she hadn't wasted her time.

"What time is it?" Joseph asked.

"About eleven," replied Mom.

"T-minus three hours to launch," he announced. "Do we really have to wait until two am?"

"T-minus three hours to walk," countered Sharianna. "We're not going to fly it tonight," she explained in response to Joseph's questioning expression.

"I thought we were going to test fly it," stated Joseph, looking from Sharianna to Dad.

"No, I agreed to a test *try*, not a test *fly*," Dad corrected.

CHAPTER SEVEN

"Look Out!"

THOMAS STRAIGHTENED UP AND LOOKED AROUND AS HE LEFT the small passageway from the control room and entered the cargo bay, which was now transformed into the kitchen and living room. He wondered why the builders of the robot had made this corridor so small. *Maybe they were small people*, he thought to himself. *Or maybe they were just conserving space.* He shrugged his shoulders to himself and let his eye scan the small, yet well organized room. It had been unusually quiet for a while. Sophia was asleep on the sofa. Joseph and Percy seemed almost enveloped in the giant beanbag. Percy opened one eye and watched Thomas with a tiny little wag in his tail. *Too comfortable to even open both eyes, huh boy?* he thought.

Sharianna was asleep on her big pillow with her old fashioned Cinderella alarm clock next to her on the floor. He remembered when she had gotten it; on the beautiful trip they had taken to Disneyland when she was only six. She was dressed in her princess dress exuding with thrilling excitement to meet the princesses and get their autographs. "I'm a lucky man," he said to himself, as he thought of all the great times spent with Sophia and their kids.

The loud clanging of the alarm clock's hammer bouncing between the two shiny chrome bells, advertising that it was five to two, shattered his reminiscence.

Sharianna jumped up, grabbed the alarm clock and rushed past Dad. "Let's go, it's almost two," she announced energetically.

Joseph continued to lay on the bean bag, he spread his arms wide with a big yawn and seemed to be falling back to sleep, when he suddenly realized what Sharianna was up to. He sprang to life so fast that he almost caught up to her by the time she leaped into one of the captain's chairs.

Thomas looked through the doorway to see who had won the coveted seat.

"Let's see if you can drive this thing as good as all your study should warrant," teased Sophia, as she came up behind him and put her hand on his arm.

"Okay, looks like Sharianna's advance planning paid off," declared Dad, as he motioned to Joseph to vacate the other captain's chair.

"Daaad," complained Joseph.

Dad motioned his head toward the empty chair next to Mom at the back of the control room.

Sharianna was smiling from ear to ear. She bounced up and down a little in her seat, overflowing with anticipation.

"Everyone put on your seat belts," instructed Mom.

"These aren't seat belts, they're just cargo straps slung under the seats," criticized Joseph.

"I'd hate to imagine what would happen if your dad tripped and fell."

"Yeah Dad, you're just a baby learning to walk," teased Sharianna.

"That's right," replied Dad. He looked back at Sophia and blew her a kiss. He knew she was as excited as the kids, but she was still willing to let Sharianna have the copilot's seat.

Sophia looked around the little spherical control room. On the view screen she could see the clear starlit sky. She was apprehensive, but her anxiety was drowned in comparison to her anticipation of adventure.

"Ready? Looks like we have a full moon tonight; I hope no one can see our silhouette." Dad very slowly pushed on the right joystick. From the view screen in front of them they could tell that the robot had sat up on the trailer, but they could feel no sense of movement. "A little bit more..." Still no sense of movement, but they heard the trailer creak. The robot was standing on the back of the trailer, which was now pushed all the way to the ground, creating a pivot point at the axels with the hitch actually lifting the back of the dump truck off the ground.

"Whoa, did you feel that? Better keep your cargo straps on," teased Joseph, as he looked at his mom for a reaction.

"Now, I think this should make it walk forward." Dad slowly pushed forward on the stick again. As the robot stepped off the trailer, they heard a loud noise as the back of the dump truck came crashing to the ground.

Their eyes were riveted to the view screen watching for any sign that the neighbors had heard the loud noise. They involuntarily held their breath.

Sharianna noticed that her hand was close to the switch on the console that had the pictures of the robot standing and flying. Almost without conscious thought, she reached out with her pinky and flipped the switch.

From the corner of his eye, Joseph saw the slight movement of her hand.

Dad breathed out, "I think we're safe, it seems that no one heard the noise." Feeling more confident, he pushed on the stick again.

Thomas was concentrating on the bottom of the screen in order to see where the feet of the robot would be placed. Suddenly, the earth under the robot seemed to melt away and was replaced by a shrinking view of the scattered lights in their neighborhood, with the city lights in the distance.

"We're flying!" declared Joseph.

Thomas eased back on the lever and the robot stopped and hovered in the air.

"Incredible," Mom gasped.

"I didn't feel any G-force at all!" observed Joseph.

"I bet this is faster than a rocket!" exclaimed Sharianna, brimming with excitement.

Dad looked at the switch on the console, and then turned to Sharianna. "Did you flip that switch?"

Before she could reply, Mom screamed: "Look out!" and pointed at the view screen.

Dad turned to see a flashing green light on one side and a

flashing red light on the other with a white light right in the middle. Within a fraction of a second he realized that a 747 was flying directly at them. Another split second and he could actually see the pilot and the copilot and a stewardess standing at the door of the cockpit. He could see so clearly that he read the lips of the copilot as he yelled: "Look out!" and saw him grab for the controls.

Joseph grabbed onto Percy's collar and winced as he braced for the impact.

I'm in trouble now. A myriad of thoughts raced through Sharianna's head: *What a stupid thought – we're all going to die and I'm worried about being in trouble? I guess it's true that time seems to slow down just before you die. Maybe your thoughts just speed up?* She shivered as she took a deep breath as if it were her last, before plunging forever into deep, dark, freezing water.

"I love you all," called out Mom softly.

CHAPTER EIGHT

Fake Moon Landings?

THOMAS SLAMMED THE CONTROL STICK ALL THE WAY Forward and the 747 almost instantly disappeared. The lights of the city dwindled to a speck and became another small point of light with all the other points of light from cities scattered across the northern hemisphere. As the earth seemed to recede, they saw the sun appear on one side of the screen with the entire outline of the earth on the other. The western United States was still shrouded in darkness, but they could see the first rays of the sun reaching the eastern seaboard and shimmering on the North Atlantic. They could see over the North Pole and, still bathed in daylight, all the way from northwestern Russia, Scandinavia, Britain, Iceland, Greenland, and the edge of Northwest Africa.

The amazing splendor of the blue ocean, the deep green near the equator and the beautiful sand color of the deserts in Africa overlaid with swirls and wisps of clouds here and there was truly astonishing. The earth continued to rapidly shrink until Dad released the control stick from his death-grip. His hand shook a little as he exhaled with his whole body.

The earth was now down near the bottom of the screen. Joseph pointed up at the ceiling. "Look at the moon; it looks as big as the earth."

Sophia's heart palpitated wildly, like an untamed animal trapped in a cage, trying to escape. She continued his thought: "If the moon is one third the size of the earth and it appears as big as the earth..."

"Then that must mean we are two thirds the way to the moon!" Joseph exclaimed.

Dad twisted the control stick ever so slightly and the robot rotated until the earth had moved to the center of the screen. It was so clear and so beautiful that it seemed they were standing outside on the hull of the ship.

They sat in stunned silence, gazing at the earth for a few minutes.

Sophia could feel the pounding of her heart begin to slow down, but the rush of adrenaline still hadn't worn off yet. *Other than the near death experience, I think I could get used to this,* she thought.

Suddenly, Sharianna thought: *maybe I'm still in trouble, now that we're not dead.* She turned to Mom. "I love you too." Turning back to Dad, "And you too Daddy, I'm sorry."

Thomas looked at Sharianna. He could see tears in her eyes. He hadn't been called daddy for several years. "It's okay princess. Maybe we can learn to fly before we walk."

"Wow! What do you think those pilots and the flight attendant are saying right now?" mused Joseph. "Uh... tower... we had a near miss with a...uh, giant man, uh, robot-thing that shot out into space."

Sharianna started laughing through her tears, followed by Mom and Dad.

"Not if they want to keep their jobs," laughed Dad.

"I'll bet *they* don't think it's funny. I hope they don't need too much counseling after tonight," Mom commented, a little bit more seriously.

Percy could sense the wild swings of emotion, from exhilaration to stark fear then relief, elation, awe and finally, laughter. He looked up at Joseph with a quick bark and a wag of his tail.

"That's right, boy, we're still alive," comforted Joseph, as he reached down and rubbed him behind the ears. "I guess we won't need these," concluded Joseph, as he released his cargo strap seatbelt. "The artificial gravity must be able to compensate for G-force. It was really strange to accelerate so fast without any sense of motion. Almost like watching a movie."

"Yeah, a movie that could kill you," replied Sharianna.

"Dad was in total control the whole time. Weren't you Dad?"

asserted Joseph.

"Yeah..." Dad agreed slowly, without a hint of conviction. He slowly twisted the control stick the other way, and the moon came back into view.

"Dad?"

"Yes?"

"You know that old movie where they faked the lunar landing..."

"Yes."

"Well, didn't they leave the bottom part of the lunar lander there?" asked Joseph.

"They left a flag too!" Sharianna added with excitement, knowing what Joseph was leading up to.

"And the moon buggy they rode in," continued Joseph.

Dad raised his eyebrows and looked back at Sophia.

"On our first trip? And that one accidental?" But she could not disguise the note of excitement that found its way into her words.

"Ah ha! You're my witnesses; Mom has turned into an adventurer!"

"Maybe you *could* use a little more flight experience before you try to land in our yard; I don't want you to smash our house. And besides, we are already two thirds the way there, right?" She looked at Joseph with these last words and he smiled from ear to ear. Looking back at Thomas, she quoted her favorite Christmas show: "George lassos the moon!"

Dad slowly pushed forward on the control stick; soon the moon appeared to be getting larger. "Look out man-in-the-moon, here we come." He pushed on the stick a little more.

"Is that a cloud?" asked Sharianna.

"There are no clouds in space," declared Joseph.

Immediately, they heard a sound like hail pounding on the hull of the ship. Dad pulled back on the stick.

Floating all around them, they saw small rocks ranging in size from basketballs down to particles of dust.

"Some of them are sparkly," observed Sharianna. "What are they made of?"

"Joseph, you're our rock expert," acknowledged Mom.

"A lot are made of iron, mica and other minerals but I think most are just rocks."

"Hey, I remember hearing something about how lucky the moon missions were that they didn't encounter any severe solar wind from sun flares or asteroid storms. If they had, they probably would have been destroyed," concluded Dad.

"How can there be wind or storms in space, if there is no air?" questioned Joseph.

"I think the wind refers to the small particles and radiation that are thrown out by the sun, especially during solar flare-ups," Thomas replied. "The storms refer to debris trails left by comets."

"Some of those asteroids look pretty big; do you think they can damage the ship?" asked Mom, nervously.

"I doubt it…" began Dad.

Joseph interrupted: "It crashed in the desert making a great big crater but there was still not a scratch or dent on it; I'll bet that was one powerful impact!"

"I guess you're right," conceded Mom.

"Can we take one of the shiny ones home?" asked Sharianna.

The thought excited Joseph. "Dad, do you think you could grab one with the robot's hand?"

"I don't know, but it would be fun to try," he answered.

"That sparkly one, over there," directed Sharianna.

Dad was having a hard time capturing the rock because the controls were very sensitive and every time he touched the asteroid, it would float away. They flew all around it several times and had to chase it each time it was bumped.

Finally, Joseph said: "Let me have a try, Dad." He used both hands and made a cage with the fingers around the asteroid, then slowly closed one hand until it gently gripped the coveted rock.

"Yeah!" cried Sharianna, as everyone clapped.

"Now what?" Dad asked.

"Put it in the cargo bay," suggested Sharianna.

"Haven't you seen the space movies?" demanded Joseph. "When they open the door to space, everything goes flying out.

56

We would lose our air, and everything else in the cargo bay."

"Well, just hold onto it until we get back home," she retorted.

"It's worth a try," agreed Mom.

"Since I'm already in the chair, can I pilot the robot to the moon?" requested Joseph.

Sharianna was quick to interject: "Hey, I've been in the chair the whole time and I haven't had the chance to fly it."

Dad intervened, "You can both have a turn, but then I will take over when we get closer to the moon."

"Be careful, I want to see the moon, I don't want to make our own crater," cautioned Mom.

"You've both had your opportunity to pilot the ship; I think I'll take over the controls now," said Dad, as they approached the moon.

"It's my turn to be copilot," insisted Joseph, while motioning to Sharianna to vacate her seat.

"I think it is Mom's turn," suggested Thomas, as he motioned for Sophia to sit down in Sharianna's chair.

"Okay, but it doesn't really matter to me." Sophia sat down in the captain's chair. As she looked at all the controls, she suddenly felt an inward craving to pilot the robot. She suppressed the desire: "Maybe I'll fly it on the return trip."

Joseph walked around the control chairs and down the steps to the seating below. From this vantage point, it felt like he was right out in space without any ship at all, because he was surrounded on both sides and the top by the curved view screen.

Sharianna joined him. "Wow, this looks even cooler than when you are in the captain's chair," she observed. "Kind of like the Soarin' Over California ride at Disneyland."

"Except it's real," added Joseph.

"I think we'll go around the back side of the moon, and then gradually approach the front. I think that will eliminate the risk of crashing straight into it," explained Dad, as he glanced at Mom.

"Okay," she agreed.

57

As they approached the moon, they could see the remarkably varied terrain, from mountains, hills and craters to smooth plains.

"Wow, it's amazing," exclaimed Joseph, from his seat down in front.

"It is so barren," observed Sharianna.

As they came around into the shadow of the moon they looked beyond, into the expanse of space, to see the most unexpected and spectacular sight they could imagine.

"Look at all those stars," exclaimed Sharianna.

With the moon blocking the light from the sun and no atmosphere to obscure the view, they could see millions of stars, brighter than they had ever seen them before.

"It's beautiful," whispered Mom.

Dad had slowed the robot down so that they would not overshoot the moon. As they slowly came around the moon, they saw the Earth rise up majestically from the horizon.

"It's a small world, after all," sang out Mom, in her soft, melodious voice. "It really is small, isn't it?"

They made a slow descent and began to realize the enormity of their search. They flew low over the mountains, craters and huge plains.

"That is a lot of area to search. Does anyone know where the moon missions landed?" asked Dad.

"If I had my computer, I could google it."

"Maybe we should bring it next time," proposed Dad.

"I doubt you could connect to the internet way out here," countered Mom.

"I guess you're right," agreed Joseph.

"But we only have to search half of the moon because we know they did not land on the dark side," Sharianna smiled smugly. "And they did not land in the Polar Regions."

"That still leaves an area probably as big as North America," concluded Dad thoughtfully.

They flew back and forth across the moon for hours searching for the lander.

"Maybe the moon landings really were fake," speculated Joseph.

Dad tried to remember a Nova show he had seen recently about the moon landings but he couldn't remember the details. Thomas and Joseph were likely Nova's biggest fans; they had probably watched nearly every show they had ever filmed. They also consumed the National Geographic movies and magazines.

"Hey, didn't they land on a large flat plain?" remembered Mom, who watched some of the Nova programs with them. "I'll bet that they chose the smoothest spot they could find. Let's go back out to space so that we can see the flattest looking place."

As they flew back out to space and looked at the moon from that vantage point, they noticed a very large level plain.

"Let's use a grid type of search pattern, that way we won't keep flying over the same area," suggested Joseph.

"Good idea, son."

After a couple more hours searching the plain, Sharianna said: "I don't know if it reflects the actual lunar landing, but I think that when we took our picture at the planetarium there were mountains or hills in the background of the display."

"Okay, we'll limit our search to a few miles from the edge of the plain," responded Dad.

"Maybe it *was* fake." Sharianna added her doubt to Joseph's.

"Don't be too fast to disbelieve something just because you can't prove it," suggested Dad.

"But what if we can't find it?" she persisted.

Dad explained: "Imagine, if you were on the beach and you had a diamond and you dropped it. Someone comes along and you tell them there is a diamond in the sand. Would it still be there even if they could not find it?"

"Yes."

"What if they did not believe that it was there, does that diminish the reality of it being there?"

"No."

"Remember, a person's inability to verify the existence of something in no way disproves the reality of its existence."

CHAPTER NINE

The Meteorite

MOM LOOKED AT SHARIANNA'S ALARM CLOCK THAT WAS still on the console in front of her.

"Well, back home it is 9:00. I think I'll make some breakfast; I've got bread, eggs, and milk. Any special requests?" asked Mom.

"We could make French toast," Sharianna concluded.

"Okay, but we don't have any syrup. Will jelly do?"

"Sure will," responded Dad.

"I'll have the eggs with toast," sighed Sharianna.

"Me too," echoed Joseph.

"I think we'll take a break. I'm going to try to land on that hill over there," announced Dad.

When the robot touched down a huge cloud of dust was kicked up.

"Houston, the eagle has landed," reported Dad, in a voice that really did sound a lot like Neil Armstrong's declaration when Apollo 11 first landed on the moon. "With this artificial gravity and counter G-force, it is difficult to tell how hard we land," rationalized Dad for his amateur landing.

As they went through the small corridor, Mom paused, "You know what is weird?"

"What?"

"To feel like we are walking on a flat level surface, while knowing that we are actually walking straight down, toward the surface of the moon. How do you think it works?"

Joseph was excited to explain his theory as they entered the kitchen and Mom began making breakfast.

"The ship has the ability to create artificial gravity..." began

60

Joseph.

"Yeah, we already know that," Sharianna interrupted. Turning to Mom, "How can you cook eggs if there is no stove?"

Sophia smiled; the investigation of the kitchen had been her personal mission. She touched a button and what looked like a cutting board slid out from under the counter. She put her hand on the stone-like material. "See, it's cold. Watch," she instructed, like a professional demonstrator, as she placed the clear container that looked a little like a frying pan on the surface. "See, it is *still* cold." Joseph and Sharianna passed their hands over the pan. Mom waved one hand over the pan and cracked an egg with the other. "Abracadabra." Instantly, as the egg touched the pan, it began to sizzle and cook.

Both Joseph and Sharianna were fascinated.

"I see your investigation of the kitchen was fruitful," observed Dad.

"How does it work?" asked Joseph.

"I don't know, but it does," replied Mom.

"I want mine scrambled," asserted Sharianna.

"Me too," concurred Joseph.

Mom quickly cracked in several more and stirred them, adding a dash of pepper and a little milk from one of the refrigerated drawers.

"There, the best scrambled eggs I have ever made," she bragged, as she slid them onto a plate. "And completely non-stick too!" The pan was clean as new.

"How did you learn that?" marveled Dad.

Mom held up a finger with an obvious red mark. "Accidentally."

After breakfast, Thomas was drawn to the big soft comfortable chairs. "About your theory..." he encouraged, as he sat down, looking at Joseph.

"Well, if real gravity is pulling from any direction that is not appropriate for the orientation of the ship then the ship automatically applies an equal gravitational pull in the exact opposite direction, while maintaining the correct amount of gravitational pull in the right direction. The same goes for countering G-force."

"Excellent reasoning and deductions. I think gravity is reduced when you sit in this chair, that's why it is so comfortable," sighed Dad, as he closed his eyes.

Percy was already occupying one of the other chairs, so Mom slipped into the third one. "I think you're right," she agreed, as she contentedly closed her eyes.

"Hey, how can you sleep at a time like this?" scolded Joseph.

"Yeah, we're on a mission to find evidence of moon landings!" asserted Sharianna.

Percy opened a lazy eye; he was enjoying the anti-gravity chair.

"Okay, let's try again," conceded Dad, as he reluctantly vacated the chair of comfort.

"Let's fly back out to space and pick the next largest plain," suggested Joseph.

"If you lived on the moon you could always see the earth, couldn't you?" observed Sharianna, as she gazed at the beauty of their home planet.

"I guess you're right; the moon always faces the earth," answered Dad, as the robot rose from the surface of the moon.

Dad slowly turned the robot back toward the moon and they looked at it in silence for a few minutes.

"Computer... scan... for any...metal... structures," directed Joseph, imitating the commanding voice of captain Kirk.

"No, you've got it all wrong. You have to talk to the ship," asserted Sharianna in mock seriousness, as she joined in the game. Looking at the moon on the view screen and mustering her most official sounding voice she commanded: "ROBO-SHIP, scan for... any metal...structures...on the surface...of...the moon."

Immediately, superimposed over the moon, there appeared on the view screen over twenty small red circles.

Mom gasped incredulously, "It's voice controlled!"

Thomas was astonished and momentarily speechless. It was inconceivable to him that the builders of the robot could possibly have known English.

62

Regaining control of his speech, he gasped, "It understands English? Incredible!" Dad waived his hand over the controls labeled with the strange writing and symbols. "Obviously, it's not their first language."

"Maybe they were studying us..." theorized Sharianna contemplatively.

"Oooo," mocked Joseph mysteriously. Then, in a much more serious voice, he pointed to the view screen, "Let's go down and see what it found."

"Let's go, maybe we can figure this out later," agreed Dad.

"Do you think we will be able to see Neil Armstrong's or Buzz Aldren's foot prints where they first walked on the moon?" wondered Mom.

"Theoretically, they should still be there, unless the dust was disturbed by something like a meteorite hitting close by," replied Dad.

"Why are so many metal structures indicated?" asked Sharianna.

"Both the United States and Russia sent quite a few missions to the moon," explained Dad.

"Except the Russian missions were all unmanned, right?"

"Yes, I don't think they ever landed a man on the moon," answered Dad.

"Where should we start?" asked Mom.

"Joseph? Sharianna? What do you kids think?" queried Dad.

"Look, one of them is in the plain that we just searched," observed Sharianna.

"I think we should start with that one," Joseph proposed.

They were able to find it quite easily by aligning the small red dot that was always in the center of the screen with the small red circle, and the robot flew directly to it.

As they approached the site, they could see that it was some type of rover.

"Hey, what kind of writing is that?" asked Joseph, when they got close enough to see the details.

"It's not English, so it must be Russian," deduced Sharianna. "Did anyone else send a mission to the moon?"

"It is Russian," confirmed Mom. "I guess they didn't fake *their* moon landings."

The next site they investigated turned out to be a crater with some metal pieces lying around.

"I think that they crashed a few rockets into the moon," explained Dad.

"Why?" asked Joseph.

"Probably to see if it could be done. You wouldn't want to attempt a manned mission to the moon if you couldn't even hit it with a rocket, would you?" reasoned Mom.

"Let's move on and find the others," suggested Dad.

The next site they chose was in the bottom of a gigantic, ancient crater, at least ten times the size of Meteor Crater in Arizona. As they hovered over the site they saw a long sloping trench cut across the bottom. Directly in line with the trench, a chunk of the crater's rim was knocked out.

"Another crash site?" assumed Sharianna.

Joseph looked at Dad. "It looks like the crater where we found the robot."

"Sure does, except it doesn't look as big," replied Dad.

"Drop down a little closer to the deep end of the trench," suggested Joseph.

"I don't see any debris," observed Mom, "could be a meteor crater."

"But the robot indicated it as a metal structure," argued Joseph, his interest mounting. "Let's dig it up!"

"What if it *is* another robot?" posed Sharianna energetically.

"Joseph used the hands so well capturing the asteroid, I think he should dig it up," reasoned Mom, as she gave her seat to Joseph.

Joseph set the asteroid that was still in the robot's hand on a large rock at the edge of the pit and using the hands of the robot like shovels he began to remove the moon rocks and dirt in the lower end of the pit.

"Look, there!" exclaimed Sharianna.

"I see it," replied Joseph, as he carefully scraped around the edges of a rough looking sphere about four feet in diameter.

"Maybe it's an iron meteorite," theorized Mom.

The robot was now on its knees as Joseph reached into the hole with both hands and carefully removed the object and held it up for a closer look. It was round and bumpy, with a lot of moon dust sticking to it.

"It's about the same color as the meteorites at the museum," concluded Sharianna.

"Yeah, but it is a whole lot bigger!" exclaimed Joseph.

"Let's take it home!" called out Sharianna and Joseph in unison.

"Okay, but how? It would be so easy to drop, especially when entering earth's atmosphere," concluded Dad.

"I have an idea." Joseph explained his proposal: "I've rethought my concern about opening the doors to the cargo area. Why would the builders of the robot make it so that you couldn't open the cargo doors in space? How likely would it be that other planets would have exactly the right atmosphere? Otherwise, you couldn't bring anything very big home." Joseph felt confident that his analysis was correct. Looking at Mom, he said: "Am I right, or what?"

"It makes sense. And the door from the control room to the cargo area really does look perfectly sealed," she responded.

"It seals perfectly, like all the other doors," added Joseph excitedly.

Sharianna added her thoughts: "That's why the kitchen and living room retract and why they have so many compartments and drawers in there, so that nothing goes flying out when you open the doors. That's why they put doors separating the cargo area from the rest of the ship! *And*, the button to open the cargo bay is right here, not in the cargo bay." Sharianna was quite proud of her deductive abilities.

"Okay, I believe," Dad capitulated.

Joseph moved his beanbag from the cargo bay to the lower observation area of the control room; it took up practically all the floor space of that level.

After retracting the kitchen and the living room and securing everything else in the drawers, they opened the cargo bay doors and Joseph carefully placed the object inside.

"Don't forget my asteroid." After a pause, Sharianna declared, "I want to try putting it in."

Dad gave up his seat and Joseph gave Sharianna some pointers as she slowly picked up her asteroid and placed it in the cargo bay. Then she picked up a moon rock about the same size and put it next to her asteroid.

"You know that we won't be able to tell anyone where we got these rocks. Don't you?" emphasized Mom.

"*Yes,*" they agreed reluctantly.

"Hey, let's take a rover home!" exclaimed Joseph.

"*That* would be a little harder to explain," cautioned Mom. "I don't think we'd better."

"Can I fly the robot now?" asked Sharianna, who was already at the controls.

"I don't see why not," replied Mom.

As they continued their search for Apollo 11, they found several more crash sites and a Russian probe.

"Hey, look at that mountain – it looks like an extinct volcano – it even has a hole in the top," observed Joseph. "Did the moon ever have any volcanic activity?"

"Yes, but not any active ones anymore," replied Dad.

"It resembles the part of the copper mine that you can see from our house," observed Sharianna.

"Yes, it does, a little," concurred Mom, as they flew past the strange mountain. "But I can't imagine there are any mines on the moon."

"What is that shadow beyond the mountain?" asked Sharianna.

"I don't know," answered Dad, in a bewildered tone.

CHAPTER TEN

The Black Obelisk

AS THEY APPROACHED, THE SHADOW BECAME A TALL, four-sided pillar with each side tapering to a point at the top.

"It's a tower!" cried Mom. "No! It's an...obelisk?"

"It's huge!" exclaimed Joseph.

Suddenly, they saw a lander next to it, and then another, and another. They looked extremely small next to the giant black obelisk.

"That one is American, see the flag on the side," called out Sharianna.

"And that one has the same flag as the Russian rover," observed Dad.

They drew closer and they could read the writing on the side of one of the landers.

"There's Apollo 12. Is that Neil Armstrong's lander?"

"No, it was Apollo 11," answered Dad.

"Wow, it's still cool," replied Joseph.

As they drew closer, the words on the side of another American lander became readable. "There it is!" exclaimed Sophia: "Apollo 11. There is a plaque on the side of it but I can't read it, we're still too far away."

Sharianna landed the robot between the American landers and the giant obelisk.

"It must be at least 1,000 feet tall," speculated Dad, as he gazed up at the shiny, black spire, "and it must be 150 feet wide at the base."

"There is *no* way they brought *that* from earth," stated Mom emphatically.

"Look, there is writing near the bottom of it," observed Joseph.

"Get closer, Sharianna," directed Mom.

Sharianna took a few steps closer with the robot. "I thought you wanted to see Neil Armstrong's footprints."

"Yeah, later," Mom replied, as her heart pounded with excitement as she realized that they must have found an alien monument.

"I guess we'll leave our own footprints," laughed Joseph.

"Yeah, huge robot-prints," added Sharianna.

Mom grabbed Dad's notepad and began copying the row of strange symbols they could now clearly see on the obelisk.

"Can you read that language?" asked Joseph.

"No, I read ancient, dead languages—not alien."

Suddenly, Sharianna remembered, "I brought my camera."

"Really?" replied Mom, as she put the notepad down.

"Yeah, I'll get it." Sharianna flipped the switch to Joseph's chair, "You take over Joseph," she said, as she ran back to the cargo bay. Returning, she handed the camera to Mom, who took a picture of the hieroglyphic writing.

"What is it?" queried Sharianna, motioning to the obelisk.

"Any ideas?" inquired Dad.

"It looks like a monument, like the Washington monument—it's an obelisk. The Egyptians built obelisks too," stated Sharianna.

"Maybe it has some kind of function, like a communication tower," suggested Joseph.

"Communicating to whom?" questioned Mom.

"Was it put here before or after the moon landings, and who put it here?" pondered Dad. "If it was before, then maybe they could see it from earth and that is why they wanted to come here so bad."

"Maybe they met the aliens who built it." Joseph gazed up at the silhouette of the spire against the background of the earth, contemplating the possibilities.

"Some of the arguments for the fake moon landings could be explained if there was a second ship–like the strange shadows seen in the pictures," mused Dad. "Perhaps that's why NASA does not strenuously refute the allegations of fake moon landings. They would rather have some people believe that they were fake than for everyone to know the real truth."

"But Dad, didn't you know that they already proved that the moon landings were real and that the shadows were normal?" argued Joseph.

"I know, but it doesn't preclude the possibility of another ship, does it?"

"I like Joseph's idea of a communication tower," said Mom. "Let's fly up and look at the top."

Mom sat down in Sharianna's chair and flipped the switch that transferred control of the robot from the right control chair to the left, and flew the robot up very slowly. There were no visible joints or seams in the glistening black obsidian-like surface of the obelisk.

"It looks as sharp as a needle," observed Sharianna, when they reached the apex of the spire.

"I guess it could be an antenna," acknowledged Dad.

"Hey, let's see if there are any alien footprints," suggested Joseph.

Mom landed the robot in almost the same spot.

"Pretty good flying," praised Dad, as Mom bent the robot down to look at the dust around the base of the obelisk.

"It is easier than you make it look," she teased, with her beautiful smile.

"Thanks...I think," he replied, a little disconsolately.

"The astronauts' footprints are still here! Unless aliens were wearing spacesuits with the same tread as the astronauts," Sophia exclaimed excitedly, as she looked at the footprints around the base of the monolith. "Too bad we don't have spacesuits – to walk in the same footprints as Neil Armstrong," she mused quietly. She had always dreamed of becoming an astronaut.

Joseph and Sharianna looked at each other.

CHAPTER ELEVEN

"What will NASA think?"

"WE DO HAVE SPACESUITS," RESPONDED SHARIANNA, WITH a huge grin.

"Where?" asked Dad.

"We found a closet," Joseph replied excitedly, as he bounded up the steps from the lower observation area, with Sharianna right behind him.

They led Mom and Dad back through the cargo area and opened the closet, revealing the suits hanging on the rack.

"How do you know they are spacesuits?" queried Dad.

"We tried them out," blurted Sharianna.

"What do you mean you *tried* them out?" demanded Mom.

Joseph and Sharianna then proceeded to relate their adventure of the previous day, while conveniently leaving out the encounter with the twins, and of course, their practical joke on their friends.

"I don't know if water is an appropriate test for them," said Dad, as another thought occurred to him. "There is oxygen in water, how do we know the suits didn't take the oxygen out of the water?"

Now it was Mom's turn to be logical: "If this is a space ship then *they* must be spacesuits."

"Maybe they are bio-suits," argued Dad.

"They must be both," concluded Joseph. "There is only one kind of suit here."

Mom continued her argument: "And why would they have a bio-suit and not a spacesuit? I agree with Joseph. They must be dual function," she insisted, with a tone of finality.

"I concur," agreed Sharianna.

"I'd bet that little room in the ankle of the robot, by the bathroom, is an airlock," proposed Joseph.

Dad began putting on one of the suits.

"So, what do you think you are doing?" questioned Mom.

"I'm going to test Joseph's theory about the airlock, and your theory about the spacesuits."

Mom grabbed one of the suits and also began putting it on.

"So, what do you think *you* are doing?" mimicked Dad.

"I'm going with you."

"And what if you are wrong and I explode into space?"

"Then we'll explode together," she said with a smile.

"And Joseph and Sharianna can take the robot home by themselves?" he replied.

Sophia relented, "I'll wait, I guess; but I'm sure it will be okay."

Dad stepped into the ankle of the robot and closed the door behind him. As he pushed the button to open the outer door there was a momentary delay. His heart started to pound as he began to second-guess his decision. He heard a sound like the rushing of wind, and then, complete silence. Slowly, he felt as if the floor were tilting; he leaned and shuffled his feet in the opposite direction, until finally, he was standing straight up on the bathroom door. He took a deep breath and looked directly overhead at the three faces scrunched up against the window of the other door, which was now directly overhead—from his perspective. All of a sudden, the outer door opened up and he stood looking directly at the great obelisk with the landscape of the moon in the distance.

"That's weird. Dad is standing on the bathroom door," observed Sharianna.

"Of course," Joseph replied. "The gravity in the airlock had to rotate in order to match the gravitational pull of the moon. Otherwise, when Dad stepped out, he would either have to twist like a cat in mid air, or he would probably fall on his head."

"There is no air on the moon," retorted Sharianna smartly.

"You know what I mean."

Thomas gave his family the thumbs up and stepped out onto

71

the top of the robot's foot. The door closed behind him without making a noise. He walked out to the end of the foot in utter silence; even his feet didn't make any sound as he walked. The low gravity wasn't the only reason he felt light footed, he was filled with the euphoria of doing something incredible that he never dreamed he would ever do. *I guess sound doesn't travel when there is no atmosphere*, he thought to himself, as he stood at the end of the foot, ready to slide down to the surface.

"Hey, Mom, I guess Dad will be the first one to walk on the moon."

Thomas heard Joseph's voice as if he were right next to him. He turned and looked at the door, but could see nothing except the uninterrupted surface of the robot. He walked back toward the leg and looked for the outline of the door but could see only the flawless surface.

"Can you guys hear me?" he asked.

"Sure can, Dad," replied Sharianna.

"Didn't we tell you, the suits have radio's, or something," explained Joseph.

Suddenly the door opened and out bounded Percy, who, with one great leap covered the distance and landed in Thomas' arms. Percy looked as surprised as Dad.

"I guess he doesn't know he can jump three times as far here on the moon," laughed Joseph.

"Where did you find the dog suit?" questioned Dad.

"Joseph said that if the same size suit could fit both Dad and me, then maybe it could even shrink down to fit Percy," explained Sharianna.

"I'll bet it will take him a while to get used to the moon's gravity," chuckled Dad.

"He'll just think he's a super-dog," said Sharianna.

"He *is* a super dog," Joseph retorted.

Percy jumped down and ran, or rather lumbered, since each step he took pushed him off the surface a little too much, toward the end of the robot's foot. He looked back and with a bark slid down to the moon's surface.

"One small step for a dog, one giant leap for..." Dad rolled his eyes as he searched for the right word.

Mom finished the new quote: "...canine."

Percy bounded all over like a new puppy, exhilarating in his newfound power of flight.

They paused on the end of the foot and looked up at the earth. Sharianna raised her camera and took a picture of it. Suddenly, she had a great thought. "Hey, smile everyone," she said, as she knelt down on the robot's foot to get a picture of Mom and Dad and Joseph with the earth and the obelisk in the background. She tucked her camera back into her fanny pack that she had strapped around her waist on the outside of her suit.

"After you, my dear," offered Dad, as he motioned to Mom with an exaggerated swing of his arm and a bow. "The first woman to walk on the moon!"

Mom slid down to join Percy, followed by Sharianna and Joseph simultaneously.

Immediately upon touching the surface, Joseph took a giant leap and cleared over twelve feet of distance. "Yahoooo."

Sharianna joined in the fun as she bounded after Mom.

Thomas looked around at the incredible moonscape, and then focused on the obelisk, thinking about all the mysteries they had encountered and the fantastic experiences of the past few days. Suddenly, the ancient pictographs and inscriptions on the rock outcropping in the desert flashed across the eye of his mind in perfect clarity. He felt the same strange feeling of familiarity that he and Joseph had felt when they first discovered them. The picture faded as fast as it had come, leaving him feeling slightly confused.

I'll have to go back there when we get home, he thought to himself as he slid down to the surface to join his family.

Sophia had already made a beeline for the base of the obelisk with slow, giant steps, each step propelling her off the surface, followed by a slow descent.

As they became used to the low gravity they were able to walk without breaking the surface.

Sophia had already circumvented the base of the obelisk by the time Thomas reached it. As Sophia came around the corner she said: "It definitely wasn't put here after the moon landings."

"How do you know that?" asked Sharianna.

Mom saw Joseph and Percy heading in the direction of the moon landers. "Don't go too far!" Mom called after Joseph.

"You don't have to yell, Mom, I can hear you no matter how far away I get. Remember the suits?" he said, pointing to his invisible helmet.

"Yeah, how do you know that?" asked Dad, bringing her back to her investigative deductions.

"The footprints."

Dad motioned for her to continue her explanation.

"The footprints go all around it in an unbroken pattern. If it were placed here afterwards, then the prints would either be disturbed or at least overlapped. You can tell that the astronauts were examining it, like we are.

"What will NASA think when they come back and see our footprints?" asked Sharianna as she lifted her foot and looked at the imprint it left in the dust.

"*That* will be perplexing," laughed Mom.

"I'm surprised that the spacesuits conform even to the bottom of our shoes," marveled Dad.

Mom held up her hand. "It even fits my hands perfectly, and yet it doesn't feel tight." She pulled on one of her fingers and the suit stretched, but when she let it go, it returned immediately to its perfect fit.

Mom resumed her investigation of the obelisk, while Dad went to keep an eye on Percy and Joseph. Sharianna picked up a moon rock about the size of a softball and followed her mom.

Sophia tapped on the obelisk with her hand – it felt solid. Sharianna banged on it with the rock. She was surprised that it made no noise. "Why didn't it make any noise?" she asked.

"Because there is no atmosphere," came the unexpected reply from Joseph, who was out of sight behind the robot.

"I asked Mom," retorted Sharianna.

"Noise has to have something to travel through, like air or water, or some other material," explained Mom.

"The flag they planted is pretty faded, and it is lying on the

74

ground, but it's still there. I think it was knocked over by the blast when the lunar module took off from the surface." Joseph looked around, "Where is the moon rover?"

"There it is!" exclaimed Dad, "over there, behind that lander."

"Cool!" cried Joseph, as he went bounding across the moonscape to investigate.

"The batteries must be dead," observed Dad, as Joseph sat in the rover and tried the controls, without success.

"It would have been so fun to go speeding across the moonscape," bemoaned Joseph.

"I don't think the rover was built for speed anyway," consoled Dad.

"I wish we had a dune buggy, or even the old truck," Joseph said longingly. "Except that without oxygen, neither would run, would they?"

"Look." Sharianna pointed to the large raised symbols on the surface of the obelisk.

The symbols seemed to use a geometric basis for their structure. Squares, parallelograms, triangles, ovals, circles, trapezoids and rectangles were used alone or in overlapping combinations.

Sharianna pointed to a round circle with a long slender obelisk extending from the top. "Do you think that one represents the moon? And that one, with the single large continent and the obelisk on the top, maybe it depicts their home world."

"Maybe," replied Mom. "Why don't you take another picture of it and we can study it later?"

Sharianna snapped the picture. She gazed at the symbols on the obelisk; she felt strangely drawn to it. A mysterious urge to touch it began to consume her. Her hands seemed to move independently of her thoughts. She seemed to have a heightened awareness of the details on the symbols and yet she felt an inability to control her fingers as they ran slowly over the symbols from right to left. *What in the world am I doing?* She thought to herself, as her mind raced, while her hands seemed to move in slow motion.

As she reached the last symbol, her fingers traced the square spiral. Suddenly, as her fingers reached the center, all the symbols began to recede into the obelisk and disappear, as if they were melting away.

"Thomas!" called Sophia.

"You don't have to yell..." began Joseph.

"Come quick!" interrupted Mom, "over here, by the obelisk!"

"What's the matter?" questioned Thomas, as he and Joseph came bounding across the moonscape in huge leaps that covered nearly fifteen feet, but still seemed slow since it took so long to return to the ground.

The faster Percy tried to run, the more difficulty he had—his timing was off.

"I don't know," replied Mom. "Just come."

"What's going on?" demanded Dad, once again, when they arrived at the obelisk.

Mom pointed to where the symbols had been, as she related what happened.

Sharianna was still standing, staring blankly at the obelisk.

Dad put his hand on her shoulder. "Sharianna?" She did not respond. "Sharianna!" Sharianna turned very slowly and collapsed into his arms.

CHAPTER TWELVE

TRAPPED

SHARIANNA IMMEDIATELY BEGAN TO REGAIN NORMAL control of her body. "I'm alright, I think," she said. "What's going on?"

"We hoped you could tell us," answered Mom.

"I took a picture of the symbols," Sharianna replied, "after that...I'm not really sure what happened," she said contemplatively, as she opened and closed her hand.

"Well, something happened," said Joseph, as he ran his hand over the smooth obelisk. "There is no trace that the symbols were ever here."

"Let's get back to the robot," said Mom.

Joseph picked up a couple of small moon rocks. "I think I'll take these home. Hey, I heard somewhere that the moon rocks they brought back from the moon are the most valuable rocks on earth."

"And how will you prove those are from the moon?" laughed Sharianna, as she regained her composure.

"Chemical analysis," replied Joseph.

"They will put you in jail because they will assume that you stole them from NASA," reasoned Mom.

As they approached the robot, Dad suddenly felt a vise-like grip on his arm.

"*Dad*," Joseph said in a strained whisper, "look at the obelisk."

Thomas could barely make out his words. He turned, and looked toward the obelisk. A tall, narrow, triangular crack had begun to appear. A dull, purple light emanated from the interior.

Mom and Sharianna followed his gaze.

"Stay here," ordered Dad, as he stepped toward the obelisk.

"No way," countered Mom. "We all stay together."

They began to walk slowly toward the obelisk.

Percy bounded ahead and approached the narrow triangular doorway.

"Percy, come back here!" commanded Joseph. But he had already disappeared into the light.

They quickened their pace and burst through the doorway.

Percy was nowhere to be seen.

The room seemed to span the entire interior of the obelisk. The floor and walls were smooth and seemed to glow, emanating the strange purple light. They could see all the way to the top of the spire.

At the exact center of the obelisk was some sort of glass-like tube, about two feet in diameter that extended from the floor all the way to the top of the spire.

"Percy!" they all called out, almost simultaneously.

Suddenly, Percy's head appeared from behind the pillar, followed by his body and his furiously wagging tail. He barked at them, turned, and again disappeared.

They ran toward the glistening pillar at the center of the floor, where they had last seen Percy, with Joseph in the lead.

"Wait, be careful," admonished Mom.

As he approached, Joseph realized that Percy had not disappeared; he had simply gone down a spiral staircase that began behind the pillar.

"Stop!" commanded Mom, as Joseph proceeded to follow Percy down. "We don't know what is down there!"

"I agree, I think we should continue with caution," concurred Dad.

"Come back here, Percy," called Sharianna.

Percy came back into view as he happily bounded up the staircase. Sharianna grabbed onto the stretchy part of his spacesuit, at the back of his neck. "You stay with us," she commanded.

They continued down as the staircase wound its way around the crystal clear pillar, which appeared to be full of some kind of liquid, all the while descending deeper beneath the surface of the moon.

Even the stairs were made of the same material as the floor and walls of the interior and emanated the same strange purple light. Thomas thought it odd that each step was so tall – about twice as high as a normal step.

"It looks like it is filled with water," observed Sharianna, as she ran her hand over the clear tube.

They continued their descent. "How far do you think we have come?" asked Mom.

Dad replied, "I would guess we have been descending for at least twenty minutes. If we are walking a normal speed of three miles an hour, that would mean we have probably gone close to a mile."

"You think we are a mile from the surface?" asked Sharianna.

"No, maybe about a half mile, since the staircase spirals down," he replied.

"Look, the bottom of the stair," observed Joseph. The small, spiral tunnel gave way to a huge subterranean chamber. It appeared to be a natural cavern. The staircase ended on a round platform, about twenty feet across that encircled the glass-like pillar.

An arching walkway with a single handrail at about shoulder height led away from the platform and disappeared in the distance.

Joseph walked to the edge of the platform and looked over. "Look, it's a pool of water." The light emanating from the platform reflected off the perfectly still water.

As Joseph peered into the water, he thought he noticed a set of faint concentric rings progressing from the darkness toward the platform, as if it were the last remnants of ripples from some disturbance on the surface of the water.

"I think it is more like an underground lake – you can't even see the end of it," said Sharianna, as she strained her eyes to see beyond the light, into the darkness.

Joseph stepped back from the edge. "I wonder how far it goes." Joseph drew back his arm and with much more strength that he would normally have on earth, flung one of the small moon rocks he had been carrying, far out into the darkness.

They all stood silent, involuntarily waiting for the familiar sound as the stone contacted the water, and yet realizing that without an atmosphere, the only sound they could hear was each other through the communication capability of their suits.

It was a total surprise when they heard the unmistakable plop as the stone splashed into the still lake.

Sophia exclaimed with excitement, "Hey! There must be some kind of atmosphere down here!"

"Shush," whispered Dad, as he put his finger to his lips. "Listen."

"Here...here...here," came back the echo of Mom's last word.

"Wow, this place must be huge!" shouted Joseph.

"Huge...huge...huge," the ghostly voice replied.

"It sounds a little eerie," commented Sharianna quietly.

The glowing walkway made a corridor of dim light through the darkness as it led away from the platform.

"What should we do?" asked Mom, who was torn by her anxiety of being so far from the robot and her intense curiosity concerning their new discovery.

"This walkway must lead somewhere interesting," stated Thomas, as he proceeded down the path, followed by Sharianna, Percy, and Sophia, with Joseph taking up the rear.

Although caution forbade Thomas to continue, he felt strangely compelled to move forward.

Soon, Thomas could see by the light emanating from the walkway, a natural looking wall of rock, with a tunnel, part way up the rock face, into which the walkway led.

Joseph got tired of holding onto his other rock. "Hey, watch this." Joseph wound up his arm like a big league baseball pitcher and let the other moon rock fly in another direction. As the rock

80

disappeared into the darkness, they heard a horrifying, unearthly wail as it impacted something other than the surface of the water. It sounded to Joseph like a cross between the terrified squeal of a pig and the metallic roar of Godzilla. It was a nerve-shattering scream.

The deafeningly intense shriek reverberated through the cavern. The placid lake seemed to suddenly transform into a raging sea. The source of the tumult emerged from the darkness a few yards away and slammed into the narrow bridge between the little group of explorers and the platform.

Sharianna screamed as she clung to the thrashing railing. Mom and Dad clutched the rail and scrambled to maintain their footing on the careening walkway.

Percy and Joseph were both catapulted into the churning water.

The creature climbed onto the walkway; it looked like an enormous glob of slimy brown luminescent jelly, pulsating as it expanded and contracted. The walkway was pushed down into the water by the weight of the enormous monster.

It sounds more dangerous than it looks, thought Thomas. At that instant, the gelatinous exterior of the creature seemed to peel away and was drawn, or sucked, into an orifice at the top of the body, revealing a hideous looking life form. It had one large foot, soft and muscular, similar to the foot of a snail. But that was the end of its similarities to the familiar mollusk of earth. It had a central large body segment with five arm-like appendages. The arms reminded Thomas of the trunk of an elephant, except that each arm terminated in a fearsome mouth with vicious looking metallic-like teeth. Above the mouth, near the end of each arm, was a single orb that emanated light. Thomas assumed these orbs were some sort of eyes. In place of the orb on the upper appendage, Thomas could see the very rock that Joseph had thrown into the lake; a sticky, bioluminescent liquid drained from behind the rock.

The surface of the monster looked as hard as a rock and was bumpy. A huge mouth with formidable metallic looking teeth opened up in the center of the body. The horrifying, bone-chilling scream again emanated from all six mouths, creating a terrifying cacophony. All four appendages turned and looked at the injured one. One of the appendages curled around and plucked the rock from the eye socket and placed it in the main mouth. Thomas could hear the rock being crushed by the powerful teeth.

Thomas wrenched his astonished eyes from the frightening scene and turned to see Sophia grab Joseph from the water and, with a single motion, lift him onto the walkway, which was no longer careening from side to side. Dad dropped to his belly on the walkway and, reaching far over the edge, grabbed Percy by his spacesuit at the scruff of his neck. Pulling Percy from the water, he stood up.

"RUN!" he screamed.

All four remaining eyes jerked to attention as the creature perceived their attempt to escape. Again, the blood-freezing scream filled the cavern as the creature crawled with astonishing speed toward the fleeing family.

Dad tucked Percy under one arm, like a giant football, as he ran behind his family. "Faster!" he yelled, as he looked over his shoulder at the monster right behind him. The last stretch of the walkway sloped up into the entrance of the tunnel, which was situated about twenty feet above the surface of the lake. He could hear the clamping of the metallic teeth only inches from his head as they flew the last few yards up into the tunnel.

The creature attempted to follow them into the tunnel, but it was too large. It began tearing at the sides of the tunnel in an effort to enlarge it. The teeth at the end of each appendage sank into the moon rock as if it were cream cheese. Each arm seemed to work independently, except the arm with the missing eye – it wandered aimlessly – but the other four were quickly enlarging the tunnel.

The family backed away from the creature, into the darkness of the tunnel. Sophia peered into the pitch-blackness and thought it strange that they were reluctant to leave the light that was emanating from the walkway, even though the monster was making surprising progress in its effort to reach them. Whenever the injured appendage bumped into the rock the beast emitted another gut twisting scream.

Sharianna clamped her hands over her ears but it was to no avail, since the helmet was hard and prevented her from plugging her ears.

Percy barked and growled at the creature, but Sharianna noticed that it seemed to agitate it more, so she knelt down and pulled Percy to her. "Shh," she whispered, as she rubbed his head. "We've got to be quiet."

Joseph noticed that once in a while the creature would deposit some rock in the large, central mouth. "It is eating the rock!" he exclaimed. The creature slowed down its excavation as it began to deposit more and more rock into its large mouth. Finally, it ceased tearing at the walls. It stood still as it peered into the darkness of the tunnel with all four of its remaining eyes. The light from its eyes lit up the tunnel for a short distance. The family quietly backed away deeper into the darkness.

Suddenly, the limbs wrapped themselves around the body, and the slime began spewing from the orifice at the top, until it was again a giant pulsating blob. Slowly, it turned and retreated to the lake, where it plopped into the water and disappeared.

Dad crept slowly toward the dull light at the entrance to the tunnel. He could see a trail of slime that was left by the monster's single snail-like foot. He looked in the distance, toward the platform and the staircase that led back to the robot. About half of the walkway was under water.

"We're trapped," whispered Sharianna from behind him.

CHAPTER THIRTEEN
The Labyrinth

"MAYBE WE COULD SWIM BACK TO THE PLATFORM," Joseph proposed, halfheartedly.

"Not with that monster in the lake," countered Mom. "Besides, I'll bet it's not the only one in there."

Dad responded: "Well, I don't want to go groping down the tunnel in the dark, not knowing where it leads or what might be down there."

Sharianna moved a little closer to the light with his last words.

"Look, the walkway is all broken up," observed Joseph.

"That's stating the obvious," retorted Sharianna. "That's why we can't get back."

"No, look, the railing is broken up too; it is made of the same material."

Dad perceived the direction of Joseph's thoughts: "Yes, if we could get some sections of it, maybe we could use it like flashlights."

"How are you going to get the pieces," asked Mom. "That creature can move through the water even faster than it can run...or crawl, on land."

"I'll bet it's not normally so dangerous," said Joseph.

"Are you crazy?" asked Sharianna. "Didn't you see those pincher-like mouths on its arms?"

"I'm just saying that if I hadn't put its eye out with the rock, maybe it wouldn't have attacked."

The last thirty feet or so of the railing had been knocked into the lake by the advance of the creature.

"I see a loose piece of railing, down where the walkway goes under water. Do you see it Joseph?" asked Dad.

"Yes, but look at that last section, the one that is closest to us – one end is loose," Joseph replied. "I wish I knew how tough that material is. Do you think it might break if we pried on it?"

"Maybe, but I'm not going to chance it. I'm going for the

one that is already loose. I don't want to waste time if I can't break the other one," said Dad. "Get ready to retreat into the cave; I'm going out to get it."

Thomas took a couple of deep breaths and braced his foot against a rock, like a sprinter at the starting line.

"I'm a faster runner than you, Dad," said Joseph.

"I'll go," replied Dad. "You stay with the girls."

Thomas burst out of the mouth of the cave and sprinted down the walkway toward the loose piece of railing.

Joseph dashed right behind Dad and grabbed onto the loose end of the closest piece of railing. He began to bend it but it would not break. Suddenly, Sharianna was by his side, and the rail bent a little more. Right behind Sharianna was Mom, who threw herself against the railing. Without warning, it suddenly snapped. Sharianna and Joseph went flying into the water, still holding onto the rail. The rail slid through Mom's hands but she clamped onto the end of it.

"Hold on!" Sophia screamed. She suddenly felt like Mrs. Hercules as she hoisted both her children from the water.

Joseph and Sharianna falling into the water was not the only disturbance upon the surface of the lake. As Thomas reached for the loose piece of railing, he felt the walkway jolt beneath his feet. He lunged onto his knees and caught the piece of railing as it rolled into the water. He felt the walkway sink a little more into the lake. He turned around in time to see his children dangling from the end of the railing as Sophia lifted them out of the water, but he could not see Sophia. On the walkway between Thomas and Sophia stood a creature like the one they had escaped from, except that this one was much smaller, but it looked no less formidable.

Sophia deposited Joseph and Sharianna onto the walkway behind her and turned toward Thomas. All she could see was the back of the creature. The lake seemed to be a cauldron of activity; the water was in turmoil and she could imagine, who knows how many other monsters, speeding toward them.

"Get back to the cave!" she ordered.

Percy raced past her toward the creature.

She leaped into action. Holding her glowing twelve-foot pole she rushed down the walkway toward the monster.

Percy barked at the creature and attempted to bite the back of its soft muscular foot. But, of course, the helmet of his space suit prevented him from inflicting any injury on the creature.

Three of the arms arched toward the back, while the other two proceeded to attack Thomas.

"The eyes!" screamed Sophia, as she swung her pole toward the end of one of the arms that was reaching for Percy. "Get back Percy!"

Rather than connecting with the eye, the monster caught the end of the pole in its pincher-like teeth. Sophia held onto the pole with all the strength she had. She was flung against the railing.

Sophia gasped as she tried to get her wind back. She was surprised to see a hailstorm of rocks suddenly pelt the monster. It screamed as one of its protruding eyes was struck a glancing blow by one of the rocks that Joseph and Sharianna were hurling. The creature bit through her metal pole, shortening it by a foot. She swung the pole at the creature again and another arm quickly grabbed the pole and pinched off another foot.

"Don't hit Mom or Percy!" cautioned Sharianna, as Joseph threw a rock the size and shape of a football with all the strength he had. The rock spiraled, like a quarterback's perfect pass as it hit the monster with a loud thud exactly in the middle of the body, about two thirds the distance from the foot. The creature seemed momentarily stunned.

Dad's pole was only about four feet long, so he had more control over it. He swung with all his might and hit the creature square on one of the eyes. As the bioluminescent fluid spurted from the orb, its unearthly shriek reverberated through the cavern, more intensely than ever. To Sophia's surprised relief, the wounded fiend plunged into the water.

The ramp sprang back up a little as Thomas sprinted toward his family. "Quick! Get into the cave!" he yelled. Miraculously, he saw one of the short pieces of railing that the monster had cut from Sophia's pole on the walkway. Without even pausing, he scooped it up and ran after his family. Thomas felt the walkway move under his feet but somehow he was able to maintain his footing.

Sophia ran headlong into the cave entrance directly behind Joseph and Sharianna.

Percy had become much more accustomed to the moon's low gravity, but he still had not completely mastered running. He was a short distance in front of Thomas as the end of the walkway began to pull away from the entrance of the cave.

"Here boy!" called out Joseph, as Percy launched himself from the end of the walkway.

Sharianna yelled, "Faster, Dad!" Her heart stopped when she saw how far the walkway was from the cliff.

At the edge of the light, she could see the wake created by what she assumed were several more of the hideous creatures coming from different directions under the water.

"Get back farther into the cave!" ordered Dad, as he leaped from the end of the walkway. Sharianna stepped back as her dad flew an amazing distance through the air.

The two pieces of railing clanged to the floor as he rolled to a stop on top of the rubble pile left by the previous monster.

Joseph picked up the four-foot pole, while Sharianna grabbed the short one. Mom still had her ten-foot pole. The light filtering into the entrance of the cave faded as the walkway was pulled down into the depths of the lake by the furious creatures. They could see the very dim glow of the platform in the distance. The only other light they had was the faint glow from their pieces of railing, but it was enough to see several yards around them.

From the light of her piece of railing, Sharianna suddenly saw a glowing orb, accompanied by the now familiar metallic teeth, appear near the floor of the entrance.

Joseph saw the eye at the same time and swung his pole with all his might. The eye popped and glowing liquid splattered against the wall of the cave. The mouth screamed as it jerked back from the entrance of the cave. A moment later they heard a splash as the creature hit the surface of the water.

Joseph held his pole over the edge to see another creature

emerge from the lake and begin climbing up the cliff. The teeth at the end of its arms simply bit into the rock as it climbed up toward the cave. This creature looked small enough to enter the cave.

"Dad, the boulder," directed Joseph, as he jumped over to a large rock that had been dislodged by the first creature.

Thomas and Joseph grabbed onto the rock, but it was so big that even with the added strength afforded them by the moon's low gravity and their spacesuits, they could not lift it.

"Roll it," directed Sophia as she joined them and pushed with all her strength. Sharianna swiftly joined the effort. Together, they quickly rolled the huge boulder to the edge. As it toppled over, they heard a crunching thud and then a splash. They could discern no more activity coming from the lake.

"I think we should get moving as far as possible from the lake; I suspect that perhaps those creatures prefer the water; if so, maybe they will stay near the lake. Surely, there must be another way to the surface," said Dad, as he turned toward the darkness of the tunnel.

"Here, Thomas, take my pole – it's producing the most light. I'll take up the rear, but I would like to have a weapon," Mom said, as she looked back anxiously in the direction of the lake, which was now quiet again.

"I'll take the rear," Joseph replied. "I know what to do if one of those creatures follows us." Joseph held his pole as if it were a two handed sword. He swung and jabbed at an imaginary monster.

"Okay, but keep your eyes and ears peeled, and keep Percy by your side," instructed Mom. "Sharianna, you follow Dad. I'll be right behind you."

"Here, boy, heel," Joseph instructed. Percy came and stood by Joseph's leg.

The tunnel led upward at a slight angle; it seemed to wind aimlessly, turning first this way and then that. The tunnel was perfectly round, even the floor was curved. It was like walking through a large stone pipe. The walls were smooth, except where there were voids or cracks in the natural rock.

Even though the tunnel was probably seven or eight feet in diameter, the curved floor made walking side by side impossible. The family trudged along in single file. Every few paces Joseph would spin around and shine his pole behind them to make sure they were not being followed.

"This cave definitely is not natural," commented Mom.

Dad stopped without warning and Sharianna bumped right into him.

"What do you think that is?" asked Dad, as he pointed to a round hole in the wall of the tunnel, a little more than two feet in diameter.

"It looks like this tunnel that we are in, except that it is smaller," observed Sharianna.

Sophia knelt down cautiously and peered into the hole. "Sharianna, let me see your light, please." She reached the light into the small tunnel. "It slopes down," she reported.

"Do you think these tunnels were dug by the creatures in the lake?" asked Sharianna.

"I doubt it," replied Joseph. "Did it look to you like that creature was too particular about the way he was tearing rock from the walls of the tunnel?"

"I agree," said Dad. "I don't think they would be capable of such precise work."

Joseph continued, "I think this tunnel was probably made by the same aliens that built the obelisk. I don't think those creatures in the lake would have built stairs, with their single snail-like foot—stairs are for bipedal creatures."

"Let's keep moving," admonished Mom, "at this rate we will never find a way out."

They continued on their way at a rapid pace. They passed several more of the small tunnels, all intersecting the main tunnel at different angles.

"What did they do with all the rock they took out of the tunnel?" asked Sharianna.

"Maybe they vaporized it," replied Joseph.

"I don't think so, the way this tunnel wanders, I would think they were following some kind of mineral deposit."

"Remember that strange mountain we saw, before we found the obelisk?" asked Mom, "I'll bet that was the tailings dump from this mine!"

"That makes sense," answered Dad, "I'll bet you're right."

"That must mean that this tunnel *does* lead to the surface," exclaimed Sharianna exuberantly.

Moments later, the tunnel widened into a cavern large enough to fit a house. Exiting the large room were several other tunnels.

"Which way?" inquired Mom, with a little anxiety in her voice. She remembered hearing stories of spelunkers loosing their way in the abandoned mines out in the desert and perishing before they could find their way out. The rumbling in her stomach added emphasis to her worry.

"Let's see if any of them slope up," suggested Sharianna.

"Great idea," exclaimed Dad, as he ran toward one of the openings, "you guys check those, I'll check this one."

There were seven other tunnels that intersected the cavern, four sloped downward, one seemed to be level, and two sloped upward.

"Which one should we take?" asked Joseph after the analysis.

"This one, we'll mark as number one," said Dad, as he jabbed at the rock next to the tunnel they had come through with his piece of railing, "then we'll number each one in a clockwise direction. That way we won't be going down the same tunnel twice – if we happen to choose the wrong one and have to backtrack."

"That still leaves the question of which one should we take?" insisted Joseph.

"That one slopes up the most," said Sharianna, pointing to number four.

"I think that one is larger than the others," said Mom, pointing to number six. "Let me have your pole, Thomas." She placed one end of the pole against the side of one of the tunnel entrances and marked the other side of the tunnel with her finger on the pole. Running over to tunnel number six she did the same thing. "See, it is several feet bigger – I think we should take this one."

90

"But that one doesn't slope up," argued Sharianna.

"It's the only one that is level," stated Joseph.

"It's just a hunch, but I think the tunnels may get larger the closer to the mine entrance we get," Mom replied.

"That makes sense to me," agreed Dad.

They hurried down the large tunnel; it seemed to wander a little less than the previous tunnel.

"There's a light up ahead," announced Dad. "It looks like a door," he declared, as they approached.

The door was closed; about five feet up it looked like there was some kind of latch.

"Open it," directed Mom.

Dad reached for the latch.

"I hear something..." whispered Joseph, who was looking the other way and peering into the darkness.

"What is it?" asked Mom quietly.

Percy began a soft, low growl, as he faced the darkness from whence they had come.

"Shh," Joseph whispered to Percy, "It sounded like a soft clicking, like the creature's teeth."

Sharianna grabbed onto her little piece of railing with both hands, but she still felt defenseless.

"Open the door!" Mom repeated in an urgent whisper.

"It's locked, or something," answered Dad.

Out in the darkness, from around a bend in the tunnel, Joseph suddenly saw five small lights; they seemed to be slowly dancing in the air.

"A creature is coming!" Joseph whispered fervently. "It must be able to track us."

Dad pulled on the handle with all his strength, but it broke off.

Dad turned in time to see all five eyes suddenly stop their slow dance. The creature began its charge with a chilling wail. Thomas put his foot against the side of the cave. Pushing off, he leaped to the other side and ran along the sloped surface until he was all the way around his family.

Sophia looked around anxiously for some kind of weapon,

91

but there was nothing to be found. Instead, she spotted one of the small tunnels right next to the door. It looked like it sloped steeply away.

Percy charged to meet the creature.

"Percy! Get back here! Now!" screamed Sharianna, as she threw her short piece of railing with every particle of strength she had toward the shrieking instrument of death charging toward them.

Joseph heard Sharianna's weapon whiz by his head.

He gripped his weapon tighter, and thought about his plan of attack. He wasn't going to hit only one of the eyes. He visualized himself hitting one and then another, and another, in rapid succession. He knew the monster would be formidably dangerous, even blind, but then at least they would have a chance. *I wish I had a gun,* he thought.

The creature's eyes fixed upon Percy, its arms lowered, ready to scoop him up.

Sharianna's projectile suddenly hit the creature, a few inches above its screaming maw. The sharp end of the broken railing pierced the tough looking hide of the creature, as if a professional knife thrower had thrown it.

The creature paused as its eyes turned from Percy to this new distraction. It plucked the projectile from its body and crushed it in two.

Mom grabbed Sharianna and shoved her toward the small tunnel. "Get down that hole!" she ordered.

As Thomas descended back to the floor, between Joseph and the creature from the lake, he saw Percy try to sink his teeth into the soft foot of the monster, but once again, his helmet prevented him from inflicting any injury. Percy immediately darted back toward the family he was trying to protect, narrowly escaping the lashing teeth as the monster reached out in retaliation. The monster let out a scream even more terrifying and nerve tearing than before. Thomas stood frozen for a moment as he held his pole toward the monster like a spear as it resumed its approach.

Percy turned and stood in front of Thomas, growling and barking at the creature. His ferocious bark sounded strangely mild and pitifully ineffectual, compared to the scream of the approaching menace. The creature seemed to be coming with a little more caution toward them, but it was still attacking nevertheless.

Mom grabbed Joseph from behind and flung him toward the hole. "Follow Sharianna!" she ordered, as she grabbed his pole from him. "I mean it!" she screamed.

Joseph obeyed the order, realizing that there was no arguing with her.

Thomas heard her directions to the children and turned his head slightly, to see what was going on behind him.

"You get down there too!" he yelled, as loud and commanding as he could. He knew Sophia would stay and fight, but he had a plan. He backed away toward the door.

"Get down there, NOW!" he ordered.

Sophia dropped her pole and reached around Thomas' legs. She grabbed Percy with one hand by the tail and pulled him toward her. She put her other hand on the scruff of his neck and shoved him down the hole after Joseph.

"You better not die!" she yelled at Thomas, as she dove into the hole headfirst.

The monster increased its speed when it saw them escaping.

In a single motion, Thomas put his long pole against the bottom of the door, placed the other end of the pole directly into the creature's main mouth and ducked. He grabbed the short pole that Sophia had discarded and dove headlong down the hole. It all happened so fast that he was right behind Sophia, sliding down with his hand pushing against Sophia's feet. They all accelerated for a while, until the slope of the tunnel began to diminish and their forward momentum decreased; suddenly, they came to an abrupt stop.

The tunnel was so small that Thomas could not even bring his arms back alongside his body. He lay there with his arms outstretched, still holding the end of the railing with one hand and his other holding onto Sophia's foot. *It's a good thing the walls of this tunnel are smooth*, he thought, *or we would be just a bloody mess.* But then he remembered the spacesuits; he rolled his arms over so that he could see his elbows from the light of the pole, where they had rubbed against the stone. He could see no damage. Pretty tough material, he thought with relief.

"Are you guys okay?" called out Mom and Dad together.

"Yes, I think so, but there is something blocking the tunnel," replied Sharianna, "I can't see what it is."

Percy whined and crawled forward onto Joseph's legs.

They could hear the maddened scream of the creature reverberating down the tunnel.

Thomas could feel rocks and debris piling up on his feet and legs. His heart was pounding wildly; the adrenaline was coursing through his veins. He could envision the enraged creature tearing at the walls of the tunnel in an effort to reach them. He had a disturbing thought: *Maybe its intent is to bury us alive.*

"Here, I have one of the poles," offered Dad, as he struggled to move the four-foot pole out from under his body and push it up past Sophia, but he could barely move his forearms and hands, which were outstretched in front of him. Finally, he was able to work the pole loose and push it up far enough for Sophia to get hold of it and push it up to Joseph, and finally to Sharianna.

The screaming of the creature had stopped, and the debris was no longer piling up on top of Thomas, but he realized that there was no way they were going to be able to climb back up the tunnel. It was deathly quiet: *Like a tomb*, Thomas thought. *I'd better stop thinking like that*, he quickly told himself.

"It's some kind of silvery metal thing, it fills the whole tunnel like a plug," Sharianna reported. From her voice, it was obvious that she was feeling panicked and claustrophobic.

"It will be alright, sweetie," said Dad, as calmly as he could, "can you push it?"

"I don't know; I think it moved a little when we hit it."

She pushed against it but it did not move.

"Put your feet on my shoulders and use your legs," instructed Joseph.

Sharianna put her head and hands against the obstruction and pushed with her legs.

94

CHAPTER FOURTEEN

"It's a Mine"

THE OBSTRUCTION BEGAN TO MOVE. THEY CREPT ALONG AT A painstakingly slow rate. It took everything Sharianna could muster in order to move the object a few short inches. It was torturous for Thomas to be stuck in the rear, unable to help his little girl at all.

Finally, the tunnel began to slope downward more, and the blockage moved a little easier; until finally, with a last shove, it began to slide on its own. The family again began to slide and pick up momentum, until they found themselves deposited in a heap in another large tunnel.

Joseph quickly picked up the only remaining piece of railing and held it up to light the tunnel, to make sure they were alone.

They examined what had been blocking the tunnel.

"It looks like some kind of robotic digging machine," suggested Joseph.

The object was cylindrical, tapering somewhat at the rear, and had overlapping metal plates of only an inch or two wide circumventing the body; it was the same diameter as the tunnel and was about three feet long. The front was the most interesting part: it had a drilling, or grinding mechanism that reminded Thomas of the triple interlocking carbide toothed wheels that are on the end of large rock drills.

Sharianna lifted up on one of the scales and the rest of them moved in a corresponding, undulating motion. It startled her.

"The scales are all connected," observed Joseph, "I'll bet that is how it moves, similar to the scales on a snake, or an earth worm—it pushes against the ground in a progressive motion that moves it forward."

"Which way should we go?" asked Joseph as he shone the light up and down the tunnel.

"Left," said Mom, "that is the direction we were going when we ran into the door."

A short distance down the tunnel, they discerned another light.

"It looks like another door," observed Dad.

"Except this one is open," said Mom, with relief.

"It's not open," contradicted Joseph, as they approached, "it has been shredded."

They could see the teeth marks around the edges of the door, where it had been torn apart.

Mom looked around nervously, "Obviously, the lake creatures have been in this tunnel."

"Let's keep moving," admonished Dad.

As they went through the doorway, Sharianna noticed a small piece of metal on the floor; she picked it up and put it in her fanny pack.

Once beyond the door, the tunnel changed; it was now about double the width of the previous tunnel and it had a flat floor.

They proceeded down the tunnel. Other intersecting tunnels joined it, but each one was smaller than the one they were rushing down.

"What's that?" exclaimed Sharianna, as they came upon an unusual looking piece of equipment.

"Looks like some strange ore cart to me, except it does not have any wheels, answered Joseph. It was about 20 feet long and 8 feet wide, shaped like a dish and it was full of crushed rock.

"How would it move?" inquired Sharianna.

"I don't know, but let's keep moving," said Mom.

As they hurried on, they came to an even larger tunnel that had many of the same kind of carts; on one side were full ones, while on the other side, they were empty.

They continued on. Suddenly, they burst into a huge open room. It was well lit because the walls and floor were made of the same glowing metal that they had found elsewhere. They could see that it must be a central shaft. It had many other

96

tunnels entering into it, like a giant wagon wheel. In the center of this central hub they saw a pile of ore carts, many of which were smashed and lying in a disorganized pile. The shaft was very tall; at the top they could actually see stars.

"There's the way out!" exclaimed Sharianna.

"Yeah, but how do we get up there?" questioned Joseph.

"This must be the volcano shaped mountain we flew over when we saw the obelisk—it's a mine!" deduced Mom.

"How far up do you think it is, Dad?" inquired Joseph.

"It must be at least one or two thousand feet," he estimated.

Thomas looked up intently at the towering walls, examining every detail. "Look, over there – there are windows up there that look out into this shaft. Maybe it's a control room."

Directly below the windows, on their level, Joseph thought he could see a doorway.

"Over there, I think it's a door!" he exclaimed.

"If there is a way up to the control room, then maybe there is access all the way to the top!" Mom nearly shouted, but she caught herself, not wanting to alert any of the creatures from the lake that might be in the vicinity of their whereabouts.

They started across the floor and wound their way around the disabled ore carts.

"Wait, I saw something move up there in the window," Sharianna said.

Everyone looked up, but the windows looked the same as they did before.

"Are you sure?" asked Mom.

"No, I guess I'm not," replied Sharianna.

"Well, let's be on our guard, anyway," cautioned Dad.

They paused near the large pile of ore carts to catch their breath.

"I'll bet these carts used some kind of antigravity technology, like the robot," theorized Joseph.

"Maybe," answered Dad, "but the metal is definitely not the same."

"I agree; judging from the smashed up condition of these containers, I would say the metal is definitely not as strong either," concluded Joseph.

"I'm getting hungry, and I'm tired," complained Sharianna.

"Me too," agreed Joseph.

"I know," said Mom compassionately, as she pulled them both to her and gave them a hug.

They continued across the huge shaft and entered the doorway, into a foyer; a hallway led directly away, and a very small room was on the left. Joseph stepped into the room.

"It looks like it might be an elevator," he said, as he motioned the others to follow. On the wall next to the door was a small knob, seated in a groove that was about two feet long. At intervals along the groove were strange alien symbols. Joseph assumed that these indicated the different levels, or floors. When they were all inside, he slid the knob up. Nothing happened.

Looking across the foyer, Sharianna saw a door. "I think that looks like stairs through the window of that other door."

"I think you're right; let's try it," suggested Dad.

They quickly made their way across the foyer. The door was slightly ajar. Dad pushed on it and it opened.

Mom looked back into the foyer. "In different circumstances, I would love to investigate some more, but right now, all I want to do is get back to the robot as quickly as we can."

The staircase led both up and down in a steep spiral, like the first staircase inside the obelisk, except this one did not have the clear tube filled with water.

The stairway was a curious work of art, because the stairwell was essentially a round shaft going straight up with flat ledges about an inch thick jutting out of the wall creating the steps. There were no handrails. The stairs and the walls were made of the luminescent metal. Joseph leaned out and looked up and down the center of the shaft. It was hard to tell the extent of the staircase because the steps seemed numberless. "At least it looks like it goes up a long way," he said, "maybe even to the top."

They climbed and climbed. It was hard work because each step was about a foot and a half high.

"Why are these steps so high?" asked Joseph.

"Isn't it obvious," stated Sharianna, "the aliens who built it were huge—at least they were very tall. Don't you think so, Dad?"

"It sure seems that way," replied Dad. He laughed with his next comment: "Or maybe they just had long legs."

"So, what happened to them?" asked Sharianna. "Mom, what do you think?"

"I'm wondering if the aliens offended the lake creatures, like we did," speculated Joseph.

"I think I agree with Joseph's premise: perhaps the lake creatures destroyed them or drove them out. Maybe the creatures became too troublesome and the aliens simply abandoned the mine," answered Mom.

Dad interjected another theory: "Maybe the mine played out."

"Played out?" questioned Sharianna.

"Ran out of ore."

"I doubt it," countered Mom, "if they left of their own volition then why are there so many ore carts piled up in the middle of the main shaft? I think the power was shut off suddenly and they all fell to the floor."

"Your logic is impeccable," complemented Dad.

"Look, the control room," said Joseph.

As they reached the level of the control room, the stairwell became open; the stairs were free standing as they continued up and disappeared into the shaft in the ceiling, like the stairs in a modern art apartment.

They could see the windows that looked out over the central shaft.

Along the windows were some table-like desks, about five feet high, with a row of tall stools in front of them.

On the floor were several peculiar balls. They were about the size of a soccer ball and, like the soccer ball, rather than being perfectly round, they were multisided. They were very shiny and looked like polished stainless steel.

This room had a high ceiling. It was long and narrow, probably three times as long as it was wide. They could see four openings, three without doors that looked like they led into other

99

rooms or tunnels, and one with a door that was closed.

Dad walked over and picked up one of the shinny balls. It was deceptively heavy. Thomas expected it to be light, because of the moon's low gravity, but to his surprise it felt like it might be solid metal. He heaved it onto one of the stools and looked out the window into the main mine shaft. "I think we are a little more than halfway to the top," he declared.

Sharianna climbed up onto one of the stools.

"It must be a control station," observed Sharianna, "look at all these levers and switches."

"Look at this, dear," said Sophia.

Thomas turned, and saw Mom and Joseph standing in front of a three-dimensional model made of a material that looked clear – something like acrylic. The whole model was over 5 feet tall.

"It's a model of the mine!" exclaimed Joseph. "See, here's the obelisk... and the underground lake... and the tunnels that we came through."

The top of the model showed in perfect detail the surface of the moon, while the extensive labyrinth of tunnels, shafts and rooms were all cut directly from the acrylic-like material.

"And here's the central shaft and the mountain," said Mom. "We are right here. Look!" she exclaimed excitedly, "We don't have to go all the way to the top! There is a tunnel leading from this control room, directly to the base of the mountain."

Sharianna pulled her camera from her fanny pack. The fanny pack was pretty shredded up, and the camera had scratches on it, but the display still worked. She took a picture of the model.

"Did you get a picture of the lake creatures?" asked Joseph.

"Do you think I had any time to take a picture?" she retorted.

"Well, let's get going!" said Dad.

"This way," exclaimed Mom, full of hope and excitement, as she ran toward the tunnel entrance.

They entered the tunnel and began to run past a small mine cart, not much bigger than a golf cart, when Joseph stopped and leaped up onto the cart. "Wait! This one has seats and controls. Maybe it still works." Joseph climbed up onto the driver's seat. "Here, hold this," instructed Joseph, as he handed the four-foot piece of railing to Sharianna.

The controls seemed simple; there was only one knob. He pushed forward on it, and back, but it did nothing, he pushed it from side to side. By this time the rest of the family was up on the cart and seated.

"I guess it lost power with the rest of them," said Mom.

Joseph got an idea. He pulled up on the knob. Suddenly, the cart lifted off the floor.

"Yippee!" exclaimed Sharianna, "get us out of here!"

"Wait," said Dad, as he leaped off the cart and ran back into the control room.

"What are you doing?" demanded Mom.

"I'll be right back," he replied.

A moment later, Dad returned lugging one of the heavy metal balls.

"Why did you get that?" asked Mom.

"I don't know, I guess I wanted a souvenir," replied Dad as he put the ball on the floor. "That thing feels like it weighs at least a hundred pounds."

"That means it will weigh six hundred pounds when we get back to earth," said Joseph.

Dad looked at the ball with a puzzled look, "I don't think even solid iron would weigh that much."

"Well, the Moon's gravity is only one sixth of earth, right?" replied Joseph.

"Yes," said Dad contemplatively.

"I think I would have chosen a souvenir that was easier to carry," said Mom.

They sped through the tunnel and onto the surface of the moon. They could see the obelisk in the distance.

The cart raced over the rough terrain, perfectly smoothly. Within minutes they had landed right next to the robot.

CHAPTER FIFTEEN

"LET'S TAKE IT HOME"

MOM GASPED AS THEY LANDED AT THE FOOT OF THE ROBOT.

"What's the matter?" asked Dad.

"The door of the robot is closed."

"Just whistle," instructed Joseph.

Mom tried to whistle but she couldn't do the catcall whistle like Dad.

Dad whistled. Nothing happened.

Mom looked at him fearfully. "Are we locked out?" she asked.

Dad whistled again. Nothing.

Dad stepped onto the edge of the cart and climbed onto the robot's foot. Again, he whistled in vain.

"Maybe the whistle only activates the main door in the control room," speculated Joseph.

"And it can't open because it's not an airlock," added Shari-anna.

Sophia began to panic. She leaped onto the foot and pounded on the hull of the ship where the door should have been with her fist. "Open," she commanded, with her anxiety clearly apparent. "The ship took verbal orders before, why not now?"

"Try being more specific," suggested Joseph. "Open the outer door of the airlock."

"Open sesame," tried Dad, as fear for his family began to wrap its bony fingers around his heart.

Perceiving their anxiety, Percy barked.

"There must be a secret latch, or something," insisted Dad, as he ran his fingers all over the surface of the ship as far as he could reach.

"Hand me the railing, please," requested Mom.

Sharianna handed her the railing.

Mom followed Dad's example and began tapping with the railing all over the top of the foot, hoping to find a hidden actuator.

When Dad was sure he had definitely pushed every square inch of the hull that he could reach, he turned back to his family. Putting his hand on Mom's arm he said softly, "I don't think there is an exterior actuator."

"What are we going to do?" she whispered, as she sank to her knees next to Sharianna. Tears of despair began to flow silently down her cheeks.

Dad knelt down next to her. "We'll figure it out."

"They're planning a permanent manned station here on the moon," proffered Joseph, trying to sound positive, as he stood next to Dad.

"When is the next mission?" questioned Sharianna.

"Maybe next year," he sighed sadly.

Sharianna put her arms around Mom. Dad continued to search in vain for a hidden actuator and tried all kinds of whistles in an attempt to open the airlock door.

Joseph tried whistling, but to no avail.

Thomas had no idea how long they had been there, the minutes may have stretched into hours; he felt weak. He stood in front of the airlock door; he could no longer whistle. Sophia's panic was beginning to take hold of him as well. The knot in his stomach seemed to threaten to overwhelm his whole being.

Tears began to stream down Sophia's face. She knew they were trapped outside, but it still seemed better than being trapped inside the obelisk, or the mine with the terrifying creatures.

Suddenly, Sharianna remembered the last time she had given the ship a command – she had addressed it specifically. She offered a silent prayer through her tears then said, "Robo-ship, open the outer door of the airlock."

The door silently and smoothly slid open.

"Thank you Sharianna," sobbed Mom, her tears of distress now turned to tears of joy as they entered the airlock.

"No, thank God," acknowledged Sharianna quietly, as she thought about her silent prayer.

"Yes, thank God," agreed Dad.

Thomas was about to push the button to close the airlock door when he remembered the metal ball in the alien cart. "My souvenir," he exclaimed, as he leaped across the robot's foot and retrieved the strange ball.

As soon as Dad crossed the threshold of the airlock, he was no longer able to carry the ball and it landed on the bathroom door with a thud.

"I guess Joseph was right – we don't even have to wait till we get back to earth for it to weigh six hundred pounds," laughed Mom.

Sharianna pushed the button and the door slid silently closed and they began to hear the air return to the airlock and the gravitational pull slowly rotated until they were all standing on the floor again. The ball slowly rolled down the bathroom door, until it also came to a rest on the floor of the airlock.

As the door to the hallway opened, Dad rushed headlong to the control room.

"I think we should get out of here," suggested Mom.

Dad lifted off and they hovered over the surface of the moon, looking back toward the obelisk. He flew the robot a few miles away and landed on top of a small mountain.

Joseph grabbed his bag of Doritos off the chair: "I'm really starving now."

Mom began to get up. "I'll make something to eat."

Dad stood up. "No, you take it easy, I'll get it."

"We'll both get it," she insisted. "I wasn't planning on an extended trip, so there is not much in the way of a real meal, but we'll manage."

Joseph and Sharianna took off their space suits. "Here, Sharianna, help me get Percy's suit off," Joseph said.

As they pulled on Percy's suit, it just stretched, but would not come apart.

"Why won't his suit come off?" inquired Mom.

Sharianna suddenly remembered when Joseph had pretended to be suffocating in the suit and she had tried to remove it. "It only responds to itself," she explained.

104

Joseph grabbed Percy's two front feet and used them to pull on the suit and it came right apart.

After dinner, they made their way to the control room.

"Where to now? Mars?" inquired Sharianna, who now felt safe inside the robot. She was half serious, as she sat in one of the control chairs and looked at the console with the depiction of the solar system.

"Yeah, right," responded Dad, with a hint of sarcasm. "I think we should go home first."

Sharianna felt a little nervous as they flew up from the surface, but her piloting skills were very good, she was a natural. She looked over at Joseph, who occupied the other control chair. She was surprised and very pleased when he looked back at her with a serious face, raised his eyebrows, and nodded his head slightly in approval. She smiled wide back at him.

"Looks like there is still one more site to investigate," observed Joseph, as he looked at the view screen in front of them.

"Okay, one last site," agreed Dad.

Sharianna lined up the last circle with the dot in the middle of the screen and flew toward the surface.

"It's another rocket," stated Sharianna, as they approached the site.

"But it's not as smashed up as the other ones," observed Mom.

"From the looks of it, they didn't have a very smooth landing," concluded Joseph.

"I'm going to land next to that big piece, over there." Sharianna pointed to a large piece that looked like part of the outer hull of the rocket.

She eased back on the controls as she hovered for a moment, while turning the robot from a horizontal flying position to an upright position, ready for landing. As she touched the surface, only a small cloud of dust was kicked up.

"Good landing," whispered Joseph. "But don't get a big head," he added quietly from the side of his mouth.

She smiled without looking at him.

Joseph read the nearly obliterated letters on the wreckage: "DIA. What does that mean?"

"I think there are two letters missing: IN," deduced Mom.

"INDIA?"

"I heard that they had recently sent a rocket to the moon," confirmed Dad.

"Were any astronauts on board?" asked Sharianna with some concern, as she looked at the wreckage.

"No, it was unmanned; I think they just sent it so they could make a claim if the moon ever became valuable real estate," explained Dad.

"Can we go out and explore the crash site?" inquired Joseph.

"I think we can see it just fine from right here," stated Mom definitively. "I think one moon walk is enough."

"Okay," moaned Joseph with a sigh.

"What then?" Sharianna wanted to know.

"Everyone's had a chance to fly." Dad motioned for Joseph to vacate his seat. "I'll take this ship home."

Joseph made his way down to the front observation area. "Better view from down here anyway. Come on Sharianna."

Mom interjected, "That's okay Sharianna, you can stay there; I haven't seen the view from down below yet." She went down the steps to join Joseph.

"Hey, what about the little hover cart that we left by the obelisk?" asked Joseph.

"Let's take it home!" exclaimed Sharianna.

"It would barely fit in the cargo bay," argued Mom. "Besides, what would we do with it?"

"I want to take it apart and see how it works," replied Joseph.

"That would be extremely interesting," agreed Dad, as he pushed forward on the stick and the robot took a step forward, flattening the large piece of debris from the INDIA rocket. "Oops, I guess I better find the right gear." He smiled amidst roaring laughter from his family.

"Where is it?" asked Sharianna, as they approached the obelisk.

Dad flew all the way around the obelisk. "It's gone," he concluded.

"The door into the obelisk is closed. Do you think the lake creatures came out and got it?" asked Joseph.

"I doubt it," answered Dad. "I would think they would have to stay down where there is some atmosphere."

"Then what?" demanded Mom.

"Sharianna did see something in the window of the control room," offered Joseph.

"Maybe someone came out and got it," speculated Dad.

"Or some-*thing*," posed Sharianna.

"It could have even been programmed to return automatically," suggested Joseph.

"We'll fly over to the tunnel and see," said Dad.

"First, let's see if there are any new footprints," said Mom.

Dad bent the robot down close to the surface; they could not see any footprints other than their own and the astronauts'.

"Nope, nothing," observed Dad.

"I don't see any slime trails either," said Joseph.

"Okay, let's take one more look at the tunnel before we go," agreed Mom.

"Hey, the tunnel is closed!" exclaimed Joseph, as they approached. "Should we fly down into the main mine shaft?"

"No way!" answered Mom. "If there is something down there, I don't want to find out if its technology is great enough to pose a risk to the robot—we're leaving."

The moon quickly receded into the distance as they approached earth. This time they didn't hit any asteroids. Thomas made a mental note to look up the asteroids on the Internet and find out more about their orbits.

"Let's fly around the earth before we land; I heard you can see the Great Wall of China from space," suggested Mom, as they made their approach to Earth.

Joseph laughed, "That's just a myth, Mom. NASA debunked it a long time ago."

"Well, we can see for ourselves, can't we?" insisted Mom.

"Alright, I don't see how it could hurt," concurred Dad.

The western hemisphere was again shrouded in darkness as they entered the orbit of the earth. Only the lights from cities were discernable from that distance.

"Can you see Salt Lake City?" asked Dad.

"I think so, but it looks pretty dim compared to Los Angeles."

"Look how bright Mexico City is," Mom observed.

"You know, that's one of the largest cities in the world," commented Joseph wistfully as he remembered a talk that the beautiful Rosa-Maria had given in his social studies class. He liked her almost as much as he liked Allison. Joseph remembered scaring Allison when he dragged her by the ankle toward the deep water of the reservoir. He felt a little guilt at scaring her so much. *I'll tell her it was me, maybe she will think it was funny. No, I'd better not; she would probably think I was immature or inconsiderate,* he thought.

He was suddenly brought back to the present: "What is that?" Sharianna pointed directly ahead at an odd-looking structure floating in space with flat panels extending from it that looked a little like wings.

CHAPTER SIXTEEN

The Ambush

"IT'S THE SPACE STATION!" EXCLAIMED MOM. "YOU'D better steer around that."

The robot was overtaking the space station so rapidly that they were alongside of it before Dad had time to push the stick sideways. The robot darted off into space. But not before they saw, in one of the small windows, the face of a female astronaut.

"Do you think she saw us?" asked Sharianna.

"I don't see how she could not have," confirmed Mom.

Dad steered back toward the earth and a few minutes later they saw the sun rising on the horizon and they were flying over the Atlantic.

"There's Europe, the Mediterranean sea, and Africa!" exclaimed Joseph.

"Slow down, or we'll blast right past China," cautioned Mom.

"Go a little lower, Dad," said Joseph.

As Thomas began his descent, they suddenly heard a loud noise on the hull of the ship.

"That sounded like another asteroid," theorized Sharianna.

"I think it was more like a metallic crunching sound," observed Joseph.

"It was a satellite," deduced Mom.

"Oops, I hope someone can do without their satellite TV," said Joseph. "Or it could be radio, GPS, Internet, or even a military satellite."

"We might as well have rung the front doorbell, if it was military," observed Sharianna.

"I'll fly down into the upper atmosphere so that we won't hit any more," decided Dad.

"Watch out for airplanes," warned Sharianna, as she remembered their near miss the day before. *Was it really only a day ago? Or was it two days?"* she thought to herself. *It seems like we have been gone so long.*

"They don't fly this high," replied Dad.

"I remember, when we went to the airplane museum at Hill Air Force Base, I learned that some of the spy planes, like the Blackbird, fly through the upper atmosphere," corrected Joseph.

"I think you are right," conceded Dad. "I think we'll just have to be careful."

Off to their right they could see the towering snow-capped peaks of the Himalayas, except that from their altitude they just looked like a little crinkle in the crust of the earth.

"There's China. But I don't see the great wall," said Joseph.

"I guess you can't see it from space after all," said Mom with disappointment. "But I would sure like to see it anyway. Maybe we could go lower?"

Dad brought the robot lower, until they were just above the clouds.

Suddenly, the Great Wall came into view, snaking its way across miles and miles of countryside, but the clouds obscured most of it.

Thomas slowed the robot some more and decreased their altitude until they were just below the clouds, to get a better look.

The view was so spectacular that Thomas brought the robot to a stop and hovered in the air. Sharianna couldn't resist taking some pictures.

"Wow, we could go anywhere we wanted to," marveled Joseph. "How about the pyramids? Those, you *can* see from space."

"I'd like to look at the Egyptian obelisks and compare them with the one on the moon," said Mom.

Suddenly, out of the clouds appeared five Mig fighter jets, only a few hundred yards away, and traveling at top speed. At that same instant, all five fired off two rockets each and veered up, back into the clouds. Dad's reflexes were quick and his thoughts just as quick. Knowing that the fighters were in the clouds and not wanting to run into one of them, he chose to dive.

The Mig commander must have anticipated the movements of the UFO because the rockets were deployed in a star pattern, with only the center rocket heading straight for them. The moment the

110

jets were in the cloudbank they fired off another ten rockets towards the rear of the UFO in hopes that if the UFO attempted to retreat it would actually run into one of them, like moving landmines in the sky.

The commander of the Migs was a very calculating man and had spaced the rockets so perfectly that they were impossible to avoid. He smiled as he watched his radar screen tracking seven other Migs who had been instructed to drop out of the clouds behind the UFO and fire all their rockets underneath it two seconds before the five Migs that had descended from the clouds in front of the UFO. The Mig commander dropped back out of the clouds just in time to see the perfect execution of his surprise attack as the UFO became engulfed in a huge explosion, as it dove directly into one of the rockets that he had shrewdly fired from behind.

The exhilaration of his triumph was momentary however, for as he watched, he saw the UFO streak toward the ground, faster than any craft he had ever seen. His delight returned fleetingly as he thought that crashing with the ground was inevitable. A microsecond before impact, the UFO made an impossible 90-degree turn and sped away only a few yards above the ground. Within moments it had disappeared over the horizon.

As they dove to miss the oncoming missiles, they heard a deafening explosion and the screen in front of them became shrouded in flames. Then the ground became the greatest threat as it came rushing toward them at an incredible speed. Thomas pulled out of the dive and the robot went zooming along the surface of the ground. The earth was all a blur.

"Look out for that mountain!" screamed Sophia.

Thomas pulled up enough to just skim the snow-covered peak. Thomas slowed the robot, in order to gain more control over his trajectory. Strangely, it occurred to him that they were flying much faster than the speed of sound and he wondered how loud the sonic boom must be along their flight path.

Suddenly, they saw water ahead as they flew over the Yellow Sea. They saw a vapor trail from a rocket that had been launched from North Korea, but they easily veered to the right, flying over South Korea, and it exploded harmlessly in the air. They crossed the Sea of Japan in just a few moments and flew right over Tokyo. As they flew out over the Pacific Ocean, they suddenly saw a huge aircraft carrier with jets buzzing off its deck like a swarm of bees. Again, Dad veered right, putting them on a course due south. The supersonic jets were quickly left in the distance.

Thomas began to realize the significance of what had just happened. As he brought the robot to a stop just above the surface of the water, he realized that the robot must show up on radar or some other tracking system.

"They must be able to track us," he said nervously, as he relaxed his white-knuckle grip on the controls. "There is no other way they could have surprised us like that."

"That was close, that rocket almost hit us," cried Sharianna.

"I think it *did* hit us!" asserted Joseph.

"Do you think the robot is damaged?" inquired Mom.

"I don't think so," responded Dad, but his thoughts were racing. He remembered hearing that radar could not track airplanes close to the ground. He hoped that they did not have any more sophisticated tracking devices than that.

Joseph must have been thinking the same things because he verbalized Dad's concern: "If the Chinese could track us so well then what about NASA, or our own military?" he paused, "How will we get back home without being detected and followed?"

"They don't know about us, they only know about a UFO. Right?" rationalized Sharianna.

"That's right," agreed Dad, as he looked around in the sky for planes and across the waves to see if there were any more ships.

"We could go back out to space," suggested Mom.

"But they would probably track us. Eventually, we would need to go home," countered Dad. "I'll bet they have satellite tracking for intercontinental missiles and who knows what else."

"They even saw us on the space station," added Joseph.

Low over the waves, they suddenly saw a formation of fighter jets screaming toward them.

CHAPTER SEVENTEEN

The Mariana Trench

"THOSE COULDN'T HAVE COME FROM CHINA," DECLARED Mom, apprehensively.

"They couldn't be from that carrier near Tokyo either—there are no planes that fast," said Joseph. "What if they fire on us too?"

Sharianna looked down. "Hey, what about the ocean?"

Immediately, Dad lowered the robot beneath the surface of the waves.

"Do you think they saw us?" asked Sharianna.

"I don't know, but we're not going to wait around to find out. Now I *know* they can track us; otherwise, they could not have found us so quickly." Dad piloted the ship through the water as fast as he dared. "I don't want to make a wake that they can follow."

"Maybe they already had an aircraft carrier in the vicinity," Mom speculated.

"They must have some sophisticated form of global positioning, or something...I wonder how they are tracking us—we don't give off any heat and we don't make any sound," pondered Dad, as he dove down even deeper.

"How deep do you think we are?" asked Sharianna.

"I don't know but we can still see, so we can't be more than one or two hundred feet."

"I think we have been oblivious tourists too long," declared Mom. "We need a plan. How are we going to get home without being detected again? I don't want them tracking us straight to the barn."

"I don't really even know where we are," complained Dad.

"We're in the Pacific Ocean," stated Joseph, proudly.

"That doesn't help much," replied Dad. "The Pacific is huge."

Joseph suddenly remembered that he had grabbed his backpack when they were loading the robot because he wanted his iPod that was in it. *I haven't even used it*, he thought. "Hey, I still have your GPS in my backpack!" He jumped up and, clearing the steps up to the main level in one leap, crossed the control cabin with two big steps. Ducking his head, he darted into the small corridor that led to the cargo bay.

"Will it work clear out here?" asked Sharianna, while Joseph was gone.

"The GPS works off of many satellites that orbit the entire earth; it should work," explained Dad hopefully.

"As long as the satellite we destroyed wasn't the key GPS satellite," commented Mom wryly.

Joseph returned with his backpack. "Look what else I've got!" he exclaimed, as he dramatically pulled from his backpack his astronomy book that Uncle Jared had given him.

"We're not in space anymore," said Sharianna tersely.

"Yeah, but look here, it's not just about space," he retorted, as he opened it up to a large fold out map of the world.

"Excellent!" praised Dad.

"Yea!" exclaimed Mom happily, as she looked at the GPS. "It works. Now we know where we are and where we are going; all we have to decide is how we are going to get there."

Joseph wrote the coordinates down on the map.

"If we lived on the coast we could stay under water the whole way," said Sharianna.

"What if we approached from the north, across the Great Salt Lake?" suggested Joseph. "There is nothing out there."

Joseph was looking at his map. "What if we came from way up north? If we flew really low, I'll bet no one would even see us crossing Canada." Joseph drew a line on the map with a pencil across the Pacific, between Hawaii and Japan, through the North Pacific, through the Bearing Straight, into the Arctic Ocean, then back south through the Northwest Passage to Hudson Bay, across the north end of Manitoba, then down through Saskatchewan, Montana, Idaho and back to Salt Lake City. "We can stay hidden under water almost the whole way."

"Yeah, but look, it's a lot farther over land from Hudson Bay than it is from the California coast," Sharianna pointed out.

"I like Joseph's idea because there are fewer people up north," said Mom.

"Look, a whale!" interrupted Dad, as he saw a large silhouette out in front and above them, coming their way.

"It must be a blue whale—it's so huge," gasped Joseph.

Suddenly, Dad was gripped with trepidation as he realized that the silhouette did not swim like a whale. He began diving deeper.

"That's not a whale, it's a submarine," Joseph corrected himself.

The submarine matched their descent.

Dad increased his speed and began to pull away.

"How deep do you think we can go?" asked Sharianna.

"Deeper than them, I hope," replied Dad. "That's a nuclear submarine – its real maximum dive depth is still classified."

The light from the surface began to fade and they could no longer see the submarine.

"Why didn't they fire on us?" asked Sharianna.

"There're probably American. And not as impetuous as the Chinese," Dad replied. "They probably want to capture us without completely destroying the ship," he theorized, as they dove deeper.

"Or maybe they just want to talk to us?" proposed Sharianna.

"They would probably experiment on us and dissect us," warned Joseph.

"They wouldn't dissect us. Would they? Dad?" inquired Sharianna.

"No, I don't think so; besides, they are not going to catch us, are they?" he replied.

"It won't matter, if the pressure crushes us," cautioned Mom, with a little worry in her voice.

"I don't hear any creaking," consoled Joseph.

"What's that supposed to mean?" questioned Sharianna.

"Submarines always creak before they are crushed," Joseph reasoned.

"How do you know that?" Sharianna probed skeptically.

"It's in all the movies," he replied matter-of-factly.

"Oh, so then it *must* be true," she answered sarcastically.

Mom looked at the GPS. It wasn't working. "At least the built in compass is still working," she said. Joseph, what were the last coordinates?"

"I think we're too deep for the GPS," speculated Dad.

Joseph looked on the map where he had written down the coordinates, "147.22 degrees longitude and 17.68 degrees North." He located the position on the map. "We're right over the Mariana trench! The map says it is the world's deepest sounding: 35,827 feet."

"That's deep," agreed Mom.

"Yeah, you could take Mount Everest, the tallest mountain on earth, and put it upside down in the Mariana trench and it still would not reach the bottom," commented Dad.

"How do you know where you are going?" asked Mom.

"I don't," replied Dad.

"It's black as pitch out there," complained Sharianna.

"What is that?" inquired Joseph, as a small light appeared on the screen. They drew closer and Joseph suddenly exclaimed: "It's a bioluminescent jellyfish! And it's huge! Mom, remember the book you got me about the creatures in the deep oceans? A lot of creatures down here make their own light."

Dad brought the ship to a stop in front of the large jellyfish, but it swam down into the deep.

Sharianna remembered watching one of the NOVA programs with Dad: "I wish we had those spotlights that the deep sea ROV's have on them." She suddenly got an idea: "Robo-Ship, light up the water in front of us."

Immediately, light shone from the eyes of the robot, lighting the ocean in front of them for several hundred feet.

There was a flurry of motion as creatures scurried to escape the unfamiliar light.

"Wow, there's a lot of life down here," marveled Mom.

Dad proceeded with renewed confidence; at least now he could see if they were about to plow into an underwater mountain or the ocean floor.

"Do you think the submarine can track us?" asked Joseph.

"I don't know what its sensor range is," answered Dad, "but I'm quite sure that we can move a lot faster underwater than they can. If we stay ahead of them and don't follow a straight line, I think we can lose them."

"And there is no way they can dive as deep as us," stated Mom. "Right?"

"Yeah, right," replied Dad, with an air of confidence that did not altogether reflect his actual thoughts.

Suddenly, there appeared a huge, unusual looking creature that extended from the top of the screen down into the murky darkness.

"A giant squid!" exclaimed Joseph.

Again, Dad brought the robot to a stop. "I think we are the first people to ever see a giant squid, this big, alive," he said. "It must be 100 feet long!"

"Look, it has something in its tentacles," exclaimed Joseph.

As they looked closer they could see that it had actually captured a shark, about six feet long, in its tentacles and was bringing it up to its mouth. They were close enough to see the light reflect from its great big eyes.

Unexpectedly, from above the squid, they saw a huge shape descend. The giant invertebrate was preoccupied with consuming its newly captured meal; it did not discern the danger that sped toward it from above.

Joseph immediately recognized the huge blunt, square head extending a third of the way down the body, and its small, under slung lower jaw. Small, was a relative thing; it was only small when compared to the total size of the head – the jaw was still over eight feet long.

"It's a sperm whale! Get a picture of that Sharianna!" he exclaimed, as they heard a very low toned reverberation that sounded a little like a sonic boom. Immediately, the squid seemed to go limp and what was left of the shark slowly drifted down into the depths, as the 60-foot whale opened its mouth and with a movement of its tongue created a vacuum that sucked the invertebrate into its mouth. As soon as the huge jaws closed on the body of the invertebrate, its tentacles seemed to spring back to life, writhing and twining themselves around the head and neck of the colossal mammal, tearing and pulling at the whale's skin, but to no avail.

With a large swish of its tail it swung its great head in the direction of the robot and seemed to pause as it observed them with its huge eyes. The great beast opened its mouth and with another sucking motion of its tongue drew in another eight feet of the giant invertebrate. Finally, the tentacles released their grip on the whale as he continued to feast. Then, with what looked like a deliberate nod of acknowledgment in the direction of the robot, it turned its immense square head and gracefully began its long ascent to the surface with the remnants of the squid's tentacles trailing from its huge mouth.

The whole family sat speechless for a moment as the whale disappeared into the darkness above. Finally, Joseph broke the silence, "Awesome," was all he could say.

"Yes, awesome," echoed Dad.

Dad pressed forward on the stick again until both small and large fauna streamed past the robot at an amazing speed. He estimated that they must be traveling at somewhere between fifty and seventy-five miles per hour, by the rate that creatures came into view in the lights and then disappeared back into the black expanse as they passed them.

Off to the right, the wall of the underwater canyon came into view. This confirmed Joseph's previous declaration that they were over the Mariana trench, for they now seemed to be deep within its walls.

"Look, the walls are alive with life," observed Mom.

Dad slowed down in order to get a better look. To their surprise, they saw a myriad of fish and other creatures: the orange roughy, with its orange skin, the snaggletooth and the anglerfish with their bioluminescent fishing lures and their enormous teeth. They saw several kinds of translucent jellyfish with their poisonous tentacles.

"Stop. There, to the right," instructed Sharianna. "That section of wall moved." As they approached closer, suddenly they saw a huge creature. "It looks like a manta ray," speculated Joseph.

"No way," exclaimed Sharianna. "Look at those huge tentacles. It looks like it has huge paws with a dozen or so sharp hooks on each of those two longest tentacles."

As they approached, they startled a large fish about four feet long from its resting place on a rock shelf. It darted past the hiding place of the colossal squid. Like a flash, it reached out and embedded its long hooks into the fish and quickly drew it in.

"It's almost as long as the robot and must weigh at least a ton," estimated Dad.

They turned away from the wall and continued their descent into the trench.

"Why are you diving even deeper?" questioned Mom.

"I still haven't heard any creaking." Dad smiled, as he looked at Joseph with a wink. "No, really, I just want to make sure we put a lot of distance and depth between us and the submarine; besides, wouldn't you like to see what is at the bottom?"

"Yes," answered Joseph. "It's even better than climbing the tallest mountain."

"But the GPS doesn't work when we are so deep," commented Mom.

"I know, we'll have to come up near the surface to figure out where we are; but in the meantime, I want to make sure we have lost them for good."

As they dove deeper and deeper into the trench they observed fewer animals, until finally they seemed to be alone in the depths.

When they reached the bottom, Dad stopped. He put a finger to his lips. "Shhh…" Dad paused as his eyes darted around at the curved ceiling. "Did you hear a creak?"

"Stop it, Dad!" commanded Sharianna.

They continued traveling south along the bottom of the trench. Abruptly, they discovered a large number of army tanks and jeeps from the World War II era strewn along the bottom. They were somewhat deteriorated by the salt water, but all seemed to be intact. They looked around for the ship that must have been carrying them but they could not find one in the vicinity.

Suddenly, Dad remembered a program on TV. "After the war, rather than bring so much equipment back home, they just dumped them in the ocean."

"That seems very wasteful," said Sharianna, as if she were scolding those who made that decision.

"What is that light!" exclaimed Mom, as she pointed toward a very faint glow a short distance beyond the reach of the robot's lights.

"How could there be any light way down here?" marveled Joseph.

As they approached the mysterious illumination, they could gradually make out the sharply defined outline of a man-made structure silhouetted against the unearthly red glow. It appeared that the structure had a few windows in the upper sections that also emanated the strange glow.

Mom put her hand on Dad's shoulder. "What is it?" she asked.

"Maybe it's a sunken city?" ventured Joseph.

"Maybe it's another space ship?" proposed Sharianna.

120

CHAPTER EIGHTEEN
Island Paradise

AS THEY APPROACHED THE STRUCTURE, JOSEPH UNRAVELED the mystery: "It's a sunken ship. But where is the light coming from?"

"It still has airplanes strapped to the deck," exclaimed Sharianna, as they got closer.

"It's a World War II aircraft carrier," said Dad.

They passed over the rusting old ship and discovered the source of the strange luminosity. A crack in the floor of the ocean exposed the molten lava below.

"Why doesn't the lava solidify when it is exposed to the water?" asked Sharianna.

"Why doesn't it spew out like a volcano?" added Joseph.

"It must be one of those peculiar balances in nature," Mom theorized. "The extreme pressure of the water from above keeps the lava down, while the extreme heat from below keeps it hot."

"Like the moon: Earth's gravity keeps it from flying out of orbit, but its momentum keeps it from crashing into the earth," Joseph declared proudly.

Dad glanced at the map, "Some of the most intense fighting during World War II took place right here, and on the islands west of here."

Joseph turned his attention back to the map. "Look, the map legend says that one inch equals 660 miles. If we went mostly straight on the route home, we would be underwater for about nine inches." Joseph was scrawling on the back cover of the book. "That is almost 6,000 miles. How fast do you think we were going Dad?"

"Probably fifty, maybe seventy-five miles per hour."

Joseph continued his math on the back cover. "At 50 miles an hour...that would be 120 hours, or..."

"Five days," interrupted Sharianna, who was happy to display her quick math skills.

"We didn't seem to be making very much disturbance; I don't

121

see why we couldn't double our speed when we're in open water," suggested Mom.

Now Sharianna was looking at the map. "There is quite a bit of information about the ocean on here. It shows where the basins are and where the mountains are..."

Joseph interrupted, "It also shows how deep the water is."

"I was trying to *say*...the basins are probably flat so we could go pretty fast without crashing into any underwater mountains."

"Good idea," agreed Dad.

Looking at the map, Dad said: "If we turn left from the Mariana Trench, we would be heading east. Then we could zigzag north in a random pattern."

"Sounds good to me," concurred Mom. "I brought some food, but I don't think it will be enough; and a lot of it is just junk food."

An exciting idea occurred to Joseph. "Why don't we catch some fish?"

Sharianna interpreted the direction of his thoughts. "We could use the spacesuits and go diving." She was not interested in fishing, but she thought it would be splendid to swim with the tropical fish.

Thomas had always dreamed of diving in tropical waters, but always had to be content with watching the nature channel, so he was an easy sell. The idea even sounded exciting to Sophia.

"Okay!" cried Mom and Dad in unison.

Mom looked at the clock. "It's almost morning."

"No, I think it is almost dusk," countered Dad.

"I'm going by our clock, and we haven't had much sleep the last few days. I'll fix something to eat; then we all better get some sleep."

Thomas rose from the anti-gravity sofa feeling more rested and invigorated than he could ever remember. He looked at Sharianna's clock as he entered the control room. "Ten hours?" he said to himself. He could scarcely believe it. He hadn't slept for ten hours straight for a very long time. He began examining

122

Joseph's book: "Earth and the Stars." He opened it up to the world map and studied it. He wondered what Columbus and the early explorers would have given to have a map so accurate and full of such an incredible amount of information.

Thomas looked up as Joseph quietly entered the control room. "Mom's fixing breakfast, and Sharianna's still sleeping," reported Joseph, in response to his dad's glance toward the doorway.

"Okay, navigator, let's plot our course," ordered Dad, with his big smile, as he handed Joseph the book.

Joseph liked the idea of being the ship's navigator. "It looks like there are a lot of little islands south of here, the Caroline Islands; maybe we can find an uninhabited shore for our fishing expedition," he proposed hopefully.

When they rose up over the rim of the Mariana Trench, they traveled south along the bottom of the East Mariana Basin and the ocean slowly became shallower. The silty mud on the bottom gradually gave way to sand as the floor of the ocean sloped up more steeply with many exposed rocks and what looked like ancient lava flows. Directly in front of them they encountered a huge cliff, fractured and broken, with many crevasses and caves. As they rose along the cliff face it gradually got brighter. When they got near the top of the cliff they could see beautiful coral attached to the rock with an abundance of highly colored tropical fish.

"It looks like a giant aquarium," gasped Sharianna incredulously.

The water was calm and so beautiful and crystal clear that they could actually see trees and the shoreline with a mountain rising up behind the trees through the water as they paused near the surface. The early morning tropical sun was beginning to rise in the eastern sky.

"I wish we had a periscope to get a better view and see if there is anyone around," commented Dad.

Sharianna couldn't take her eyes off the pretty fish. "I sure hope the colors are as bright in the pictures," she said, as she snapped several shots. Then she noticed a large, bare rock right at the edge of the cliff. "Why don't we park the robot on that big rock over there?" she suggested. "That way we won't crunch any of the coral reef and the robot could stay hidden under the water while we explore the shore; it doesn't look very far to the beach."

"We swam a lot farther than that when we wore the space-suits in the lake," added Joseph, who was eager to get out and explore.

"I can't see any people, or any sign of civilization," observed Mom.

"Okay, but we'll leave the robot here, just to be safe," determined Dad, as he maneuvered the robot over to the large rock. While standing upright on the rock, the surface of the water was only ten or fifteen feet above the robot's head.

"No, not you this time boy," Joseph rubbed Percy's ears and head, as they proceeded to get into their spacesuits. Joseph emptied everything out of his backpack and put it on, before donning his spacesuit.

"The water might come rushing in when we open the outer door," cautioned Dad as they all stood in the airlock.

Mom looked at Dad's strange metal ball, "Shouldn't we put that in the cargo bay?" she asked.

Dad tried to pick it up without success.

"Don't you remember, Dad, it weighs at least six hundred pounds now," Sharianna reminded him.

Thomas began rolling the ball down the hallway to the cargo area. *Even if this were solid steel, I can't imagine how it could weigh this much,* he thought.

"Everyone ready?" asked Dad when he got back to the airlock. He pushed the button to open the door, but instead of it opening, water started to rise up from the floor until the little room was full right up to the ceiling.

Mom felt a little nervous as the water was rising in the airlock, but then she realized how silly it was. *We just escaped from monsters on the moon, what could be more dangerous,* she thought. Percy barked from the other side of the hall door. Joseph swam over to the window in the door and looked out to see Percy sitting in the hall; he waved as the outer door opened.

Sharianna was the first one out. She swam toward the beach, looking down at the beautiful coral and brightly colored fish. Joseph quickly caught up to her and they swam side by side.

"Come on you guys. What are you waiting for?" called out Joseph, as he motioned them to follow.

"It's even more beautiful than I've ever seen in the pictures and the movies," marveled Sharianna, as they swam over the reef. Anemones waved their colorful tentacles slowly with the gentle movement of the water. A myriad of colors were boldly displayed on sea cucumbers, starfish and innumerable tropical fish that danced in and out among the pretty coral.

"This must be the most colorful place on earth," exclaimed Joseph softly. The clear, sparkling water seemed to only enhance the bright colors.

"I heard that there are more species of animals in these waters than anywhere else on the planet," commented Dad. "And I believe it."

As they left the reef and swam toward the beach, Joseph and Sharianna noticed many beautiful seashells lying on the sandy bottom. Joseph picked up a delicate looking spiral, cone shaped shell. Sharianna spotted a huge shell, larger than a grapefruit, with pretty white, pink and salmon colors. Carrying the shell made it a little harder to swim but she figured it was worth it; besides, she could put it in Joseph's backpack when they got to the beach.

Mom and Dad caught up with the two explorers as they reached the shallow water at the edge of the beach. As they stood up and looked around, they realized that they had entered a sheltered lagoon. Directly in front of them and curving around to their left was an expanse of pristine, undisturbed, white beach, bordered by many species of tropical plants, blooming with beautiful, colorful flowers. At the head of the lagoon it looked like there might be a small stream flowing from amongst the trees. Palm fronds swayed gently in the morning breeze.

Not more than a few hundred yards from the beach rose up a steep, cone-shaped mountain, the slopes of which were covered in verdant vegetation more than a third of the way up, then giving way to steeper, rocky terrain and finally, nearly vertical, barren cliffs up at the truncated summit.

"It looks like an old volcano," observed Sharianna.

"Most of these islands are," agreed Mom.

"Even Hawaii," added Joseph.

Off to the right, they noticed an old lava flow about ten feet high extending from the base of the volcano, through the lush vegetation and out into the ocean, protecting the lagoon from the waves, like a breakwater. It appeared that a few very enterprising plants had begun to colonize the rocky flow, but for the most part it looked like a very bumpy highway leading from the mountain all the way down to the ocean.

As they gazed over this tropical paradise, Joseph smiled as he imagined that they were the Swiss Family Robinson. Over by the stream, Joseph noticed a stand of giant bamboo.

"Come on Dad, let's go make some fishing spears," invited Joseph, as he headed toward the bamboo.

"I'm going to search for some more seashells on the beach." Sharianna pulled off her spacesuit and slung it over a small palm tree that was growing almost horizontal to the ground. She kicked off her shoes, and ran back toward the water's edge through the soft white sand.

"Go ahead and explore; we'll be on the beach," said Mom, as she followed Sharianna's example and removed her spacesuit. The fresh breeze coming in from the ocean was invigorating. She took off her shoes and ran toward the water's edge, feeling euphoric, like a little girl.

"Oh yeah, I almost forgot about the spacesuits," said Joseph, as they added theirs to the pile on the tree.

As they approached the stand of giant bamboo, they realized how big they really were. Some of the canes were over twelve inches in diameter and over 50 feet tall. "It's hard to believe that this is grass, isn't it?" queried Dad.

Putting a hand on Joseph's shoulder, "Wait," instructed Dad earnestly, as he stared at the bamboo.

"What is it?" inquired Joseph apprehensively, as he peered into the stand of bamboo, wondering what could be hiding in there.

After a long pause, Dad continued: "I heard that bamboo is the fastest growing plant, and that you can actually see it grow, sometimes two or three feet in a day."

Joseph breathed a sigh of relief, "I'll bet that observation was made by a really bored person," concluded Joseph, after staring for only a few moments.

"I'll bet you're right," confirmed Dad, as he grabbed onto one of the small canes, only about an inch and a half in diameter, and tried to break it off, without much success.

"Wait a minute, Dad." Joseph pulled from his backpack a short knife that he had taken from the kitchen of the robot. The entire knife was made of a strange, clear material with silver crystal flecks throughout. Joseph drew the knife across the base of the cane and it immediately cut through the tough fibers with only the slightest effort.

Dad looked at the cut end in amazement. He flipped the cane around and measured two arm lengths from the base. "Did you know that most people's stretched out arm length is the same as their height? That means this stick is twelve feet long, if you cut it right there."

"Let's explore the jungle," suggested Joseph, after selecting a suitable cane for his own fishing spear.

Sharianna looked up from scouring the beach for beautiful seashells to see Joseph emerge from the trees carrying a huge armload of what looked like strange looking footballs, followed by Dad carrying some shiny greenish, leathery looking, pear shaped objects, larger than grapefruit.

As they approached the tree where they had left their space-suits they saw a small pile of the most exotic seashells they had ever seen, carefully piled up next to Sharianna's shoes.

"Wow, I have only seen most of these in expensive gift shops," declared Dad.

Sharianna came running up the beach. "Look at this one!" she exclaimed, holding up a shell that looked like a delicate red and white spiraled corkscrew.

"What are those?" asked Sharianna, pointing to the burdens they had been carrying.

"Coconuts!" answered Joseph, as he picked one up and quickly cut through the stringy fibrous husk, revealing the familiar brown nut inside. "Look," he directed, as he pierced one of the 'eyes' of the nut and drank some of the sweet milk inside. "Here, try some." He handed the nut to Sharianna.

"Did you see any animals in the jungle?" asked Shariana.

"Just lots of pretty birds," Dad replied.

"And lizards," added Joseph.

"You won't believe this," said Joseph, as Sharianna handed the nut back to him. With all the flare of a professional demonstrator, he easily sliced through the hard shell of the coconut, revealing the beautiful white meat inside.

Mom looked at the knife. "How does it cut so easily?"

"I wish I knew," replied Dad.

Joseph put on his suit and grabbed his long sharp bamboo spear. He had ingeniously fashioned a barb out of a long, curved thorn, which he had accidentally found on a formidable tree; he proudly showed them the wound in his arm like a warrior exhibiting his battle scars. He had carefully cut a small hole at a steep angle near the point of his spear and pushed the thorn all the way through until it was wedged in tight, then he shaved the thick end flush with the spear.

"Robinson Crusoe!" exclaimed Mom.

Dad put his suit on, picked up his spear and brandishing it like a primitive hunter exclaimed: "We bring back meat!" Joseph followed suit, and the two hunters then sprang toward the water yelling like primordial savages.

Sharianna winced. "Why can't we just sneak into a restaurant, or a supermarket, on the way home?"

"Good idea," agreed Mom, as she donned her suit. "I'd sure like to explore the reef some more."

"Me too," said Sharianna, as she picked up her suit.

Sharianna swam over to explore the reef near the ancient lava flow. As she was reaching out to touch an interesting looking piece of coral, she was startled when it suddenly swam away. She raised her hand instinctively. Suddenly, the piece of metal that was attached to the wrist of her suit flipped open right into her hand. She looked at it and discovered a button. She curled her hand all the way toward her and the handle flipped back onto her wrist. Then she flipped her wrist back all the way and it flipped out again. Carefully, she put her thumb on the button. It was round, like a roller button. As she pushed the button slowly forward, her whole body began to move in that direction. Immediately, she released the button and her forward momentum stopped – it seemed to be spring loaded.

Joseph approached the reef in anticipation of spearing a fish. He was surprised to find that the reef seemed unusually still.

"Must be pretty smart fish to know that we were coming," chuckled Dad.

They swam on toward the drop-off in hopes of finding some game there. Joseph went left along the edge of the cliff, while Dad went right. Joseph spied a rather large silvery fish hiding in a cavity under a rock. Slowly, he inched closer and finally, with a strong thrust of his spear, impaled the fish and, with some difficulty, pulled it out of its hiding place. "I got one!" he exclaimed.

Mom turned from examining a blue, multi-armed starfish in time to see Joseph freeze as a large tiger shark flashed up from the edge of the drop-off and clamped its jaws onto Joseph's wiggling fish, biting off the end of his spear.

"*Thomas!*" Mom called frantically for aid as she began swimming toward Joseph.

Suddenly, three more large sharks appeared and competed for the scraps from Joseph's fish.

Joseph was right in the middle of a feeding frenzy. Joseph had seen this shark behavior on TV and knew that he was in extreme danger. He could feel his body tighten with fear.

CHAPTER NINETEEN

The Volcano

JOSEPH TRIED TO SWIM BACKWARDS WHILE KEEPING HIS
blunt spear between himself and the sharks.

Several sharks turned toward Joseph and, seeming to perceive
his fear, swam toward him. Joseph jabbed at them with the blunt
end of his spear. The sharks approached, as if testing for
vulnerabilities, and then turned suddenly away and swam in
circles around him, only to return to test him further.

Sharianna pushed the button and sped toward him. "Joseph,
look!"

Joseph looked to see Sharianna speeding through the water
like a torpedo.

"Fling your wrist back like Spiderman and a button will flip
out that makes the suit power you through the water."

Joseph followed her instructions. When he saw a gap in the
circle of sharks around him he went shooting toward the beach.
Sharianna met him about halfway to the shore.

Mom and Dad also followed Sharianna's instructions and
came speeding toward them. Dad was still holding his spear and
he turned to face the sharks, but they were nowhere to be seen.

"Where did they go?" asked Mom.

In fact, they could not see any fish at all; the reef seemed
strangely devoid of all life.

Suddenly, they noticed a strange undulation in the sand
beginning from the shoreline and progressing underneath them
and quickly going out to sea, accompanied by a strange, muffled
rumbling sound. The sand puffed up a few inches as the
vibration moved through the seafloor.

"It's an earthquake!" announced Joseph. Then, remembering
that volcanoes and earthquakes often go together, he exclaimed:

130

"The *volcano*…"

They turned and looked up through the water in the direction of the volcano but the shaking of the lagoon floor had stirred up some of the sediment from the bottom and their view was cloudy. They quickly swam to the surface and looked toward the mountain to see a thin cloud of black smoke belching from its flat top.

"Oh, no," cried Mom.

"No wonder there were no people here," groaned Sharianna.

"We'd better get back to the robot," declared Dad, as he turned out toward the ocean and, using their newfound method of propulsion, headed in the direction of the robot. Dad looked down into the cloudy water to see the bottom but he could only see a few yards down. As they approached the place where he thought they had left the robot, he looked down but could not even see the reef.

"Wait here," he directed.

"We'll all come," Mom countered.

"Okay," but stick together, I don't want to get separated, the vision is limited down there," he cautioned, as they ducked beneath the surface.

Sharianna couldn't believe how much their underwater paradise had changed. "Do you think the fish are okay?" she asked, with genuine concern.

"Yeah, it seems that they could sense the earthquake coming and they all swam out to deeper water," replied Dad.

When the reef came into view, Dad turned toward the ocean to find the edge of the drop-off. "Can everyone see me?" asked Dad as he swam out in front.

"Yes."

When he reached the edge of the cliff, he looked both ways.

"Where is it?" queried Sharianna.

"Joseph, you go with Mom, that way. Sharianna and I will look in the other direction. Stay at the edge of the cliff, we can use it as a reference so we don't get lost."

Sharianna knew it was only a few minutes, but it seemed like a long time as she peered through the murky water that only a little while ago was as clear as crystal. Each moment she expected to see the robot rising like a welcome monolith from the edge of the cliff.

"This is the easy way to swim, huh Mom?" Joseph said, as they sped effortlessly along the edge of the precipice.

"Sure is."

Sharianna thought it was weird to be able to hear them so perfectly, knowing that they were quite a ways away and going in the opposite direction.

Suddenly, she saw a dark mass in front of them. "There it is," she declared. Almost instantly, she realized her mistake.

"No, it's the lava flow," observed Dad, with obvious disappointment. "How far have you guys gone?"

"I don't know, but it seems like a long way," Mom replied, trying to disguise her apprehension.

"Wait there, till we catch up to you," directed Dad.

They turned around and Dad increased his speed as his apprehension mounted. Suddenly he stopped. A piece of the reef seemed missing. He turned around and hovered over the spot. The whole edge of the drop-off was expectedly uneven and broken, but the transition from coral to bare rock was a natural one all across the reef. Here, the coral stopped abruptly. As he looked closer, he noticed that the coral at the edge of the barren hole was broken. Suddenly, he felt sick as he realized that the rock the robot had been standing on had been right there.

Sharianna also saw the broken coral, and the worried look on Dad's face. "It fell off the edge, didn't it?" she questioned.

"What do you mean, it fell off?" demanded Mom, from her distant position.

"I think the rock it was standing on broke away from the cliff during the earthquake," reported Dad.

"Oh no!" came Mom's agonized cry.

"Percy!" cried Joseph.

"I'm sure he's okay – come back toward us and we'll figure something out," comforted Dad reassuringly, but he knew the drop off was hundreds of feet deep. Unless the robot landed on a shelf or otherwise got hung up on the face of the cliff he knew there was no way he was going to be able to reach it.

"Stay here and wait for Mom," he instructed Sharianna. "I'm going to go down to find the robot."

"Be careful," cautioned Mom.

"Yes, be careful, Daddy," added Sharianna.

As he descended along the face of the cliff, the water turned from cloudy to dark, as the light from the surface dimmed. He continued slowly to descend through the darkness in the hopes that the lights on the robot were still on. He reached out and felt the wall of the cliff. Here and there, he banged into a protrusion jutting out from the face of the cliff. The first time it knocked the air out of him and he began to panic, feeling like he would suffocate. When Sophia heard his groan she asked him if he was okay, but he didn't respond until he got some air back in his lungs. She was about to leave the kids and go search for him when he finally responded. Now, he was being more careful, but as he went deeper, the water pressure on his body continued to increase. The helmet part of the spacesuit seemed to be holding, but the rest of it was stretchy and flexible and didn't seem to resist the pressure of the water.

Finally, when the pressure became so great that he could hardly expand his lungs, he began to retreat with great disappointment from the depths. As he ascended, he suddenly stopped. A strange tightness in his chest was accompanied by an unfamiliar feeling of panic as he remembered hearing about the bends. In his mind's eye he imagined the nitrogen in his bloodstream suddenly expanding from the change in pressure, as he got closer to the surface and forming small bubbles in his bloodstream and flowing to his heart and brain. He realized that the result would be severe pain and damage, or death.

He didn't want to alarm his family, so he simply said, "I'll search around some more, don't worry I'll be a little while." He slowly ascended in a long zigzag pattern along the face of the cliff so that his body could adjust to the changes in pressure. Finally, the darkness began to dissipate. He sighed with relief but knew that the danger was still menacingly present, so he continued his slow, indirect ascent, all the while searching the cliff for any sign of the robot. His heart sank as he thought about poor Percy, who was trapped in the robot.

"Where are you now?" asked Mom, who was anxiously waiting on the edge of the precipice.

"Still searching," he replied.

Finally, after what seemed like hours he reached the top of the cliff and peered through the cloudy water to the left and the right but could not see his family.

"Maybe you should go back to the beach and wait for me there," he suggested, as he swam the last few feet toward the surface to look around and get his bearings.

Suddenly, as his head pierced the surface, he heard a loud noise, like a bomb going off. Almost simultaneously, he felt another percussion move through the water.

"I don't think that is a good idea," countered Sophia, sounding very stressed.

He looked toward the island, expecting to see the lagoon, but instead looked upon an unfamiliar shore. A giant cloud of smoke and gas belched forth from the throat of the volcano and billowed its way high into the afternoon sky. An ominous red glow emanated from the top of the mountain as searing hot magma poured over the rim. Lush, green trees strangely burst into flame as the burning river of death slowly meandered down the slope.

Off to his left, Thomas noticed another ancient lava flow. Immediately, he realized that it was the same flow that bordered their lagoon – he was on the other side of it.

"I am on the other side of the ancient lava flow," he tried to say calmly. "Swim over to the tip of it, where it goes over the drop off and I'll meet you there."

Thomas quickly made his way to the end of the breakwater created by the old lava flow. He was very impressed by the suit's capability to propel him through the water so quickly. He felt like a body surfer who didn't need a wave to surf. He continued to rack his brains for a way to save Percy.

His heart leaped when he saw his family skimming across the surface toward him.

"Daddy!" exclaimed Sharianna with relief, as she wrapped

134

her arms around his neck.

"We're so glad you are safe. We were very worried," sighed Mom.

"Did you see any sign of the robot and Percy?" asked Joseph.

Thomas shook his head sadly. A tear welled up in Joseph's eye and rolled down his cheek, quickly followed by another.

Sharianna sobbed.

Hot ash began to fall around them like large snowflakes.

"I think we had better get away from the island," admonished Dad.

Dad turned toward the open ocean, "Follow me," he directed, as he sped away from the island. His mind raced as he tried to figure out what to do next. He thought of their situation – in the middle of the Pacific, without any food or water, without any idea where the closest land was. Then he remembered from Joseph's map that they must be somewhere in the Caroline Islands. At least we have the suits, he thought. When he felt they were safely far enough from the island he stopped.

"What's the plan?" inquired Mom.

"Did you go all the way to the bottom?" asked Joseph.

"No, the pressure was too great," replied Dad sadly.

"Maybe we could get an undersea ROV?" Joseph proposed, hopefully.

"That's a great idea, but it could take weeks, even if we could find this island again," bemoaned Dad. "I don't know if Percy could last that long," he added softly, as he put his hand on Joseph's shoulder.

"I don't think finding the island will be a problem, simply ask about the one that blew its top," Mom reasoned.

"He'll starve," Sharianna sobbed – she couldn't bear to think of the dog she loved starving to death all alone at the bottom of the ocean. "Oh, Robo-ship, I wish you were here," she whispered to herself through her tears.

"He won't starve," consoled Mom. "I'm sure he'll eat the rest of Joseph's Doritos, and I left out some bread and cookies."

"It will be okay, princess, we'll figure out some way to find Percy," promised Dad.

"I think we should go south until we find another island," Mom suggested.

Joseph spoke up, "When I was looking at the map, I noticed that the Northern Mariana Islands belonged to the United States – there must be people who speak English. I think we should go west."

"There might even be a research station that has an undersea ROV," said Sharianna hopefully.

Dad looked up at the sun, then toward the pillar of smoke coming from the island. "I'm sure the island is south, so that must be west," he said, pointing off to the right.

Sharianna suddenly grabbed Dad by the arm and pointed.

"Something big is coming toward us under the water!" shouted Joseph in a frightened voice.

"Hurry, that way!" commanded Dad, pointing to the west. "And fast!"

Apprehension gripped Joseph as he speculated what could be chasing them. His mind was called involuntarily to the old shark movies with the great white shark that relentlessly pursued its victims.

As his family sped across the water with Thomas taking up the rear, he looked back, expecting to see the distance widening, but discovered that it was actually narrowing.

Joseph looked over his shoulder. Their pursuer was now making a large wake and the water was spraying off of its head like the hull of a speedboat as it bore down on them.

CHAPTER TWENTY
Salvage operation

SUDDENLY, THROUGH THE WATER SPRAY, JOSEPH recognized their pursuer's round head. He was instantaneously filled with euphoria.

"Wait, it's the robot!" he exclaimed, incredulously.

As they stopped, the crest of the robot's head rose from the water a few feet away. The water spilled off of it as it rose up into the air until the top of its feet were level with the surface of the water.

The family quickly clambered onto the top of the foot.

"It must have heard my wish," rejoiced Sharianna.

"Robo-ship, open the airlock," ordered Joseph, filled with elation.

Percy wagged his tail and barked a happy hello when they opened the door from the airlock to the hallway, completely oblivious of his near death experience.

With Dad at the helm, the robot again slid beneath the waves of the Pacific.

"Where to now, navigator?" Dad asked, looking at Joseph.

Mom interrupted, "I think we had better get some food from somewhere. We left the coconuts and mangos on the beach…"

"And most of my shells," interjected Sharianna as she pulled several beautiful seashells from her pockets. "But not all of them." Her smile looked a little out of place on her tear-streaked face.

"And my backpack," added Joseph.

"My point is," continued Mom, "even if we ate all the junk food, it would only last a couple of days."

Joseph examined the map, "What about Guam, or Saipan? The map shows them as American possessions. That's where we

137

were going before the robot showed up."

"Is there any fast food there?" asked Sharianna.

"I doubt it," answered Mom. "Besides, even if we hid the robot and went in on foot, I think if we showed up in some small village store to buy food they would ask a lot of questions."

"I heard they have American restaurants in Japan," proposed Sharianna hopefully.

"I think they might still be looking for the UFO that flew over Tokyo," cautioned Dad.

"Hey, what would they call an unidentified object in the water?" posed Joseph.

"What?" inquired Mom.

"A UFO."

"Why is that?"

"An Unidentified Floating Object."

"Was that a joke?" jabbed Sharianna.

Dad pulled out his wallet and counted out the small bills. "Seventeen dollars. You kids have any money?" he asked hopefully.

"I have the credit card," offered Mom. "I think *this* qualifies as an emergency."

"Yeah, I think it does," replied Dad.

"I think Hawaii is the logical choice," concluded Mom. "I'm sure they will take the credit card."

"Japan *is* closer," argued Joseph.

"We don't just need food," countered Mom.

"What else?" inquired Dad.

Mom sniffed the air. "I think a change of clothes would be a good idea."

"And some shampoo," added Sharianna.

"And a razor," laughed Mom as she rubbed the stubble on Dad's chin.

"Joseph found something even sharper than a razor, didn't you Joseph?" commented Dad.

"Yes, the kitchen knives," he replied, as he pulled the small knife from the sheath he had fashioned from a piece of green bamboo and attached to his belt.

138

Mom continued, "On second thought, we can skip the razor, I kind of like it," she pulled on his chin and gave him a kiss. "Although the fresh clothes and soap wouldn't hurt."

"*Hey!*" protested Dad, feigning injury. "Hawaii, here we come!"

They proceeded rapidly in a northeasterly direction across the bottom of the East Mariana Basin. They zigzagged in a random pattern, all the while heading in an overall easterly course for Hawaii. At, or near, the point of each zig and each zag they came up near enough to the surface to get a reading from the GPS.

Joseph looked up from the map, "Hey, it's now yesterday," he declared.

"*What?*" asked Sharianna.

"We just crossed the International Date Line."

"Are we going to go to Honolulu?" asked Sharianna. "It's the capitol, you know."

"*No way,*" asserted Dad. "Not unless we want to encounter the whole fleet of nuclear subs all at once. Honolulu is on the island of O'ahu and overlooks Pearl Harbor, which is one of the largest U.S. Navy bases in the Pacific."

"Joseph, what is the next largest city?" queried Mom.

"Looks like Hilo, on the Big Island of Hawai'i."

"Is it on the coast?" asked Dad.

"Yeah. It is on the east side of the island. If we go around and approach from the west, we can probably avoid the submarines," suggested Joseph. "Especially if we circle around and keep to the bottom – it is 17,000 feet deep there."

"Thanks, Navigator," acknowledged Dad. "Any suggestions on how we get to shore without being seen?"

"If the Hawaiian Islands were created by volcanoes then I'll bet they have pretty steep drop-offs into the ocean, right?" asked Sharianna. "Like the last island. We could get pretty close while staying deep. Then, while staying close to the drop-off we could come up to a safe depth, go out the airlock in our spacesuits and speed in to shore."

"If we went early in the morning, just before dawn, we would be hidden and anyone seeing us come up from the beach would think that we had been out for an early morning swim," added Mom.

"In our street clothes?" questioned Joseph.

"Okay, an early morning *stroll* along the beach," corrected Mom. "Anyway, then we would have a whole day to get the food and other shopping done that we need. We could even find a nice seafood restaurant in the evening and be back at the robot that night." Mom smiled as she thought of all the great shopping there must be along the beach.

"Remember, we can't carry that much back with us when we swim back to the robot," asserted Dad, in an attempt to preempt the big shopping spree.

"I know, I thought if we all had backpacks, we could carry the stuff we need under our spacesuits, like Joseph did when we went to the island," suggested Mom. "I'll only buy what we need...unless there is a really great deal."

"We had better take something to put the spacesuits in once we get to the beach," concluded Dad.

"I still have my backpack," suggested Sharianna.

"Okay, we'll spend the night at the bottom, then we'll park the ship up on the shelf in the morning, in shallow water," agreed Dad.

"Everybody ready?" asked Dad, before opening the airlock the next morning.

"How far is it to the beach?" asked Sharianna.

"I don't know, but we can't risk going into any shallower water," replied Dad.

"Let's stick together, and we'll be fine," instructed Mom.

"We'll go straight up to the surface so that we can get a reference from the shore; that way we'll be able to find the robot tonight. Then we'll go under the surface to the beach."

"If we can't find it we could call it to us again," said Sharianna.

"Oh, yeah, I can see the headlines now: WITNESSES SAW A GIANT MONSTER-ROBOT RISE UP FROM THE DEPTHS

OF THE OCEAN," teased Joseph.

The sun was barely beginning to illuminate the buildings on the shore as they sped along, a few feet below the surface, toward the beach.

"Now we really look like tourists," complained Sharianna, as she looked at the new clothes that Mom had bought. "Why do we all have to wear the same goofy Hawaiian shirts and shorts?"

"Because we are *in* Hawaii and we *are* tourists," replied Mom.

"And they were on sale," added Dad.

"We can do some other shopping later," Mom whispered in Sharianna's ear.

Dad got a map from the city tourist information shop. "Let's take the bus tour out to Hawai'i Volcanoes National Park."

"No, I think I have seen enough volcanoes for one trip. Thank you," asserted Mom.

"I'll go with you," offered Joseph.

"Make sure we meet back here by seven o'clock at the latest," instructed Dad.

"I'll stay with Mom," elected Sharianna.

That evening they met back at the tourist information shop. After dinner at the wonderful seafood restaurant that Mom and Sharianna found during their shopping expedition, they went for a stroll on the boardwalk along the beach. When they looked out from the boardwalk toward the place where they left the robot, they noticed a flat-decked salvage ship with two huge cranes in the distance.

"What's going on out there?" Dad asked a man who was manning a kiosk on the boardwalk. Dad tried to keep his voice sounding mildly curious, but inside he was frantic.

"Some treasure hunter thinks there is an old wreck out there with a lot of gold on it; he's been scanning the shelf for weeks. I

141

wonder if he finally found something?"

"I think we had better get out there quick, before they get their cables on the robot," whispered Joseph, as they walked down the steps to the beach.

"It's not even dark yet," groaned Sharianna. "And look at all the people – someone will see us for sure."

"Over there, we can put the suits on under the pier," suggested Dad.

They quickly put on the spacesuits, out of sight of all the people playing on the beach, and made their way toward the water's edge, while staying under the pier. They could see the people on the beach every now and then between the pylons.

As they neared the water, they realized that two boys were playing in the rocks near the water's edge, under the pier.

"We should have bought swimsuits," lamented Mom. "That way we would blend in as we entered the water."

"Follow me," instructed Dad, as he waded out into the water. He went behind one of the large pylons and disappeared, followed by Sharianna, Joseph and Mom.

"Hey, where did they go?" exclaimed one of the boys, after a few minutes.

As they neared the place where they left the robot they could see it lying on its back on the bottom, right where they left it. However, they could also see two divers working on getting a cable around the neck – they already had a cable around the feet. The divers seemed completely occupied with their task, so the family quickly jetted toward the robot.

At that moment, another diver appeared who was bringing the end of the cable up from the other side of the robot. He looked up and saw them as he clipped the hook onto the cable. They were still about a hundred and fifty feet from the robot. He quickly motioned to his two companions, who looked with incredulous eyes to see a man and a woman with two teenagers speeding straight through the water in their matching Hawaiian shirts and shorts, each wearing a bulging backpack, without any scuba gear. The first diver began swimming for the surface, while the other two swam in an effort to intercept the family.

"Robo-ship, open the airlock," commanded Joseph, as they raced toward the ship.

Suddenly, they saw the slack go out of the cables as the robot was hoisted slowly off the ocean floor.

"Hurry, get into the airlock," ordered Dad, as he turned to face the divers who had come to cut off their escape.

The divers suddenly stopped and looked at each other incredulously when Dad turned around and faced them with his fists up, as if he were in a boxing match.

Dad took the opportunity to drop down into the airlock and push the button to close the door. As the door closed, the faces of the two bewildered divers appeared above it. Sharianna smiled sweetly and waved goodbye.

"We've got to hurry," asserted Dad nervously, as he waited impatiently for the water to drain out of the airlock so that he could open the door to the hall. When the door finally opened they rushed into the control cabin.

Above them they could clearly see the hull of the salvage ship. They could also see the two divers swimming toward the surface.

Dad and Joseph jumped into the captain's chairs and Dad began to pull away.

On board the salvage ship the winches groaned and the crane booms bent toward the water. The barge began to list as the tips of the cranes dipped beneath the waves. Men yelled as they hung onto whatever they could grab. "The cable is breaking!" screamed one of the crane operators, when he heard the pinging sound as each of the strands that made up the huge cable stretched and broke in rapid succession. Suddenly, there were enough strands broken that the rest gave way all at once. The whole ship swung around in an arc wildly as it pivoted on the remaining cable. The men continued to cling to their precarious handholds.

"Wait!" yelled Mom, as she saw the ship above suddenly lurch onto its side and then swing around wildly as the cable around the robot's neck broke.

Dad reversed his direction, creating some slack in the cable.

The barge suddenly slapped back down onto an even keel.

Dad tried to grab the cable that was still around the legs of the robot.

"Let me," offered Joseph.

Dad flipped the control switch and Joseph quickly grabbed the cable with both of the robot's hands and pulled it apart as if it were a piece of yarn.

Joseph then piloted the robot toward the drop-off and descended down into the depths of the ocean.

The divers witnessed the incredible underwater drama in stunned incredulity as the robot disappeared into the dark depths.

"Do you think they will report this to the military?" asked Sharianna.

"I don't know, but we're not waiting to find out," replied Joseph, as he reached the ocean floor and headed in a very fast northerly direction across the Northeast Pacific Basin, toward the Bering Sea.

"Good piloting. I think we should still move in a random pattern," cautioned Dad.

"That was close," sighed Mom.

"That was exciting!" exclaimed Sharianna, as she threw her suit on a chair and took off her backpack.

"I think I may have squashed the bread," confessed Joseph, as he leaned forward in the captain's chair.

"I'll take over for you while you take off your spacesuit and backpack," suggested Sharianna sweetly, as she saw an opportunity to pilot the ship.

Joseph realized her designs, but relinquished his seat nevertheless. He picked up Sharianna's suit and backpack and headed for the cargo bay.

Sophia's heart was still pounding as she followed Joseph into the cargo bay.

Dad joined them as they were hanging up the spacesuits in the hallway closet. "I'm real proud of you son; I think you can handle the robot better than me."

Joseph was beaming from this compliment – he knew his dad was sincere and it made him feel good. "I guess it's from playing computer games. You know, the controls are almost the same."

They returned to the control cabin and Sharianna continued their random zigzag pattern for a few hours, without returning to the surface for a GPS reading.

Mom yawned, "I think we ought to stop for the night. I'm looking forward to that shampoo we bought today."

Sharianna set the robot on the bottom for the night.

Joseph awoke early the next morning and rubbed Percy behind the ears. "I think we should get going," he whispered.

Joseph made his way into the control room without making any noise and sat down in the captain's chair.

"What are you doing?" whispered Sharianna quietly from the doorway.

"I'm going up to get a GPS reading," he replied softly.

Sharianna sat in the other chair. "Okay, let's go."

At the bottom, they could only see as far as the lights, but as they rose toward the surface, the ocean changed from pitch black to a kind of twilight that slowly got brighter as they neared the surface.

Joseph recorded the GPS reading on the map. They looked up to see a large, long shadow silhouetted against the light above.

"Another submarine," speculated Sharianna fearfully.

CHAPTER TWENTY-ONE

The Leviathan

JOSEPH LOOKED AT THE SILHOUETTE; HE NOTICED THAT IT WAS slowly undulating. "No, this one has a tail – it's a blue whale!"

"And a baby!" exclaimed Sharianna. "Get a little closer."

Upon their approach, the 100-foot leviathan turned its giant head and the calf moved to the other side of its mom. The whale showed no other signs of distress; Joseph moved in a little closer. They could see the long, powerful tail gently sweep through the water as the whale glided effortlessly through its environment. As they neared the surface, they suddenly saw the huge tail give a powerful thrust as the giant mammal, more than twice as long as the robot, lunged through a school of krill, leaving the baby behind. They saw the huge lower jaw expand as it engulfed thousands of tiny fish.

"Wow, Mom and Dad should see this," declared Joseph.

"We did," came the reply from the doorway behind them.

The majestic mammal made a couple more passes through the school of krill and then dove back down and swam serenely away with her baby.

"What is that noise?" pondered Mom.

They listened intently and heard a sound through the water that definitely sounded mechanical.

"Is it another submarine?" asked Sharianna.

"No, submarines are designed to run silently under water," replied Dad.

As they looked, they saw a rusty old hull, with barnacles clinging to its side, through the water above them.

"It's definitely not a military ship," stated Dad. "They never let them get that bad."

"It's heading in the same direction as the whale," observed Mom. "Do you think it's a whaler?"

"I thought blue whales were protected!" asserted Sharianna.

"They are!" confirmed Mom.

"Match its speed and stay underneath the ship," directed Dad. "Let's see if we can determine what kind of ship it is."

As they drew close to the ship, they could see a large, sloping ramp cut into the side of the ship extending up onto the deck. It was streaked with red that was slowly draining into the ocean.

Mom's heart started to pound as her anger mounted.

"A little faster, Joseph," she instructed.

As they looked up along the bow of the ship, they saw the huge harpoon loaded and ready to fire, with two men out on the platform. Suddenly, one of the men looked into the water and, motioning to the other, pointed directly at them.

"They saw us!" exclaimed Joseph.

"Good, I hope they're scared," replied Mom.

"Are they going to shoot the mother whale?" asked Sharianna distressfully. "What about the baby?"

"They'll take it too," cried Mom angrily. "We've got to do something!" she almost shouted.

"There they are!" Sharianna looked through the water out front and could barely discern the shadow of the two whales returning to the surface.

Joseph got an idea; he suddenly slowed the robot down.

"What are you doing?" asked Sharianna, as the rusty old hull passed over them.

"Watch," was all that Joseph had time to say as he reached out with one of the hands of the robot and caught the ship by the giant propeller. The ship came to a grinding halt as Joseph reached out with the other hand and squashed the blades like a ball of tinfoil. Then, while still holding onto the propeller, he swung the ship around like a top, and pushed it in the opposite direction, while accelerating to a speed at least twice the capability of the whaling ship. Joseph was as angry about the illegal killing of the whales as Mom. He didn't let go of the whaler for a few miles while traveling at a break neck speed.

"Be careful, don't sink it," cautioned Dad. "The men who work on it are probably just trying to feed their families. It's the owners of the ship that should be sunk."

Realizing that Dad was right, he finally let the ship go and the robot quickly retreated to the depths of the ocean floor.

"I'll bet that will take a while to fix," exclaimed Sharianna exuberantly.

"As superstitious as sailors are, they might have a hard time getting enough men to crew it once that story gets around," concluded Mom triumphantly.

"Incredible," declared Dad, as Joseph brought the hands of the robot up into the light and looked at them. They were still flawless. "How did you know the ship's screw wouldn't tear through the hands of the robot?"

"I didn't," replied Joseph, his voice trembling slightly.

"Did you get a GPS signal?" asked Dad.

"Yes," answered Joseph. "You take over, Sharianna," he flipped the control switch to her seat and, using their most recent GPS reading and the compass, plotted their course on the map, through the Aleutian Islands and into the Bearing Sea.

"I think we'll have to slow down a little, once we pass the Aleutian Trench in order to navigate through the islands," observed Joseph, as he examined the map.

After they passed over the Aleutian Trench, Sharianna slowed down and looked for any sign that the water was getting shallower, or a cliff, or shelf indicating that they were near land. Finally, she saw what looked like the base of a barren mountain rising up from the sea floor.

"This might be one of the islands," postulated Joseph, as they rose along the slopes of the mountain. As they ascended past the twilight layer of the ocean they could see that there was land at the top of the mountain.

"Which way should we go?" queried Sharianna.

"Left," directed Joseph, as he looked at the map. "If it is the Alaskan Peninsula and we were to go right, then we would be following the coast toward Canada."

"Left it is," concurred Sharianna. They turned southeast and

148

followed the shoreline for about a half hour; slowly, they began to turn northeast as they rounded the tip of the island.

"Let's go up and have a look around," proposed Joseph.

The robot's head pierced the surface of the water just enough for them to see that the island was barren and windswept, nearly devoid of plant life.

"Look at all those seals," marveled Mom. "There must be thousands of them."

Joseph looked at the GPS, then the map. "That must be the Bering Sea," he concluded, as he pointed north.

As they proceeded along the shallow rocky bottom near the island they saw something that looked strangely out of place. In the distance, off to the right, they could see something that looked geometric, in the watery world of jagged rocks and boulders.

CHAPTER TWENTY-TWO

The wreck

"WHAT IS THAT CIRCLE-THING?" QUESTIONED SHARIANNA, AS SHE steered the robot for a closer look.

"It's a paddle wheel steam ship!" exclaimed Joseph.

"What is it doing way up here?" asked Sharianna. "I thought they were only used on the Mississippi river."

"No, I think they used a similar type for ocean travel for a short time," replied Dad. "I'll bet they used these ships during the height of the Alaskan gold rush."

"Let's explore it!" said Joseph. "Oh, to explore a sunken ship!" he added longingly.

"That water is probably very cold," warned Mom, in an attempt to dissuade Joseph from his goal.

"The spacesuits protect you from the cold," he replied.

As they approached, they could see a great hole that had been ripped through the wooden hull, right into the cargo hold. The huge metal smoke stack lay rusting away a short distance from the wreck, lying wedged between two boulders. Part of the bulkhead was missing and they could see in to the huge steam engine with its enormous flywheel and long piston rods still attached to the massive shaft that turned the paddle wheels. They could tell that it had once been a magnificent ship with its ornate carved railings and teakwood decks. As they peered through the broken windows, they could see into the bar and dining area.

"Look, the mirror above the bar isn't even broken! And some of the bottles and glasses are still intact," observed Dad, incredulously. "This was one lavish boat," he said, looking at Mom. "The cold water must have helped preserve it; otherwise I think it would have disintegrated long ago."

"I'll bet it's not more than seventy-five feet from the surface," estimated Dad.

"Think of all the history," reasoned Joseph, realizing that Mom was the one he had to convince.

"And the artifacts," added Sharianna.

"And the skeletons," interjected Mom. "And the ghosts...Oooo," she added, in her most mysterious and chilling voice.

"I don't see any lifeboats, maybe the passengers and crew all escaped," Dad rationalized.

Without warning, Sophia felt the lure of the adventure begin to grip her, like it did when they first explored the robot. "Okay, Dad and I will go. You two stay here and take care of the robot," she teased.

"*No!*" they cried in unison.

Mom paused for a moment, looking at her kids as she thought about how brave they had been.

"Okay, you can come too, but no goofing around!" she ordered, gravely.

Sharianna quickly set the robot down a few feet from the wreck.

They were in their spacesuits in record time.

Mom went over to the counter and dumped out everything that was still in her backpack and slung it over her shoulder. "Artifacts," she said simply.

They entered the wreck through the main doors into the dining hall. There were windows on both sides and across the front of the room with a view of the side and the front decks – all of which were broken, except one, which was etched with the image of the mountain peaks above Anchorage, Alaska.

Several of the round mahogany tables were still bolted to the walnut floor, the others had tipped over on their sides as the bolts that held them slowly rusted away. Immediately to their right was a flight of stairs leading to the upper deck and another flight leading down into the hold.

Sharianna looked down into the darkness of the hold and felt a shiver run through her body, even though the spacesuit completely insulated her from the cold water. She grabbed onto Dad's arm, "Let's look over there by the bar."

The mirror behind the bar was beveled and etched with a beautiful pattern all the way around; above it, hung a golden plaque. In large raised letters was the name of the ship: "The Golden Alaskan." The brass trim on the bar and on the stools was tarnished, but still intact, even though the finish on the wood was deteriorated and peeling. The leather seats on the stools were mostly gone, but the ornate wooden backs bespoke of their original elegance.

Sharianna looked under the bar and saw many glasses still not broken. Some of them were etched with the name of the ship. She put two of them in Mom's backpack.

Above both ends of the bar, still hanging from large brass chains, were two beautiful, ornate brass and red crystal lamps, and an even larger one still hanging from the center of the dining room.

Joseph swam over to the antique brass cash register and pulled on the lever to open the drawer, but of course, the mechanisms were all rusted together. To the right, and behind the bar was a door with a large gold door handle that was hanging by one tarnished brass hinge.

Dad swam over to the door and pulled on it. The brass screws holding the hinge to the jam pulled right out of the deteriorated wood and the door settled slowly to the floor. Dad paused as he entered the room, to let his eyes adjust to the darkness. *I wish we had some waterproof flashlights*, he thought to himself. He could barely make out through the gloomy darkness, a large desk in the middle of the floor. Behind the desk he saw the remains of a large leather office chair. Behind the chair, he could barely discern the outline of a large rectangular box about six feet high and three feet in width. Sharianna was right beside him as he swam over the desk to get a better look at the box. It was pitted and cankered with rust, but he recognized it as the ship's safe from the large, rusted, combination dial set in the front panel.

"It's a safe," concluded Sharianna, when her eyes had become adjusted to the darkness. "Do you think there is anything in it?" she asked with excitement.

Dad pulled on the door of the safe but the iron was so thick that it had not yet rusted all the way through.

"You found a safe?" asked Joseph, as he swam into the room. "Can you open it?"

"No," replied Dad. "It is pretty thick iron...but maybe we can move it." He put one hand on the back of the safe and with his other pushed against the wall. The safe began to tip when, suddenly, his hand went right through the deteriorating wall.

"Let's work together," suggested Joseph, as he tapped on the wall and found a spot that seemed stronger than the rest. Dad and Sharianna did the same, and they all pulled together. To their surprise, the safe tipped and then fell. As it hit the floor, the deck boards gave way in between two structural members and it fell down into the hold.

"I guess these suits do enhance your strength," acknowledged Dad. "But they definitely don't make you superman," he added, as he looked through the hole in the floor.

Joseph voiced what Dad had thought earlier as he peered down into the darkness: "I wish we had some flashlights."

Mom swam into the room with a huge smile on her face, wearing her now bulging backpack and carrying the large chandelier from the center of the dining room. "I always wanted lamps just like these, and these are real antiques." She almost giggled with delight. Sophia looked down at the dark hole in the floor. Suddenly, an almost tangible gloom seemed to emanate from the hole. She consciously shook off the unexpected feeling. "Hey, what about the lights on the robot? You could shine them through the hole in the hull. Then you could see what is down there."

"And it might not be as scary," concluded Sharianna, as she gazed down into the darkness. Suddenly, she thought she saw some movement. "Something moved down there!" she declared.

"Probably fish," consoled Dad.

"I've got to make a trip back to the robot, so I'll shine the

153

lights for you," proposed Mom.

"I'll go with you," offered Sharianna.

Joseph made an exaggerated, scary sound.

"Stop that!" rebuked Sharianna.

"That's not very nice," scolded Mom, who felt a little spooked herself.

While Mom and Sharianna hauled their newfound treasures to the robot, Joseph and Dad busied themselves investigating the room. Joseph opened the desk drawers, or rather, he pulled off the drawer fronts and reached into the drawers, since the wood had swelled up with the water and the drawers would no longer slide. He found an old pistol that was cankered with rust, but the pearl handle was still perfect, and a bunch of old papers and documents.

They looked out the small window of the ship's office to see the robot bend down as Mom directed the light into the hold.

"There is a lot of stuff down there," reported Mom.

"Are you still wearing your spacesuit?" inquired Dad, when he heard her voice.

"No, but we can still hear you perfectly," she replied.

They looked through the hole in the floor and saw the safe lying on top of a pile of flattened barrels. The water was a little murky in the hold, probably from the debris that was kicked up when the safe crashed to the floor. They dropped through the hole and swam down toward the safe. Joseph noticed that the hold must have been used for transporting both animals and cargo, because there were several partitions that looked like pens, and on the opposite side of the ship there was a large door ajar in the bulkhead about halfway up from the floor, with a ramp extending up to it that looked like it was for loading livestock. They swam around the hold examining the cargo.

"I think they were on their way back from Alaska," deduced Dad.

"How can you tell?" asked Joseph.

"Because there are no cattle skeletons, only a few horses'."

"What's the significance of that?" asked Sharianna from her position in the control room of the robot. She could see Joseph's

154

and Dad's shadowy figures swimming around in the murky hold.

"On the way up they would probably take cattle to sell to the miners. On the way back they would only have a few horses that belong to the passengers," explained Dad.

Joseph pointed to the smashed barrels that the safe had landed on. "Pickled herring – that comes from up near Alaska too, doesn't it?"

"I think so," replied Dad.

At one end of the hold, Joseph saw a large cage with old rusty iron bars. As he swam closer he could tell, through the murky water, that it was divided by iron bars into two compartments or cells. Suddenly, he swam backwards with a startled shout.

"What is it?" asked Dad, as he swam toward Joseph.

"What's the matter?" asked Mom, anxiously from the robot.

"A skeleton," answered Joseph, trying to regain his composure.

"It's the brig," explained Dad. "Looks like they forgot to release the prisoner."

"That one's not a man," said Joseph, as he pointed through the rust cankered bars of the other cell.

"It looks like it is either a polar bear, or a grizzly bear; I'll bet they were taking it down to the states for a zoo, or for some other kind of exhibition," speculated Dad.

"How did they get it in there?" asked Joseph. "And how were they going to get it out?"

"Good question," replied Dad.

"He gives me the creeps," shuddered Joseph, as he looked back at the prisoner, the bones of his arms still extended between the bars. "I hope he deserved it. Let's get the safe and get out of here."

"Be careful," cautioned Mom.

Joseph wondered if he and Dad would be able to pick up the safe.

"Ready? Heave!" grunted Dad, as they lifted the safe from the floor.

Even with the added strength from their suits they had to rest several times before they got it to the hole in the side of the hull.

"Mom, put the foot of the robot right here, so that we can step out onto it."

As they carried the safe across the top of the foot, Joseph thought he saw, from the corner of his eye, something move within the hold.

Finally, they had the safe in the tiny airlock; they had to lay the safe on the floor lengthwise and there was still barely enough room.

"I'm beat, let's have some lunch," suggested Dad, as he pushed the button to close the airlock.

In the kitchen, they made sandwiches for lunch from the groceries they had purchased in Hawaii.

"I'd still like to get the name plate of the ship that's above the mirror," said Joseph, as he took another bite from his sandwich.

"I want to explore the upper deck," declared Sharianna. She felt a little apprehension at the thought of going back into the spooky ship, but she quickly suppressed the feeling, realizing that if she expressed it, Joseph would likely exploit her fear, just for the fun of it.

"I think it would be real cool to explore the engine room." Joseph paused, "What about you, Mom?"

"I think I'll have a look at that engine room too."

As they exited the airlock, Sharianna and Dad swam directly to the upper deck. Joseph and Mom entered the hold through the hole in the hull.

Joseph made his way to the engine room with Mom following.

"They are pretty scary looking," commented Mom, as they swam past the brig with its skeleton prisoners. A strange shiver made its way through her body, but she shook it off.

"Look at all those gages," said Mom, when they entered the engine room.

It was pretty dark, but a little light from the robot filtered through the murky hold and illuminated the room.

As they looked around the engine room, they could see the huge boiler tank and the big firebox where they burned the coal or wood to make the steam that turned the huge crank shaft that powered the paddle wheels.

Sharianna felt a surge of excitement as she swam over the railing of the upper deck and saw the ship's bridge, with the ship's wheel still intact. She swam through the large front window, being careful not to snag her suit on the broken glass that was still clinging to the edges of the frame; she looked around. Next to the ship's wheel was a tall desk, almost like a podium with a sloped top. Attached to the side of the desk was a tarnished brass funnel with a brass tube attached to it. Sharianna swam over to the funnel and called down into it. "Jooseph, caaan yooou heeear meee?"

"Of course I can hear you. Why are you talking so strange?"

"Oh yeah, I forgot about the radios in the suits. We're in the bridge and there is a communication funnel with a pipe, I think it goes to the engine room."

"Oh yeah, I see it," Joseph grabbed a large rusty old wrench that was still hanging on the wall and tapped the edge of the brass funnel. "Did you hear that?"

"Yes."

On the back wall of the bridge, in a brass frame, was a large map. The glass covering the map was still unbroken. It showed all of Alaska, the Aleutian Islands and the west coast of Canada and the United States all the way down to San Francisco.

"I can't believe how well preserved this map is," commented Dad. "I wonder how well it would survive in the air if we were to take it home?" he mused, as he pulled it off the wall.

"Hey, if you guys are done looking at the engine room, you should come up here - we're going to explore the rest of the upper deck," suggested Sharianna.

"Okay, we're coming," replied Mom.

"Let's go out the loading ramp, then we can swim straight up the outside of the ship," suggested Joseph.

Sharianna swam out the door of the bridge and looked over the railing. What she saw made her blood feel chill. She opened her mouth, but her larynx seemed stuck.

157

Three sleek gray torpedo-like forms swam in the water below; one was at least twelve feet long. The largest seemed to slide effortlessly through the water, when suddenly, it disappeared through the large loading door, into the hold.

"Look out!" Her voice had been stuck for only a fraction of a moment. "Sharks!"

The two smaller sharks seemed to hear her scream as they fluidly changed direction and efficiently swam up toward her. Sharianna felt very exposed, clinging to the railing.

Joseph looked toward the loading door and saw the massive creature as it silently glided into the hold and turned to look at them. "It's a Great White!" he exclaimed.

"Quick! In the cage!" ordered Mom, surprisingly cool, as she grabbed the bars and pulled on the door. It did not move. She looked down at the lock, then looked at the perfect killing machine that was gracefully making its way toward them.

Joseph struck the lock with the large wrench that he still had in his hand with all the force that both he and the suit could muster.

Mom grabbed the only weapon within reach and turned to face the fearsome predator. Her weapon seemed severely puny as she held it up to face the approaching menace.

The rust weakened mechanism inside the lock finally gave way under the immense blows delivered by Joseph and the lock opened up. Joseph pulled on the door with all his strength and the huge rusty hinges capitulated.

Mom threw the prisoner's arm bone in the direction of the approaching danger and it floated harmlessly to the floor.

They darted into the cage behind the door and tried to pull it shut but the shark was already there. Its eyelids rolled back as its lips seemed to recede and huge jaws with innumerable teeth protruded, expecting to tear away the flesh of its victims. Somehow, remembering that sharks have a tender nose, Joseph pulled on the door with his left hand and swung the wrench as hard as he could at the carnivore's nose with his right hand.

Instead of impacting his intended target, the wrench struck the upper gums and large triangular teeth of the upper jaw, breaking several of them away. Joseph released his grip as the jaws slammed together, clamping the wrench in its grasp. The shark, realizing that it had not grasped onto soft warm food, quickly darted away and they slammed the door shut.

Sharianna's heart leaped when she felt something grab her by the ankle and pull her away from the railing. She looked back to see her dad pulling her toward a door behind the bridge.

"Hurry, get into that hallway!" admonished Dad fervently.

As they closed the door behind them, they saw, through the broken window in the door, the two smaller sharks rise up and swim over the railing toward them. One of them put his nose near the broken window and nudged the door, as if testing it. The other shark seemed to swim away.

Sharianna looked down the hallway. There were several doors along the hall that led to the passenger cabins, some of which were closed, while others were open. The door at the end of the hallway opened up onto the opposite side of the ship. She could see the railing through the open door at the far end of the hall.

Dad continued to hold the door as his mind raced, trying to think of a solution. Suddenly, he felt Sharianna grab his arm in a viselike grip. He turned his head toward her and saw the other shark entering the far end of the hall.

Sharianna quickly opened the closest cabin door and pulled her dad inside.

Thomas felt a sense of surprised relief as he slid the brass dead bolt latch into place.

"A huge shark went into the hold," Sharianna declared as she tried to catch her breath.

"Sophia? Joseph? Are you okay?" asked Dad anxiously.

"Yes, we're in the brig, but there is a huge great white shark swimming around the hold, waiting for us."

Dad looked toward the small window and saw a shadow as

one of the sharks swam by. "There are two sharks up here, but we are safe in one of the cabins.

Dad looked around the room, searching in vain for something to use as a weapon.

"They will probably go away when they realize that there is no food for them here," reasoned Dad hopefully.

It seemed like a long time had passed, but the sharks continued to linger about the ship. Soon they were joined by three more. It seemed that they knew there was prey, and it would have to come out eventually.

"Are the other two sharks still up there?" inquired Mom.

"Yes," replied Dad. "It looks like they have been joined by a few more. How about the big one?" queried Dad.

"Yep, he's still here," answered Joseph. "I thought great whites were supposed to be solitary creatures," he added.

"I guess not always."

Sharianna looked out the window toward the robot. She couldn't see any sharks. She flipped her wrist back and pushed the button. Barely squeezing through the window; she shot toward the robot.

"Sharianna!" Dad cried, as he rushed to the window. It was too small for him to follow.

"I'll get the robot," Sharianna called out.

Dad rushed to the door and quickly drew back the bolt. Suddenly, the nose of a shark pushed through the opening. Dad hit the nose with his fist and it withdrew. He slammed the door and refastened the bolt and raced back to the window. Sharianna was more than half-way to the robot with three sharks close on her tail.

"Faster, Sharianna!" he cried, frantic for her safety.

"Robo-ship! Open the airlock!" ordered Sharianna.

Dad began kicking at the windowsill in an effort to enlarge the opening. Suddenly, another shark descended from above and made an attempt to feast on his foot.

"What's going on up there?" demanded Mom.

Sharianna dared not look back. She was going full speed. Realizing that she would slam into the back wall of the airlock, she pulled back on the button. Reaching around the edge of the doorway, she pushed the button to close the door. Finally, she looked back to see the lead shark only feet away. As the door began to close, it turned with all the grace of a figure skater and swam back toward the ship.

"I'm in the airlock," she announced, as she impatiently waited for the water to drain out of the little room.

As she leaped into the captain's chair she reached toward the sharks with the arms of the robot.

The most fearsome predators of the ocean scattered like frightened minnows in a pond. The giant great white made a beeline for the hole in the other end of the hold and followed the example of his companions.

Dad opened the door of the cabin and, seeing no sharks, swam toward the robot. He waved at the robot, knowing that Sharianna could see him. "You're so brave, honey." He went into the bridge and emerged with the map in the brass frame.

Joseph picked up the three huge shark teeth that had fallen to the floor and pushed open the door of the cage.

As Mom and Joseph swam through the doorway of the loading ramp toward the airlock, Joseph stopped. "I'm going to grab the nameplate."

CHAPTER TWENTY-THREE

Orca!

MOM WAITED IN THE AIRLOCK UNTIL DAD AND JOSEPH entered with their treasures. She put her arms around the two men. "We're all safe."

"Yep," Sharianna replied proudly from the control cabin.

Dad and Mom took the captain's chairs and they headed north across the Bering Sea. Joseph and Sharianna sat in the lower observation area.

"It looks like it gets a lot shallower as you approach the Bering Straight," reported Sharianna, as she looked at the water depths shown on the map.

It was a welcome change to be traveling through the upper layer of the ocean that was lit by the sun's rays, rather than the pitch black depths along the deep ocean floor.

It was amazing how much sea life there was in the northern oceans. Salmon, steelhead, herring, and many other fish flourished in the cool water. It is true that they were not as colorful as the tropical fish around their island paradise, but they seemed to be as plentiful.

As they traveled through the Bering Straight, they began to see more marine mammals like seals, and even walruses.

"I think we should continue north for a while, because it looks from the map that the water is a little shallow along the northern coast of Alaska, and we wouldn't want to risk detection," admonished Joseph, as they left the Bering straight behind and entered the frigid waters of the Arctic Ocean.

"Look, over there, the water looks cloudy," observed Mom.

Dad slowed down to take a look.

"It's a school of small fish. There must be millions of them!" exclaimed Sharianna.

"They are being herded."

Seven black and white whales were circling the huge school of fish, while expelling streams of bubbles, condensing the swirling mass of fish tighter and tighter.

Dad stopped the robot in order to watch what the killer whales were doing. As the whales swam around and under the fish they condensed them into a tight, almost solid mass, right up against the surface. Then, five whales would stay in the herding pattern, while two dashed into the swarming mass of fish with their mouths wide open, shooting straight to the surface, and jumping clear out of the water. They continued this – taking turns herding and feeding, until the school of fish was decimated and the orcas had their fill.

"Hey, they are coming toward us." Sharianna felt a surge of excitement as the huge, graceful mammals glided through the clear arctic water. Sharianna remembered their California trip when they went to Sea World in San Diego. She loved to see the killer whales perform and especially liked to see them through the glass wall of their tank as they swam underwater. While they were feeding, the orcas seemed to ignore the robot, even though they were now somewhat close. Now that they were done feeding, they seemed to be curious. The whales swam around the robot, nudging it now and then with their noses. They didn't seem to be the least bit scared. Dad began to slowly move away in a northerly direction and the whales followed, swimming alongside the robot, as if they had found a new friend.

"This is incredible," marveled Sharianna, it's like being at Sea World, except that these are wild whales, and they are just as playful! Talk about whale watching, I'll bet you never see anything like this from a boat!"

"Did you know that killer whales really aren't whales?" asked Joseph.

"Then what are they?" demanded Sharianna skeptically.

"They are in the dolphin family."

Dad slowly increased the speed of the robot and the orcas matched its speed for a while; then finally, they had enough fun and dropped out of the race.

"I think we ought to continue north for a while," suggested Dad. "I think I would feel safer traveling out in deep water."

"Did you know that my great Uncle Rex was the only man from Utah that was on the Nautilus, the first nuclear powered submarine to go to the North Pole, under the polar ice cap?" bragged Mom. She paused for a moment. "Funny, he never talked about it much. Joseph, how far are we from the North Pole?"

Joseph looked at the GPS. "186.42 degrees west longitude and 74.11 degrees north. We could be there in less than two hours."

"We're so close…" Mom looked at Dad with raised eyebrows and a questioning look.

"I guess a small detour shouldn't hurt," conceded Dad.

As they made their way north, Dad continued to follow the random zigzag pattern, rising only long enough to take the GPS readings. They were now under the permanent pack ice that covers the extreme northern tip of the planet.

"We must be getting pretty close, judging from the last GPS reading and the heading we took since then," said Joseph. "Let's rise near the surface and see how close we are."

The lights from the robot were a small prick of light in the dark depths of the Arctic Ocean.

"What is that?" asked Sharianna.

"What?" replied Joseph, peering into the darkness.

"Over there to the left. I saw something black."

"Everything is black," replied Joseph, "How could you see something that is black?"

"It was sort of shiny black and it looked geometric."

"There it is!" exclaimed Mom, as the object came into the view of the ship's lights. "Oh, my goodness, it can't be…can it?"

"It's another obelisk!" confirmed Dad.

"It looks like it is made of the same material as the one on the moon," observed Joseph.

"What in the world is it doing submerged under the ice at the North Pole?" puzzled Mom.

"I still want to know who built them," wondered Dad thoughtfully.

"Why did they put it at the North Pole?" inquired Joseph.

"I wonder if it is exactly at the North Pole," said Dad. "Let's go up a little and see if we can get a GPS reading."

"It is exactly at the North Pole all right," Joseph announced, as he looked at the GPS.

"Let's find its base," directed Mom, "and see if it has the same writing on it as the one on the moon."

"Good idea," agreed Dad, as he descended to the bottom.

The lights of the robot shone on the glistening surface.

"Look, there are no crustaceans, barnacles or other sea life attached to the surface," observed Joseph. "What does it mean?"

"It's either brand new, or it is so smooth that nothing can get a grip on its surface," concluded Dad.

As they circled the base of the obelisk, it became apparent that it truly was much larger than the one on the moon.

"It must be four or five times as big as the other one," commented Dad, in absolute awe.

"There is writing on it!" exclaimed Mom. "Sharianna, show me the pictures of the other obelisk."

Sharianna scanned through the dozens of pictures that she had taken and found those of the obelisk and handed the camera to Mom.

"It's the same," she declared breathlessly.

"Pangea!" Mom suddenly exclaimed excitedly, as she examined a round symbol that looked like a world with a single continent and a slender triangle extending from the top.

"What's Pangea?" questioned Sharianna.

Joseph remembered watching a PBS program about continental drift and plate tectonics; he showed her the map of the world. "Look, if you fit North and South America to Africa and Europe, pull in Australia and Antarctica, you get one great big super continent – Pangea."

"It sure does look the same," concurred Dad contemplatively, as he looked from the map back to the symbol on the obelisk.

"It's a depiction of Earth!" asserted Mom. "Why didn't I see that when we were on the moon?" she asked herself.

"Except that it is Earth millions of years ago," amended Dad.

"I wish we knew what the rest of these symbols mean,"

pondered Mom.

"Wait a minute," gasped Joseph. "Look, over there, the last symbol. Shine the light over there, Dad. That one wasn't on the moon's obelisk."

"It's the continents as they are today!" exclaimed Sharianna.

Sophia was bursting with unanswered questions: "Were the obelisks built during the age of dinosaurs, or more recently? Who built them? Why did they come? Why did they leave?"

Mom felt compelled to investigate. She flipped the control switch to her side and reached out with the robot and gently ran the finger of the robot around the edge of the square spiral.

"I don't know if you should..." began Dad.

Mom then touched the center.

"Why did you do that?" asked Dad.

"I don't know," she replied.

"Oh, oh," moaned Joseph, as the row of symbols began to disappear. They expected the obelisk to open up like the one on the moon. They were surprised when it began to slowly rise from the floor of the ocean. The silt on the ocean floor around the base of the obelisk was sucked up as the obelisk accelerated, causing the ocean to be murky, instead of clear.

"Oh, no!" exclaimed Sharianna, as they sat in stunned silence.

"Let's follow it!" cried Joseph.

Mom piloted the robot, following the wake left by the obelisk, but it was already out of sight. Suddenly, they heard a sharp cracking sound travel through the water as the point of the obelisk penetrated the thick layer of ice covering the ocean, followed by a powerful percussion reverberating through the sea.

"That last noise sounded like an explosion," said Sophia nervously, as she peered into the darkness above the robot.

Without warning, she saw a long cylindrical object in the darkness above.

"A sub!" exclaimed Joseph incredulously. "How did they find us clear up here?"

They veered off to the left, in an effort to avoid the submarine.

"Oh Oh," groaned Sharianna, as she saw another cylindrical

166

shape emerge from the semi-darkness directly in their path, heading in their direction quite rapidly.

"Don't worry, I think we can evade them," declared Mom, as she turned the robot with the intention of diving off into the depths.

Suddenly, off to the left, a third submarine emerged from the shadows below, also making a beeline for the robot.

Mom turned the robot again, searching for an avenue of escape, when a fourth sub appeared and effectively cut off their flight. The first three subs were closing fast when the fourth one abruptly fired an extremely fast torpedo directly at the robot.

In a split second Mom made her decision and looked up at the solid ice above. The light from the sun barely penetrated into the water below the permanent ice cap that floated on the Arctic Ocean above the North Pole.

"It looks pretty solid," cautioned Dad, as the robot shot toward the barrier of ice. As they got closer, he amended his first assessment of the ice. "No, I think it's fractured from where the obelisk went through not too far from here."

The robot hit the ice with such an immense impact that the primordial ice shattered and huge chunks went flying into the air. As the robot burst through the thick ice, it was followed by a huge vortex of water that was drawn high into the air, followed by an enormous explosion that enlarged the hole in the ice even more, as the torpedo detonated.

They looked up in the sky, but could see no sign of the obelisk. "No telling which direction it went," declared Dad, "we might as well continue home."

Mom brought the robot back down so close to the surface, that the wind created a mini snowstorm as they sped across the frozen north.

Realizing that the subs would be linked to the tracking satellites, they decided not to travel too far on the surface before coming to a stop over the ice.

"That was close," sighed Mom, her heart still pounding. "What now?" she asked.

"I think we are safer way down deep, where the subs can't go,

167

and the satellites can't track," Dad replied.

Mom flipped the switch back to Dad. "You take over."

"Are we going to crash through the ice again?" asked Sharianna.

Suddenly, Joseph got an idea. "What about the laser; you could cut a hole in the ice and we could drop down through."

"Great idea," acknowledged Dad, as he activated the laser and cut a circle through the ice a little bigger than the widest point of the robot. Then, by landing the robot on one edge of the circle of ice, it tipped down as the robot slid through, like opening and closing a door.

"I'll bet they won't even be able to see where we came through the ice," said Joseph as he looked up and saw the huge disc of ice rotate back into place. Dad continued to descend until they reached the bottom.

"How in the world did they know we were there?" asked Sharianna.

"They must have somehow been able to track our every movement," theorized Joseph.

"I don't think so," replied Mom, as her deductive abilities kicked into gear. "Otherwise, I think they could have easily caught up to us in Hawaii – we were there a whole day, and I'm sure there were submarines at Pearl Harbor that could have intercepted us, if they had known where we were. I'll bet Uncle Rex saw the obelisk when the Nautilus first went to the North Pole. Maybe that's why he didn't talk about it very much..."

Joseph interrupted, "And that is why the submarines were waiting for us at the North Pole: They knew the obelisk was there, and the one on the moon...I'll bet they assumed that we are the aliens who put them there! And they assumed that when we came back we would return to the obelisk!"

"Maybe we are!" declared Sharianna.

Everyone looked at Sharianna incredulously. "Well, maybe the same aliens who built the robot also built the obelisks?"

"Maybe. But the question still remains: What happened to them and where are they now?" Mom's analysis continued as she looked at the picture of the writing on the obelisk. "I sure wish I knew what this said. The material that both the robot and the obelisks are made of is hard, but the similarities end there: the obelisks are pure black, while the robot's appearance depends on how close you are to it and seems to encompass many colors."

Joseph continued the comparison, "The obelisks are geometric with sharp angles, while the robot doesn't have any sharp angles at all. And none of the symbols inside the robot look like the symbols on the obelisk." He said, as he waved his hand over the symbols on the console for added emphasis. "And these chairs are made for people our size, while the steps inside the obelisk were obviously designed for creatures much taller." He smiled with this last gesture, feeling like he had irrevocably disproved Sharianna's theory.

"Your argument seems convincing..." agreed Dad.

"That's not proof," argued Sharianna.

Dad continued: "I was about to say, I think I will reserve my opinion until we have further information."

"Well, a few days ago, I wouldn't have believed that anything that has happened to us in the past few days could ever happen, so I'm fine with a little mystery...for now," stated Mom.

"Do you think that second loud noise was a torpedo fired at the obelisk?" asked Sharianna.

"Do you think NASA tracked the obelisk into space?" asked Joseph.

"I don't think they could miss something as tall as a mountain shooting up from the North Pole," commented Dad.

"I wonder if its propulsion is the same as the robot," pondered Joseph.

"We don't even know how the robot works," Mom reminded him.

"To answer Sharianna's question: I think they did fire on the obelisk, like they fired on us," responded Dad.

"Do you think there are aliens inside the obelisk?" asked Sharianna. "Maybe we should try to find it."

Mom quickly responded: "No way! We have no idea where it went or what technology or weapons it might have—we're going home."

169

"Why did the submarines try to destroy us?" asked Sharianna.

"I couldn't really tell for sure, but the fourth submarine seemed different than the first three. I suspect that the first three were American, and the fourth one might have been Russian," theorized Dad.

"You wouldn't want to let your enemies get their hands on alien technology, would you?" reasoned Joseph.

"But I thought the cold war was over," stated Sharianna.

"Yeah, but we're still not best friends," counseled Mom.

They quickly made their way across the bottom of the Arctic Ocean, following a course southward, directly toward Heiberg Island in the extreme northern territories of Canada.

"We are about to pass the magnetic North Pole," commented Dad, as he looked at the map.

"I didn't know there were two North Poles," said Joseph.

"Yeah, the magnetic North Pole is a few hundred miles from the geographic North Pole," said Dad. "It has even moved during the history of the earth," he added. "In fact, at least once, the poles actually reversed their polarity."

"Why would it move?" inquired Joseph.

"I think the scientists believe it is because the earth's magnetic field is generated by the movement of the earth's liquid iron core. Changes in its flow, due to the slow cooling of the earth over millions of years, affects the magnetic field. The movement of the continents across the globe may even have an effect."

"The earth's magnetic field is what protects us from the sun's solar wind. Without it, the atmosphere would be stripped away and life could not exist." Dad loved to throw out little tidbits of scientific information.

"I thought there was no wind in space, because there is no air," challenged Sharianna.

"That's true, but solar wind refers to small particles and radiation thrown out by the sun."

Joseph continued Dad's lecture. "That's what probably happened to Mars: it lost its magnetic field, and then its atmosphere, and consequently, its life." Joseph had watched the same program as Dad.

They stayed under water and snaked their way among the islands, through the gulf of Boothia and into Hudson Bay.

Joseph was looking at the map. "Hudson Bay should be called a sea, because it's bigger than the black sea and it's even wider across than the Mediterranean Sea."

"Hey, there is a big river that leads up to Reindeer Lake, in Saskatchewan," said Joseph. "I think that is as close to home as we can get while staying under water."

Dad acknowledged Joseph's suggestion. "Okay, we'll go up the river and wait for nightfall in the lake. We'll have to go overland once we leave the lake. I think from here on out we should only travel at night, and below the sound barrier to try to avoid detection."

Upon leaving Reindeer Lake that evening, they flew low to the ground, making sure not to travel faster than the speed of sound across Saskatchewan and into Alberta, where they found a railway that led south.

"What if we followed the railroad really low and went about the same speed as a train?" proposed Mom.

"Yeah, that way, even if we were detected, they would probably think it was a train," added Joseph.

"Great idea," complimented Dad.

The moon was still almost full; they could see the moonlight reflecting off the top of the rails where the wheels of the train had made the metal shiny.

It wasn't very long before they caught up with a freight train headed south. They followed it so close that it appeared as if they were part of the train.

"I'm glad that trains don't have cabooses with brakemen anymore," commented Dad, as he followed the blinking red light at the back of the train until close to dawn.

Sharianna, Joseph and Percy fell asleep on the huge beanbag on the lower observation level of the control cabin.

CHAPTER TWENTY-FOUR

"RUN!"

As THE TRAIN CLIMBED OVER A MOUNTAIN PASS, THE moonlight revealed a large lake, lying serenely off in the distance a few miles from the track. "That's a fairly large lake," whispered Dad. "We could hide at the bottom for the day; I'll bet we could be home sometime tomorrow night."

The robot silently veered from the tracks and glided over the forest to the lake and slipped unnoticed beneath the water.

"Great breakfast, Mom," complemented Joseph.

"Are we just going to sit here all day?" complained Sharianna.

"Don't you think we have had enough adventure for one week?" queried Mom. "Maybe we should just rest for the day."

"We might as well go for a swim and a hike," suggested Joseph.

"Well, you guys got some sleep last night, but Mom and I have only had a couple of hours. I'd like a nice quiet nap."

"We'll be careful..." Sharianna trained her magical blue eyes on Dad.

"Okay, but take Percy with you," he admonished them.

"Do you think he will be okay swimming in the space suit?" questioned Joseph.

"I think he'll be alright if you both hold onto him until you get to the surface. He did fine on the moon," replied Dad. "He deserves to get out and run; he's been cooped up inside for days."

"At least there won't be any sharks," commented Joseph.

Percy seemed anxious to get out and run around. He even cooperated quite well when they put the spacesuit on him. He was a little apprehensive when the water began to fill the airlock, but Joseph and Sharianna held onto him and talked to him reassuringly.

When the airlock opened up, they could see surprisingly far through the clear glacial waters of the lake. They swam with Percy up to the surface and looked around. Percy struck out for the nearest shore the moment they reached the surface.

They could see the entire shoreline of the lake. It was bordered on one side by a mountain with jagged cliffs that rose directly up from the surface of the water. On the other side of the lake, the ground sloped up gently with a mixed conifer forest of spruce, pine and fir with a few stands of deciduous maples and quaking aspen that came nearly to the water's edge, with small clearings of meadow grass visible here and there.

From the north, a small river flowed into the lake, creating a shallow, marshy area with tall grasses and reeds, as it deposited sediments carried down from the mountains.

On shore, they removed Percy's space suit and put their own on a large, rounded boulder. Joseph stood on the boulder and surveyed the scene. The air was crisp and clear. He took a deep breath and exhaled slowly, enjoying the feeling of such incredibly clean air, and the fragrances from the pine trees and wild flowers that surrounded him.

The robot was completely hidden beneath the water, although Joseph thought he could see a faint dark spot where he thought it would be.

Sharianna gazed at the cliffs across the lake. There were several small, off-white patches set against the darker stone. One of the white patches moved. "Look, Joseph, over on the cliff. That white spot is moving."

"Mountain sheep," Joseph stated, almost casually. "I saw a bunch of them when camping with the scouts in the Uintah Mountains." He suddenly pointed at the head of the lake, "Look there! Moose!"

In the shallow marshy part of the lake they saw two Bull Moose, knee deep in the lake. As they raised their heads, water plants hung from their huge antlers.

"Do you have your camera?" asked Joseph.

"Of course," Sharianna replied, matter-of-factly as she reached into her pocket to retrieve it. She zoomed in on the mountain sheep as much as her small camera would allow, but they still looked like indiscernible white splotches on the cliffs.

"Here, let me take one of the moose," requested Joseph, impatiently.

Sharianna quickly snapped her own picture of the moose, and then handed the camera to Joseph.

"Where do you think you are going?" asked Sharianna, as Joseph began to make his way stealthily toward the feeding moose.

"I'm getting closer, to get a better picture; the zoom on this camera is not powerful enough."

"Don't you remember Yellowstone?" she called after him accusingly.

Joseph felt a pang of old humiliation: last year, on a family trip to Yellowstone National Park, Joseph had recently gotten a cheap little camera and aspired to get some award winning photographs of a huge bull elk as he protected his herd from the other bulls. Joseph had crept increasingly closer to the magnificent bull, which was preoccupied with chasing away the younger competition. The master of the herd suddenly spotted him and charged with his formidable antlers lowered. Providentially for Joseph, when the huge bull was only a few yards away, he suddenly stopped, turned, and chased after another, younger bull who was trying to steel some of his herd.

Joseph remembered the embarrassment he felt as the other onlookers told him how stupid he was, and the scolding he got from his frightened mother. He wasn't going to repeat his mistake.

"But I got a great picture!" he retorted, as he tried to play down his previous foolishness.

Sharianna followed him along the edge of the lake, staying within the cover of the trees, so as not to spook the feeding moose. She knelt down and grabbed Percy's collar and rubbed his ears. "Now, you have to keep quiet," she admonished,

174

looking into his eyes. She kept hold of his collar.

As they neared the moose, they came to a meadow that extended from the trees at the bottom of a hill to the marsh grasses at the edge of the lake where the moose were still feeding. A small stream meandered its way through the middle of the meadow. Purple and yellow flowers dotted the green grass. The scene was so peaceful and serene that Joseph felt comfortable stepping into the clearing. He raised the camera – as he did so, the largest of the bulls raised his head and looked directly at Joseph, sniffing the air. Joseph's heart leaped and he froze in his tracks. The huge animal was probably only about a hundred and fifty feet away. Sharianna stepped behind the trunk of a large pine tree and watched, her heart pounding.

Joseph snapped the picture, but otherwise remained motionless.

He didn't know if it was true or not but he thought he remembered hearing that moose had poor eyesight. He hoped it was true.

The bull lowered his head and continued to feast on the lush water plants.

"See, no problem." He turned to look at Sharianna as a mother moose with two babies enter the meadow only a few yards away. She stopped and sniffed the air. She lowered her head and turned toward Joseph. Suddenly, she leaped forward into a full charge, her sharp front hooves flailing formidably, intending to stomp to death any threat to her babies.

Joseph sprinted for the trees that, luckily, were only a few steps away. Percy broke free from Sharianna's grip and ran toward the charging mother.

"RUN!" yelled Joseph.

"Percy! Come back!" she shouted.

Avoiding the dancing hooves, Percy nipped at the moose's nose, ran a circle around her, and then darted for the trees. They ran for fifty yards, until they realized that the moose hadn't even entered the forest. Joseph sat down on a fallen tree while Sharianna bent over with her hands on her knees to catch her breath.

175

"You crazy dog," she softly scolded, as she knelt down to give Percy a big hug and rub his ears.

"Too bad we didn't have a stop watch; I'll bet we set a new fifty yard dash record," gasped Joseph, in between breaths.

"Yeah, and you don't have to dodge trees and leap boulders on the track at school."

"And it's not uphill either," Joseph huffed with a smile, as he handed the camera back to Sharianna. "I got a great picture!"

"Let's see…" Sharianna pushed a button and looked at the screen on her camera. "I guess you did."

A tree squirrel began chirping a warning to its friends in a nearby tree. A small stream flowed close by and they could see the water and hear its soothing sound as it tumbled over the rocks toward the meadow that they had so hastily retreated from.

Joseph bent over to tie his shoe, when he noticed some red fruit growing on some low-lying plants. "Look, wild strawberries."

"Don't eat them, they might be poisonous." She was too late, Joseph had already plopped them into his mouth.

"Mmm, they are small, but sweet. Don't you know that strawberries are indigenous to America? There aren't any poisonous varieties."

Joseph got up from his log and started looking for more. Sharianna joined him for the delicious harvest. Their strawberry picking led them up the hill.

"I think it would take all day to get enough for a meal at this rate," complained Joseph, as he straightened up to stretch his back. Through the trees, a little further up the hill, right at the base of a cliff he saw a very old log cabin. "Hey, look at that."

"Cool, let's take a look."

The roof was in severe disrepair, but was mostly intact with only a few cracks here and there between the thick, hand-split, cedar shingles. There was no glass in the single, small window and the door was lying on the ground, its old leather hinges fallen apart long ago. They peered through the small doorway; the interior was lit by the window and door with some shafts of light streaming through the cracks between the logs where the mud chinking had fallen out.

Sharianna stepped into the interior and looked around, quickly followed by Joseph.

The floor had been simply hard packed dirt; the grasses and other vegetation had encroached into the cabin wherever enough light and water would allow their growth.

Below the window, against the wall was a narrow rough-hewn table. On the table was a tin washbasin accompanied by a pie tin, a tin cup, a rusty old bowie knife with a horn handle and a large spoon. In front of the table was a section of log that served as a stool.

On the opposite wall rested a rusty old rifle on two wooden pegs driven into a crack between the logs. Two more pegs, directly below, held a double-edged axe. The rest of the wall was covered with an assortment of old jaw traps ranging in size from one a trapper might use to catch a bear, or a cougar, to one small enough for a squirrel or a muskrat.

"It must be an old trapper's cabin," deduced Joseph.

The cliff face actually served as the back wall of the cabin. In the middle of the back wall stood a rustic hand-hewn cabinet with several shelves, holding two antique oil lamps and a few tins of lamp oil, along with some deteriorated blankets and clothing. The cabinet seemed to be hung on the wall with the bottom only an inch or two from the dirt floor and reached to a height of about seven feet.

To the right of the cabinet, in the corner, was a small stone fireplace, its chimney extending up above the roof. It had a single large flat stone for a hearth. A black kettle lay in the old ashes where it had fallen when its supporting stick had long ago broken.

Along the wall, near the fireplace were the remnants of a narrow makeshift bed.

Joseph picked the old rifle from its resting place on the wall and examined its mechanism.

Sharianna stepped across the small room; bending down, she looked into the small fireplace. Suddenly, she heard a noise from inside the chimney. She jumped to one side and accidentally banged into the cabinet on the back wall; it swung away from the wall, like a door, revealing an opening in the face of the cliff behind it.

The cause of the noise burst from the fireplace and ran across the floor, onto the table, and leaped out the window.

Percy, who had been at Sharianna's side, streaked after it, leaping from the floor to the table and then out the window.

Joseph burst into laughter as he stepped to the table and set the rifle down on it. "It's only a squirrel," he teased, as he stood watching Percy tree the squirrel in a nearby pine tree.

Sharianna returned her view to the opened cabinet; she could see a short distance into the passageway behind the cabinet. She took a couple of steps into the cave to get a better view, when the cabinet suddenly swung closed behind her. An involuntarily cry escaped her lips as she stopped in the darkness and turned back toward the door.

CHAPTER TWENTY-FIVE

EL DORADO!

JOSEPH TURNED TOWARD SHARIANNA WHEN HE HEARD her scream, but she was gone.

"Sharianna..." he called, apprehensively. *She couldn't have gone out the doorway, I would have seen her,* he thought.

He heard a muffled voice: "Here I am, behind the cabinet." At the same time, he saw the cabinet begin to move. He grabbed onto it and helped swing it open.

The cabinet was easy to open but it was hung in such a way that when it was released, its own weight swung it back into place against the wall.

"The hinges must have been sticky when I first opened it," deduced Sharianna, as she swung the cabinet back and forth, trying to figure out why it stayed open and then closed by itself. "It took a few seconds for gravity to overcome the sticky hinges and make it close."

"Or maybe it was a ghost," teased Joseph, as he rolled the stump over and propped the cabinet in the open position.

"Like there were ghosts on the wrecked steam ship?" she retorted calmly. Sharianna felt the same shiver she had felt on the ship, but she kept her feelings to herself. The last thing she wanted was for Joseph to think he could scare her.

Joseph went a few steps into the cave. "It looks like a natural cave – like a crack in the mountain." The cave tapered from about three feet at the bottom to a thin crack in the ceiling. The light from the doorway penetrated the blackness only a few yards. "I wish we had some flashlights," he commented.

"Or the piece of railing from the moon," said Sharianna. "Hey, what about the old lanterns?"

"I'll bet those old things don't even work. Besides, we don't have any matches."

"I saw some in the cabinet," Sharianna replied, as she stepped around the end of the cabinet and picked a box of old wooden stick matches off the shelf.

179

"There's no way…" began Joseph.

Sharianna struck a match on the side of the box and a small trail of smoke rose from the match. "You were saying?"

He continued his thought: "…no way those are still good."

She struck another match on the box and a small flame appeared momentarily but flickered out before it could ignite.

"Try two together," suggested Joseph, as he found a lantern that still had oil in it and removed the glass top.

Sharianna did so, and the two matches flamed together. She touched the flame to the wick of the lantern and it sputtered and flared brightly, as Joseph replaced the glass top. She put the box of matches back on the shelf.

The other lantern was empty, so Joseph popped a small hole in the top of a can of lamp oil, using the tip of the old bowie knife, and filled the other lantern. They used the flame from the first lantern to light the other.

Percy returned from terrorizing the squirrel and sniffed the air at the entrance to the cave. He whined as his two friends entered the darkness of the world underground, armed only with their puny, temperamental, fragile, antique sources of light.

Sharianna thought about the mine they had escaped from on the moon. "I don't think I want to do any more cave exploring."

"At least we know there are no moon monsters in this cave," replied Joseph. "Let's go in a little, we ought to at least see if there is anything interesting."

"I guess you're right, there can't be anything as dangerous as those creatures on the moon."

"Come on boy, aren't you coming?" called Sharianna, as she motioned for Percy to follow them. "Why do you think the entrance to this cave was hidden?" she asked.

"Whoever built the cabin must have been trying to hide something in this cave," Joseph replied.

"I know, but what?" she insisted. "And what happened to him? It looks like he left all his stuff in the cabin."

"Maybe he got eaten by a mountain lion, or a grizzly bear?"

The cave began to get narrower and shorter, until finally, Percy was the only one who could continue comfortably.

"I don't want to go any further," complained Sharianna, whose knees were getting sore from crawling on all fours.

Carrying the lamp made crawling even more tedious. As the ceiling got lower, Joseph began to reach out ahead and place the lantern down, and then he could use both hands to crawl with, instead of holding the lamp with one and hobbling along with the other.

"There must be something valuable in here for the trapper to conceal the entrance," Joseph encouraged.

"What if he used it to hide his furs, or his food? It is pretty cool in here," proposed Sharianna.

This thought hadn't occurred to Joseph – he had assumed that the trapper must have found something worth concealing in this cave–treasure, perhaps.

"I'm going back," Sharianna announced.

Joseph looked at the tunnel ahead, "I think someone else has been down here, there are tool marks on the ceiling. I'll bet it will get bigger soon. It's a long way back, crawling backwards. There is no way to turn around in this small space. I'm going forward."

Sharianna reluctantly agreed, even though she was feeling a little bit claustrophobic. It did give her a little comfort knowing that Percy was bringing up the rear.

Joseph would never admit it, but he was feeling a little bit apprehensive also.

They continued on, it seemed like hours must have gone by. Joseph automatically reached out for the numberless time to place his light ahead. As he began to crawl forward, he looked up just in time to see the lamp teeter. He reached out to catch it, but it was too late. The lamp fell over, but to Joseph's surprise, it toppled clear out of sight. The light from the falling lamp revealed a large cavern.

"We made it!" he exclaimed. At that moment, his lamp hit the rocks below and the glass chimney shattered on the rocks as the rusty metal split open and spilled the flammable liquid, erupting into a large, smoky flame that illuminated a large portion of the cavern.

The flame quickly burned down in a few minutes as the fuel was consumed.

While the flame was still burning, Joseph looked for a way down. To the right of the tunnel, and less than a couple feet away, was a tall stalagmite rising up from the floor, ever attempting to connect with its counterpart, the stalactite reaching down eternally from the ceiling. Geologically speaking, their meeting was imminent—a few thousand more years, give or take a few hundred.

Joseph looked at the glistening, conical pillar. He contorted his body, until he was crouching uncomfortably at the tunnel's entrance, hanging onto a rusty old spike that had been driven into a crack in the stone sometime long ago. With Sharianna's lamp on the floor behind him, he half leaned, half jumped out toward the stalagmite; wrapping his arms and legs around it, he slid down the moist, slick, yet bumpy pillar, all in one motion.

Sharianna stuck her head out from the tunnel entrance, holding her lamp, as the flame from Joseph's broken lantern flickered and went out.

"Come down the way I did."

"And how are we going to get back up?" retorted Sharianna. "And how do you propose to get Percy down?"

Joseph looked around at the pile of rubble he was standing on, "We could pile up this rubble against the base of the cliff." Once Sharianna realized that his plan would work, she hung her lantern on the rusty spike and slid down the stalagmite to help him.

"Someone has definitely been here," Sharianna said, pointing to a pile of rotten rope at the base of the small cliff, "an old rope ladder."

"Looks like he is still here," Joseph whispered as he suddenly saw, at the edge of the light, a skeleton curled up at the base of the cliff, with the remnants of an old trapper's attire still clinging to his bones.

Sharianna gasped when she saw him.

Joseph took a step toward the hapless miner and interpreted the evidence to come to a conclusion as to what had taken place such a long time ago.

"The rope ladder broke, and he fell, accidentally impaling himself on his pick," Joseph deduced. "See, there are two broken rib bones and there is the pick, still lodged in his ribcage."

Sharianna was full of compassion for the long dead trapper. "It must have been terrible to die here all alone."

"Well, we better start piling up the rocks," said Joseph, trying to change the subject.

Finally, their makeshift staircase was tall enough that Joseph could reach up and lift Percy down.

Joseph handed the remaining lamp down to Sharianna.

They proceeded to make their way through the seemingly endless cavern. Many of the stalactites and stalagmites had merged together to form pillars from floor to ceiling like some eerie subterranean cathedral of the underworld.

The floor of the cavern was an uneven maze of boulders and rocks intermixed with a few broken stalactites and stalagmites, evidence of long ago seismic activity.

As they explored the cavern, they came upon a large skeleton, with the bones scattered around and a few even broken.

"From the skull, it looks like a giant bear – like the one on the steamship – except that this one is much larger and it has extra huge fangs." Joseph remembered reading a book about prehistoric creatures. "I think it might be an extinct cave bear."

A short distance from the bear skeleton, they came across an even more exciting skeleton; it was complete, and the bones weren't scattered around like the first skeleton.

Sharianna recognized this new skeleton from the long, distinct fangs. "It's a saber tooth tiger!" she exclaimed.

"Maybe the tiger was hunting the cave bear and they both got trapped in here," speculated Joseph, as he imagined the saber tooth stalking the huge bear through primordial forests and the bear taking shelter in its cave, the giant tiger in pursuit. He imagined a rock slide closing up the entrance to the cave, leaving the two enemies to battle it out, both of them inevitably dying in the darkness of the cave.

"Look, a tunnel," stated Sharianna.

"It is definitely man-made," observed Joseph, as they entered the mineshaft.

The floor was smooth and flat and devoid of rubble and debris. The walking was quite easy. They passed several side tunnels; each time they chose to continue straight. Joseph assumed from the quartz filled cracks in the ceiling that the original miners must have been following veins of gold or some other precious mineral, since quartz and precious metals are often found together.

Without warning, they suddenly found themselves at the edge of a cavernous room. Their lantern barely penetrated into the darkness of the great expanse. The interior of the mountain had been excavated for several hundred feet, except for three foot pillars about every thirty feet.

While exploring the room, they found many artifacts made out of copper. The most interesting of these was a pick. There were also sledgehammers and chisels of various sizes. Joseph picked up one of the smaller chisels and put it in his pocket.

"Why would anyone make a pick out of copper?" wondered Joseph. "It's a very soft metal, it wouldn't hold up to continuous use digging in rock."

After discovering that the tunnel which led them to this great room was only one of several tunnel entrances, Joseph began to worry about finding the right tunnel on their way back. They had not marked it, thinking that they could go straight back, but it turned out that the pillars were not all lined up as Joseph had originally assumed. As they progressed through the huge room they could not tell exactly which way they had come. Joseph's worry was forgotten when he noticed that the quartz and granite of some of the pillars and one of the walls looked like it had golden wire woven throughout its structure. The gold veins on the back wall radiated from a central vein in the middle of the wall that was several inches wide and extended from the floor all the way to the ceiling. Using the ancient copper pick, Joseph began picking at the main vein. After a while, he was able to extract two large chunks about the size of apples.

"Hey, hold the light so I can see."

"I am, I think it is running out of oil," Sharianna replied apprehensively, as she swished the small amount of remaining oil in the lamp.

Joseph turned to see the lamp flickering. "We'd better get out of here before it quits."

Joseph handed one of the chunks of gold to Sharianna and began to make his way quickly across the huge main room of the mine.

"There, there's the tunnel." They entered the tunnel quickly and hurried along; the floor began to slope up and they came to a Y.

"I don't remember a Y in the tunnel."

"Neither do I," replied Joseph.

"The floor of the tunnel that we came through before was flat," decried Sharianna.

The old lamp began to sputter more. Suddenly, they were enveloped in the utter darkness of the mine. Joseph felt a strange sense of despair grip him, as he felt helpless and completely lost. He reached out with one hand and grabbed onto Sharianna at the same time she was reaching for him. He put the chunk of gold in his pocket and with his other hand he reached out for the wall, in order to give himself some sense of location.

"What do we do now?" Sharianna cried, as the same feelings of foreboding and helplessness began to overwhelm her.

Sharianna set the lantern on the floor and reached for Percy's collar. She rubbed his fur and somehow it gave her a little comfort to know that Percy was right there beside her.

"Let's keep going – it is sloping upward – it must lead to the surface, eventually," she suggested.

In the complete darkness, it did not matter whether they had their eyes closed or open, they still could see absolutely nothing. Time seemed to be lost as they slowly groped their way along the rough wall of the tunnel. Suddenly, Joseph stopped. "Your camera!" he exclaimed.

"What? You want to take a picture?" asked Sharianna incredulously.

"No, the flash will light up the tunnel."

185

"Yeah, even the screen might give us some light." She retrieved the camera from her pocket. "Smile," she said, as a painfully blinding flash of light momentarily illuminated the tunnel.

"That didn't do me much good," said Joseph, rubbing his eyes.

"Look, the screen does emit light." A feeble glow extended a few feet into the darkness.

"I guess it is better than nothing," said Joseph gratefully.

They passed many side tunnels and each time they had to guess which way to go. They wandered their way around the labyrinth, while the battery on Sharianna's camera slowly went dead.

Joseph couldn't tell if they had been stumbling along in the darkness for minutes, hours or days – except that his hand began to feel raw and painful from touching the wall of the tunnel, and his legs were weak.

He was about to complain about his discomfort when Sharianna said: "I'm tired and hungry, let's rest."

They sank to the floor, still holding tightly to the other's hand, each fearful of becoming separated and left alone in the darkness and the silence. Sharianna put her arm around Percy's neck and pulled him close. His warmth gave her the reassurance she needed.

The only sound they could hear was their own breathing.

In the darkness, Sharianna suddenly felt Percy stand up and face down the tunnel in the direction that they had come from. She moved her hand to his collar. "What is it boy?" she asked soothingly, as she felt the muscles of his body quiver slightly as he whined softly.

She began to fear more than the darkness and the silence, as she imagined what else might be living down there in the depths. "Do you think anything else could be down here?" she asked nervously.

Joseph's imagination was conjuring up the spirits of long dead miners and other ghostly denizens of the darkness. He remembered the stories he had heard, that dogs could sense the

186

spirits of the dead. He tried to shake off these disturbing thoughts.

"No, I doubt it," he forced himself to say, but Sharianna could feel his hand begin to sweat and knew that he was scared, despite his attempt to sound strong, brave and optimistic.

"What about bears, mountain lions, or other wild animals?" she asked.

Joseph hadn't even thought about the possibilities of these other dangers yet. He reached over and put his other hand on Percy's back. It also gave him some courage, knowing that Percy was there and would protect them, no matter what might come down the tunnel in the darkness.

Joseph reached into his pocket and pulled out the ancient copper chisel that he had taken from the main chamber and held it like a weapon.

Sharianna heard the sound first. It was a low-volume high-pitched noise; she shuddered. "Could there be rats down here?" Moments later, she could hear a soft flurry of movement as well. She reached into her pocket for the lump of gold to use as a weapon, if need be, when her finger touched something else.

"My gecko," she exclaimed softly.

"Your what?" Joseph whispered, as he tried to prepare his nerves for whatever was coming down the tunnel. *I wish we still had the spacesuits*, he thought, as he pictured them lying uselessly on the boulder by the lake where they left them. *I'll bet Mom and Dad have found them by now*, he thought.

Sharianna pulled from her pocket the key chain Mom had bought her while they were in Hawaii; it had a small, silver gecko attached to it. She pushed the tiny button on the top of the gecko's head and it seemed to Joseph that a huge spotlight burst forth from Sharianna's hand, but in reality it was a small LED light. The light was so welcome that Joseph had to quickly suck back the sob of relief that nearly escaped his lips.

"I had forgotten all about it," Sharianna exclaimed excitedly.

As their eyes followed the beam of light toward the ceiling, they suddenly saw the source of the strange noises.

"Bats." Joseph's voice was full of relief as he realized the

187

implications. "It must be getting dark outside and they are headed out to feed!"

"Hurry, let's follow them!" Sharianna jumped up and, holding her precious little light, led the way, but the bats were quickly out of sight.

As they hurried along, they came to a small side tunnel, barely big enough to stand up in.

"Which way now?" asked Joseph, as he strained his ears to hear the sound of the bats.

"Which way boy?" asked Sharianna, bending down close to Percy. Percy seemed confused as well; he sniffed around on the floor, but of course there was no trail left by the flying bats.

Suddenly, a single straggler appeared out of the darkness and fluttered down the side tunnel.

"This way!" ordered Joseph quickly, as they tried in vain to keep up with the bat.

The tunnel became smaller and they had to run half crouched down.

Unexpectedly, they ran into a dead end. Sharianna spun around, shining her dim light on the walls. "Where did it go?" she cried desperately.

Joseph looked up at the ceiling, and to his surprise, he could see at the end of a vertical shaft, a small, round patch of the night sky with a few stars shining like eternal beacons of hope. "Look! It must be a ventilation shaft," he declared, with enormous relief.

"But how do we get up?" questioned Sharianna.

"Let me see the light."

Joseph reached up into the shaft with Sharianna's light: "It has handholds and footholds cut right into the walls of the shaft – I think we can climb up."

"What about Percy? We can't just leave him down here," insisted Sharianna.

"I've got an idea." Joseph handed the light back to Sharianna, pulled off his shirt and began putting it on Percy, with his front legs through the armholes. "Give me your belt."

Sharianna handed him the belt. Joseph looked at it; it was made of cheap vinyl. "I don't think this will hold," he said, as he handed it back to her. Removing Percy's strong leather collar, Joseph squatted down over Percy and, putting the collar through the neck of the shirt that was now on Percy, he threaded it through his own belt and buckled it. He stood up and was able to pick Percy up. Joseph reached up and grabbed hold of the first handholds in the shaft and put his foot on one of the niches in the back wall. "Help me lift Percy."

Sharianna helped lift Percy until Joseph was fully in the shaft with Percy dangling below. At first Percy didn't seem to be that heavy but by the time they were halfway up the shaft, Joseph's arms and legs were trembling from the strain; he stopped to rest.

"I don't know if I can make it," he said.

Sharianna was right below. Suddenly, Joseph felt the weight lifted. He looked down; Sharianna had the key chain in her teeth and from the dim illumination he could see that she had followed him up the shaft and had Percy's belly resting on her shoulders.

They continued to struggle up the shaft; luckily, Percy sensed that they were helping so he didn't wiggle or struggle too much.

Finally, weak from hunger, stress and muscle fatigue they reached the top and Joseph crawled out of the hole with Percy and then reached down and helped Sharianna.

They sat on the ground trying to recoup their expended strength.

They were well over a mile from the lake; they could see the robot flying low around the shore of the lake with its lights illuminating the trees.

"They're looking for us." Sharianna flashed her little light in the direction of the robot, but there was no response.

"Do you still have any matches?" asked Joseph, as he put his shirt back on.

"No, I left them in the old cabin."

By the moonlight they could see the lake and the small river that flowed into it and the small stream that flowed by the cabin.

"Look, there's the stream that leads by the trapper's cabin!" exclaimed Joseph jubilantly.

"And the cliff above it," added Sharianna.

They carefully made their way down the mountain by the

light of the moon – Sharianna's little light was not producing very much light by this time. She carefully put it back in her pocket. *I'm not going to lose this after it saved our lives*, she thought.

Sharianna quickly got the matches from the cabinet while Joseph got another can of lamp oil.

"Grab those old rotten clothes too," instructed Joseph.

Out in the clearing in front of the cabin, Joseph doused the rags with the fuel. By striking two matches at the same time on the side of the old box he was able to get the fire going.

The fire burned rapidly, creating an eerie light across the front of the old cabin and dancing shadows on the surrounding trees.

They could no longer see the robot in its search, but suddenly, it appeared above the trees and landed right in front of them. It bent down with its hand directly in front of the foot to create a step. Percy and his best friends bounded up the foot as the airlock opened with Mom and Dad standing in the doorway.

"Where have you been!" chastised Mom with a sob, as she embraced her children. "We have been frantic for hours."

"We found an ancient gold mine," explained Joseph.

Sharianna pulled the chunk of gold out of her pocket. "Look what we found."

"Is it gold?" asked Mom.

"Sure looks like it," commented Dad, as he hefted it in his hand. "Sure is heavy, like gold."

"How much do you think it is worth?" inquired Sharianna.

"I don't know, I guess it depends on how heavy it is and how pure it is, but I would suspect that it must be worth thousands of dollars," replied Dad.

Joseph pulled the other chunk and the copper chisel out of his pocket. "We've got another one. And check this out Dad," he said, as he handed him the chisel.

"It's copper," observed Dad.

"Yeah, but it's as hard as steel," replied Joseph. "There were picks and other tools made out of the same stuff."

"I heard that the ancient Americans had some way to harden

190

copper—modern scientists still haven't figured out how they did it." Thomas examined the chisel with great interest. He pounded on the chunk of gold with the chisel. "It's malleable, I'm sure it is gold."

Joseph marked the GPS coordinates of the mine on his map.

"When you did not respond, we realized that you must have taken off your spacesuits," said Dad.

"We found them right where you left them," explained Mom.

"I guess if we had left them on, we would have been able to communicate with you," Sharianna concluded. "We're sorry we made you worry."

They followed the railroad tracks all the way into Utah. Sharianna and Joseph told Mom and Dad all about their experience in the mine as they traveled.

The monotony of watching the shinny tracks and the rhythm of the railroad ties flash by in the moonlight forced Joseph's weary eyes to droop as he laid his head back on the giant beanbag. Sharianna had already succumbed.

"I can't stop thinking about all that has happened to us," whispered Sophia. "Especially the obelisks. I wish we had some more batteries for Sharianna's camera—I'd sure like to look at those alien symbols again. I think the strangest thing we have encountered—and it has been a strange few days—is the obelisk at the North Pole. What was it doing there? How long has it been there? Why in the world did it take off? Just because we touched it? Now, I'm kind of wishing we had followed it like Sharianna suggested. Where did it go? Could there have been aliens in it, or was it automated?"

"I think the moon monster was very strange, and completely unexpected—everyone knows there is not supposed to be any life on the moon," replied Thomas.

He continued, "Did I tell you that both Joseph and I had a strong feeling of déjà vu?"

"No. When?"

"Out in the desert when we found the pictographs. There was

some form of ancient writing on the rocks too."

"You never mentioned that before," chastised Sophia.

"Sorry, I guess I forgot in all the excitement of the robot. Anyway, I had the same feeling on the moon, except even stronger. For a moment, I could see in my mind the rock art perfectly. The robot was depicted on the rocks, you know."

"Yeah, I remember you telling me that," replied Sophia.

"I think there was even an obelisk, and maybe a round circle that depicted the moon. Joseph thought that the human stick figures on the mural represent us."

"Do you think it is possible?" replied Sophia.

"I don't know, but if we had dug where I wanted to, we would never have found the robot."

"What do you mean?" asked Sophia.

"I wanted to dig into the side of the gully, but Joseph wanted to dig right in the bottom—where he found the spearhead. He said maybe it was a good luck charm. Now that I mention it, I think there was also a spearhead in the pictograph," commented Thomas.

"As soon as we get home and settled, I want to take a drive out there and see those pictographs and the writing—I did not think there was any written language among the ancient natives of North America," said Sophia thoughtfully.

Suddenly, her face got very serious: "Do you think we were *meant* to have the robot?"

"What do you mean, *meant*, to have it?"

"You know, fate, destiny," she replied.

"I don't know; I've always thought that we could make our own destiny—we are free to choose, after all."

"I guess you're right, but I can't help feeling like there is some meaning or reason for all of this," agreed Sophia.

"I'm just grateful that we are all together and that we are almost safely home. Look, there is the Great Salt Lake."

Thomas remembered hearing that the lake was very shallow, so he decided that they would fly slowly over the lake, skimming the surface, so that they might look to any observers on the shore to be simply one of the brine shrimp boats coming in late.

Once across the lake, they flew about a foot or two above the deserted back roads, traveling at the speed limit and finally arriving home at 3:30 in the morning.

"Let them sleep," whispered Thomas, as he looked at Percy with Joseph and Sharianna on either side of him.

"Do you think the robot is safe here in the barn?" asked Sophia quietly.

"I think so, even if they were looking for the UFO, I'll bet they weren't looking for it on the back roads. With the lights of the robot turned down, we probably looked like a truck to any surveillance they might have had."

"A very quiet truck," Sophia added, as they entered the cargo area.

They surveyed the room. On the left was the kitchen. On the right was the living room with the sofas and chairs. In between the chairs, up against the curved wall were the treasures the kids and Thomas insisted on bringing home: the strange metal ball, the small asteroid from the asteroid field, Sharianna's moon rock, the glowing piece of railing, the map from the Golden Alaskan bridge and the large bumpy but oddly uniform meteorite from the moon crater. On the counter were the smaller treasures: Mom's chandeliers, Joseph's shark teeth, the rusty old pearl handled pistol and the golden name plate, Sharianna's piece of the shredded door from the mine on the moon, her shells from their island paradise, Joseph's small copper chisel and their two chunks of gold from the Eldorado mine.

"I think I could handle one more night on the anti-gravity couch," yawned Thomas, as he laid down on one of them.

"I wonder why there are no beds in the robot," mused Sophia, as she took the other sofa.

Thomas sighed as he lost himself in the perfect comfort of the sofa. "Good night sweetheart."

"Good night."

As Thomas began to slip into sleep, he gazed at the meteorite. *It seems to have changed color*, he thought groggily to himself, but welcome sleep had already claimed him.

CHAPTER TWENTY-SIX

"That's no Meteorite"

JOSEPH FELT SOMETHING WET AND WARM ON HIS FACE. HE recognized the sensation even before he opened his eyes. "Percy!" he whispered, as he grabbed him around the neck and they wrestled off the beanbag onto the floor.

Sharianna opened her eyes to see the ceiling of the barn displayed on the view screen. "We're home," she sighed, with both feelings of relief and a hint of sadness, simultaneously.

Joseph stopped wrestling and looked around at the view screen. "We must have gotten here sometime in the night. I guess we made it."

"Where's Mom and Dad?" asked Sharianna, as she went up the steps and made her way toward the back door of the control room. Joseph and Percy followed her. As they passed the captain's chairs, Joseph glanced at the princess clock on the console. It read: 9:47.

As they entered the cargo bay, the first thing that Joseph noticed was the meteorite. Instead of being the brownish black color from yesterday, it now appeared to be more orange. The coloration seemed to follow the texture of the meteorite. The high spots were blacker, while the low spots blended into a rusty orange color.

"It's pretty; I guess the colors were revealed as the moon dust fell off of it," whispered Sharianna softly, trying not to wake up Mom and Dad, as she looked at the gray dust on the floor around the meteorite.

Percy planted a great big slobbery kiss, or rather a lick, across Mom's face from her chin to the tip of her nose.

"Ugh, Percy!" exclaimed Mom, as she immediately awoke and wiped her lips on her sleeve. "What did you let him do that for?" asked Mom, as she looked at Joseph.

"I didn't know he was going to do it," Joseph replied, laughing.

Percy then turned his diabolical attention on Dad, who was still sleeping.

Dad awoke with a start as the enthusiastic dog leaped on top of him.

"Look, Dad, how pretty the meteorite is." Sharianna looked at the meteorite again and was even more impressed with the change. She stepped over and put her hand on the meteorite. "It feels warm," she observed.

"It almost glows," added Joseph.

"After I get a nice hot bath, I'm going to town for some groceries; who's coming?" asked Mom.

"Me," Sharianna replied.

"I'll come," offered Joseph.

Dad declined the invitation: "I think I'll stay and start fixing the hole in the side of the barn. How about a hand, Joseph?"

"I'll stay and help you, Dad," offered Sharianna.

"While you are out, stop off and get a gallon of paint for the barn," suggested Dad.

By the time Mom and Joseph got back from shopping, Dad and Sharianna had the repairs to the barn well under way.

"Guess what we saw on the way to town?" asked Joseph, as he handed Dad the paint.

"I don't know. What?" queried Dad.

"A great big army truck set up with a whole bunch of satellite dishes and twirling radar antennae."

"Do you think they are still looking for us?" asked Sharianna.

"I'm sure they are," concluded Dad. "I'm sure glad we came in last night along the back roads."

"They must have thought we were a truck," theorized Mom.

"They may not have even been scanning the surface at all, because they were looking for an unidentified *flying* object, right?" reasoned Joseph.

Sharianna interjected: "We may not be so unidentified anymore. A lot of people have seen the robot: the pilots and the stewardess, the astronaut on the space station, the Chinese military, the Koreans, a lot of people in Tokyo, both U.S. and

195

Russian subs, the salvage ship's divers, and the harpooners on the whaler.

"Just more tabloid fuel," commented Joseph.

"Nevertheless, I think we had better keep the robot hidden for a while," cautioned Dad. "Here, give me a hand nailing up the rest of these boards."

Suddenly, Joseph remembered the safe. "What about the safe?" he asked, excitedly.

"Sharianna and I already got it out, by using the engine hoist. It's over there."

The rusty old safe lay on its back on the floor near the welding torch.

"I didn't want to wait for you, but Dad said that Mom would want to see it opened up," Sharianna informed Joseph.

"Well, what are we waiting for?" asked Mom eagerly.

"Do you want to do the honors?" asked Dad, as he handed the torch to Joseph. "Let's start by cutting off the hinges; then we can try prying the lid up."

The metal popped and spattered as the rusty scale on the safe resisted melting. Joseph turned off the torch and grabbed the sledgehammer to bang off the thick scale. Once the scale was knocked off, the torch cut easily through the remaining metal.

Dad got two large crowbars off the wall and handed one to Mom.

"Pry it up," instructed Joseph, as he lifted his welding hood. "Careful, it's still hot." Mom and Dad pried up on the hinge side of the door. Joseph grabbed a chisel and a hammer from the drawer and tapped it into the crack opposite of the hinges, pushing the door with the locking pins away from the jamb. The heavy old plate of iron slid, and then clanged to the floor, revealing the contents of the safe.

Mom gasped in disbelief.

Dad let out a whoop of excitement.

"Joseph, please go get the scale out of the bathroom," Mom asked breathlessly.

"And a calculator," called out Dad, as Joseph went tearing out of the barn toward the house.

Lying in jumbled disarray, with deteriorating record books and documents, were many solid gold ingots. And even more, larger bricks that looked kind of black.

"What are these?" asked Sharianna, as she hefted one of the black bricks.

Dad took the chisel that Joseph had used to open the safe, and scraped the brick. A shiny streak of metal was revealed: "Silver. It tarnishes when in contact with salt water."

As they began to empty the safe, they also found a number of gold coins and antique silver dollars interspersed with coins of varying denominations. Mom reached in and picked up a deteriorating leather pouch; opening it, she discovered a stack of both silver and gold certificates, still damp, but intact.

Joseph returned with the scale and set it on the floor and they began to stack the gold ingots on it.

Dad took the two large nuggets from the ancient American mine in Canada off the workbench and placed them on the top of the pile.

Mom looked at the scale incredulously.

"Hey, eighty-seven pounds. That's how much I weigh," commented Sharianna.

"Oh, my goodness," whispered Mom, as she sat down on the floor next to the scale and looked at Dad. "How much is gold worth right now?" she asked, in a soft whisper.

"About seventeen hundred...per ounce," answered Dad, in an even softer whisper.

"How many ounces in a pound?" asked Sharianna.

"Sixteen," Mom replied.

Joseph still held the calculator. "Let's see, eighty-seven pounds, times sixteen ounces per pound, equals: one thousand three hundred and ninety two ounces. Multiplied by...how much?" asked Joseph, looking at Dad.

"Seventeen hundred."

Joseph typed in the numbers, "One, seven, zero, zero. That equals..."

Sharianna looked at the calculator and they read the numbers in stereo: "Two million, three hundred and sixty six thousand,

and four hundred dollars!"

"And that doesn't count the silver and the coins, or the paper money," exclaimed Mom, in delighted disbelief.

"I'll bet these coins are collector's items too," declared Joseph, as he picked up some of the gold coins.

"We're rich, aren't we?" concluded Sharianna.

Suddenly, Percy jumped up from where he had been comfortably sprawled on the cool cement of the barn floor and ran toward the robot. Dad had turned the robot onto its side in order to get the safe out easier and it was still in this position. The ankle door was only a couple feet off the floor. Percy leaped through the door and let out a yelp when he experienced the shift in gravity and slid "down" the wall to the floor of the air lock, then charged down the hall toward the cargo area. Joseph was close behind, followed by the rest of the family.

Joseph stood in the doorway and pointed at the large meteorite as Dad burst into the room. The meteorite had divided into two hollow halves. It was hinged like a huge interlocking locket. On both halves they could see small blinking lights, almost like LED lights.

"That's no meteorite!" exclaimed Mom.

Directly above one half, suspended a few inches in mid-air, was what looked like a flat, round, red cushion about eighteen inches across and several inches thick, with a depression in the middle.

"It's an eggshell," breathed Sharianna.

On the cushion, cradled by the depression, sat the broken pieces of a beautiful blue-green eggshell, about twice the size of an ostrich egg.

"It must be an alien egg! The meteorite must be some sort of incubation chamber," assumed Joseph, as he looked around apprehensively for the alien that must have emerged.

"More like a stasis chamber," commented Sophia. "Who knows how long it sat on the moon."

Suddenly, the colored lights on the inside of the meteorite went out and the cushion dropped, spilling the remnants of the shell onto the floor.

Percy started sniffing the floor as if he were following a scent. Joseph grabbed him by the collar, and followed him toward the control room.

"I'll go first," insisted Dad.

Percy whined as he tried to squeeze past Dad's legs in the small passageway to the control room, but Joseph held tightly onto his collar.

Dad looked through the doorway, but could see nothing unusual. He stepped down onto the main level with Joseph and Percy by his side and looked over the console, down into the lower observation area. There, curled up on Joseph's huge beanbag was the little alien.

"It's some kind of reptile," assumed Mom.

Sharianna pushed past Mom to get a better view and stood on the top step leading down to the lower level.

"It looks more like a dinosaur, to me," concluded Joseph. "Maybe a baby T-Rex, or a velociraptor."

"Sharianna! It might bite!" whispered Mom anxiously.

As Sharianna approached, the alien opened its eyes, raised its head and stood up on two legs on the beanbag. Sharianna smiled and reached out her arms. She looked into its large, beautiful, brilliant turquoise-blue eyes. "It doesn't look dangerous to me." She moved down the steps toward the alien. "It's just a baby."

"Hi there, cutie pie," she consoled in a soothing, sweet voice.

The alien mimicked her motions, seeming to smile, while reaching out with its arms and making a soft, melodious, crooning sound.

Sharianna picked up the baby alien and cradled him in her arms.

"It's a baby dragon!" exclaimed Joseph softly, as he saw the wings slowly unfold from the alien's back.

The end of the Beginning

POSTWORD

Long before the beginning of the beginning

A BONY, AGED, FINGER POINTED TOWARD THE CLEAR MORNING sky. "Look." As the word passed the wrinkled lips, it carried an unexpectedly vibrant tone of confidence and power.

Two pairs of eyes followed the trajectory indicated by the finger.

A small speck appeared above the desert's horizon and quickly grew larger as it rapidly and silently approached the three diverse friends, who stood unflinching as it passed directly overhead. It was close enough that the old seer could have easily hit the strange object with an arrow from his bow, had that been his desire.

The silence and welcome tranquility of the morning was supplanted by a thunderous shock, as the huge object collided with the sand a few miles away. A great cloud of dust erupted from the desert and lingered in the still air.

"Shall we fly to the point of impact and discover what manner of creature hath fallen from heaven?" inquired Draco. His powerful voice retained its characteristic absence of all apprehension as it reverberated softly from deep within his cavernous chest.

As the trio approached, Draco was the first to see the long shallow impact crater, since his eyes were much more powerful than those of his companions'.

The dust had fully dissipated by the time they arrived at the deep end of the crater; they gazed incredulously at the object.

The sand and rocks at the head of the crater buried two thirds of the object. The dust refused to cling to the portion that was still exposed; its dark surface glistened in the sunlight.

"I cannot comprehend how an object of such size could be hurled through the sky," commented the seer thoughtfully. "It must have fallen from the stars."

"Yes, it must be from another world," observed the man who was dressed in a fine white linen shirt and woven cloth britches

200

tucked into fine, black leather boots. He looked at Draco, "Perhaps even from your home world."

The ancient seer, in his traditional deerskin and handmade beads, placed his hand on the object. It was cool to the touch and felt smoother than frozen water on a still pond. He leaned forward and gazed intently at the object as if he would peer into its depths. Suddenly, he fell slowly backward. Draco reached out and caught him gently before he reached the ground and carefully carried him out of the pit and into the welcome shade of a tall rock outcropping that had been pushed up by the tremendous force of the strange object.

The man in the white shirt was a wise man of many years experience, but obviously not as ancient as the seer. He quickly removed his long cloak from his shoulder and placed it upon the ground.

He knelt down as Draco gently placed the seer upon the cloak. "Are you well, my old friend," he asked softly.

"I am well," spoke the seer after a few moments. "I have returned from another place."

"What place?" asked Draco.

The seer looked up at the stone. "I'm not sure," he replied. "May I use your long knife?" he asked, as he stood up.

The well-dressed man quickly drew his dagger and handed it to the seer, who began to use it to etch the descent of the object from the sky into the rock outcropping.

The seer finished his carving and looked out over the crater. His companions noticed a faraway look in his eyes.

"What do you see?" asked Draco, who could obviously see much farther and with much greater clarity than the old seer. Draco saw in the distance a hawk souring through the sky. On the ground below the hawk he could see a jackrabbit resting in the shade of a small shrub. Farther in the distance, almost at the horizon, he saw a lone antelope; but he knew the seer could not see these things.

The seer looked into the distance and forward through time. He saw what he thought was a whirlwind in the distance. As the plume of dust drew nearer, he imagined it to be a small herd of

201

bison stampeding across the desert, except that bison did not frequent the desert.

The unusual dust cloud approached the place where he stood. He was surprised to see, in the leading edge of the dust cloud, four persons. They were riding astride – no, they were within – a strange beast with round feet. The beast came to rest only a few steps from the rock outcropping. The sides of the beast sprang open and its occupants spewed forth and ran to the rock outcropping and stared at his freshly finished carvings; their mouths were moving and he could tell that they were speaking, but he could not hear their words.

The fair-haired woman pointed to some strange scratches at the bottom of his carving. Suddenly, he could hear her words, but she spoke in a strange tongue that he could not understand–it sounded much like the language of his two companions. Even though he could not understand the words, he somehow comprehended their meaning.

As the words faded, so too did the woman and her three companions—and the beast that they were traveling in.

The seer turned to his companions. "You once said that your people could draw words?"

"Yes, we have a written language."

"Will you draw these words here at the bottom of my drawing?"

"Can you read the inscription, Mom?" inquired Sharianna.

"Yes, but it's very strange–it is an ancient Gaelic form of Latin. How could an ancient language from Scotland end up on a rock in the middle of the West Desert?"

The inflection in Sophia's voice and the expression on her face reflected the query carried by her words. She continued: "These words, 𝔍𝔞𝔱𝔲𝔪 𝔄𝔩𝔞𝔰𝔱𝔯𝔦𝔬𝔫𝔞 are interpreted: Defenders of mankind's destiny. These other words are: 𝔄𝔰𝔱𝔯𝔬 𝔏𝔞𝔯𝔦𝔰, which mean star tool."

"Astrolaris," repeated Joseph thoughtfully. "That's what we should call the baby dragon."

BOOK TWO, CHAPTER ONE
THE baby *ALIEN*

The alien made another soft, melodious, crooning sound; it reminded Joseph of the purring of a kitten combined with the gentle cooing of a dove.

Mom anxiously, yet cautiously, went down the four steps to the tiny lower observation level of Robo-ship's control room. She was worried that her movements might startle the baby alien that was encircled in the protective embrace of Sharianna's arms.

Dad articulated Mom's concern, his soft whisper seemed to reverberate in his ears because of the small spherical space of the control room as he cautioned, "Don't make any sudden movements or loud noises."

Sharianna turned around. "See, he's not dangerous," she said tenderly.

"It *is* a dragon," gasped Mom, in an almost inaudible, incredulous whisper as the baby's wings gently refolded inconspicuously onto its back. Her thoughts were in ultra-high-speed: *What was a mythological creature's egg doing in an incubation/stasis chamber on the moon? It must have been there a very long time before we dug it up. Maybe dragons weren't myths. That's quite obvious – I'm standing here looking at one.* She looked at the sharp little claws, six on each hand and foot. The creature seemed to smile, revealing two rows of innumerable sharp gleaming teeth. *It's definitely designed to eat meat*, she thought with fearful horror, as she saw how close it was to Sharianna's tender throat. All these thoughts flashed through her mind in the moment it took for Sophia's eyes to meet the big beautiful turquoise blue eyes of the infant dragon. Somehow, her heart seemed to connect with the dragon through those gentle orbs. Her anxiety miraculously and instantaneously morphed into a motherly manifestation of warmth and tenderness. "No, he's not dangerous," agreed Mom kindly, as she reached out her hand and gently caressed the cheek of the baby dragon. Its nearly scarlet skin felt surprisingly soft...

"I wonder if he is hungry?" wondered Sharianna, as she threaded her way through the ship's living room and entered the hallway that led down to Robo-ship's ankle door.

"That reminds me," said Mom, "we bought a bucket of KFC while we were in town."

They sat down at the kitchen table; Sharianna had the baby carefully cradled in her arms.

"Here you go little guy, do you want some chicken?" asked Joseph, as he handed a drumstick to the little dragon. It reached out and took the chicken with its mouth. To the family's surprise it reached up with one of its front feet and held the chicken, just like a person would. This was the first opportunity the family had to get a close look at its feet.

"Those are more like hands, than feet," exclaimed Joseph.

"You're right. Look, it has six fingers, but two of them seem to be opposable thumbs, one on each side of the hand, instead of only one, like us," observed Dad, as he held up his hand and wiggled his thumb.

Suddenly, they heard a crunching sound as the baby bit all the way through the bone of the drumstick. The dragon made a strange growling sound from deep within his chest. It was definitely different than the cooing sound they had heard before, and yet, it was not alarming. It was as if the infant were saying "mmm," like a person when they really like something they are eating.

The baby finished off the chicken leg, bone and all, and then crawled out of Sharianna's arms and onto the table. Reaching into the bucket of chicken with his hands, he pulled out another piece. He squatted on his hind legs and using his tail for balance he began to devour the chicken, he seemed to relish the bone and gristle just as much as the meat.

When he was done eating, he crawled back into Sharianna's arms, closed his eyes and went to sleep.

DON'T MISS THE REST OF BOOK TWO!!

Astrolaris grows surprisingly fast, he is an incredibly intelligent pet...or is he more?

Realizing that Astrolaris must be kept as close a secret as Robo-ship, they only go outside to play at night. Despite their precautions, an amateur cameraman inadvertently captures Astrolaris on his night vision video camera and posts it to the internet.

They begin to wonder if there are any more stasis chambers to be discovered; but is it wise to take Robo-ship on another adventure in search of more dragons while the world's militaries are scanning the skies and oceans for UFOs?

Unaware of NASA's true capabilities, they court disaster and begin their exploration. While scanning for stasis chambers, they discover that the thick layer of ice encapsulating Europa, Jupiter's large icy moon, conceals an ocean of liquid water warmed by volcanic activity. It is an incredibly beautiful world, full of colorfully vibrant, bioluminescent plants and creatures. They find a friendly technologically advanced sentient species with a lingering, dark, past. Their fate has become intertwined in the struggle of this spectacular world of water, fire and ice. Agony and anguish cry for them to abandon their quest, as home gently summons them back to Earth.

Destiny is renewed as the quiet sound of a computer keyboard reverberates fatefully through the silence of the stone chambers and passageways of an ancient monastery in a remote region of the Himalayan Mountains. The Tibetan monks faithfully fulfill their sacred oath which their brothers had sworn centuries earlier: to guard and defend the secret of Draco...

Your friend in reading and writing,
Brenton Barwick

Visit brentonbarwick.com to order books and download eBooks.
I host FREE school assemblies and literacy night book signings.
You can also use Defenders of Destiny books for your school fundraiser.
Email me if you have a comment or question: brentonbarwick@hotmail.com